HONEYMOON BLISS

HONEYMOON BLISS

HONEYMOON SERIES, BOOK 4

LILY ZANTE

AUTHOR'S NOTE

'*Honeymoon Bliss*' is the fourth book in the '*Honeymoon Series*'.

I have written a spin-off series called the '*Italian Summer Series*' which tells the stories of some of the minor characters who first appeared in the '*Honeymoon Series*'.

The timelines of both series are connected and you can find the recommended reading order here.

Honeymoon Series:

Honeymoon for One
Honeymoon for Three
Honeymoon Blues
Honeymoon Bliss
Baby Steps
Honeymoon Series (Books 1-3)

Italian Summer Series:
(A spin-off from the Honeymoon Series)

It Takes Two
All That Glitters
Fool's Gold
Roman Encounter
November Sun
New Beginnings
Italian Summer Series (Books 1-4)

CHAPTER ONE

"Nico, I'm sorry but I won't be able to make it to your wedding."

Hot on the tails of Bruno telling him about the problems with the treatment rooms in the new spa center, one of his closest friends not coming to the wedding was the least of his problems.

"That's a shame," Nico replied, slowly. He'd been looking forward to meeting his friend.

"I hate to let you down like this, especially since you asked me to be your best man, but Chiara's ankle is bad, she was lucky not to have broken it, and there's no-one to look after the twins."

"Your wife comes first," replied Nico, understanding the man's dilemma. "Don't even worry about the wedding. What happened?"

"She fell down the stairs last night while carrying up the laundry. She's resting now but the twins are running riot. You know what they're like. I'm sorry if I've left you stranded."

"No," said Nico, closing his eyes. "Please don't worry about it." He wondered who else he could ask. "You take care of Chiara and the twins and you take it easy." If such a thing were possible. "I hope we can all meet up sometime."

Nico didn't have such a tight knit circle of friends; from his younger days he'd had many hangers-on, had known many women, but when it came to close friends and people he could trust, he could count them all on one hand. Romano was one such person, they went back a long time, and had been his first choice for a best man.

Now he was a best man short.

He stared at the wall in front of him, at the picture of his father that hung there, as he adjusted the cuffs of his shirt. He tried to think who else could stand in Romano's place.

The memory of his father still held strong in this room which had once been Edmondo's office before Nico had taken it over. He felt his father's spirit strongly in here, as if his essence was imprinted everywhere within the four walls and ingrained upon the leather chair in which he now sat. Deep in thought, he clasped his hands together; not quite praying, but sitting in silent remembrance.

A faint knock at the door was followed by the slow opening of it and instead of Ava entering, as he'd expected, he was surprised to see his future mother-in-law, Elsa, walk in.

"There you are," she said, as if she expected him to be

somewhere else. "Why so glum? That's not how a prospective bridegroom should look. It's time for you and Ava to get ready for this big day of yours."

He attempted a smile and watched as she walked over to examine the photo of his father. She always did this, as if she was drawn towards it. He'd put it up there but wasn't sure he liked to see his father staring back at him all day long, watching over him with an almost stern expression on his face. Yet sometimes, even looking at that stern face gave Nico comfort.

Edmondo was never far from his thoughts, and having that photo close by always took Nico back in time to memories that were tinged with sadness. He tried not to show his grief to others, but he missed his father sorely and knew that only time would heal the wound left by his untimely death.

"There is so much of you in him," Elsa said quietly, still staring at the picture.

"There is so much of him I want to be like."

She turned and faced him. "You *are* like him," she insisted. "You have his warmth, his eyes, his ability to make people feel at ease, and to trust in you. You are already so much like him, Nico. Perhaps you don't see it, but I do. I'm sure others do, too."

He remained silent because nothing would ever bring his father back. Even though four months had passed since his death, sometimes Nico imagined his father sitting in the kitchen or the study at home and tortured himself with the thought of Edmondo walking through the door to his office. Of course, that would never happen. But it didn't stop him from wishing.

The absence of the man he had clashed with for so long— and whose respect he had at last begun to earn—was sometimes hard for Nico to acknowledge. And there wasn't a damn thing he could do about it. It made him want to hold onto Ava more tightly than ever. It taught him how much could change in one second and this thought frightened him. It was a constant reminder to him that nothing lasted forever. Even the new life Ava carried, and the new start he'd been given, could all be taken away from him in the blink of an eye.

Sadness surrounded Elsa too. This gentle woman, the mother of his fiancée, tried to mask her grief, even from him, yet it was plain for Nico to see straight through it because their grief was almost identical. He knew she still missed Edmondo and her visits back to Verona were hard for her because she lived alone and had nobody to spend her time with, nobody to distract her from her sorrow and only the memories of the golden days she'd shared with Edmondo months earlier to haunt her.

"Look at you, Nico," she said, disapprovingly. He unclasped his hands and picked up a pen, twiddling it around in his hands. "Your father wouldn't have wanted you to sit here like this. You can't bring him back, Nico. And you mustn't let the darkness of his passing pull you down. Your father would have been happy that you and Ava were getting married."

"I know," replied Nico, remembering how much his father had adored Ava. "I wish he were here, that's all."

She looked down and nodded. "I wish he were here every day. We would have been outside the whole time. Or he would have shown me more of Verona." She chuckled softly to herself. "If there was anything else left to show me."

Nico swallowed. His father had died a happy man—happy for Nico, for he had seen the effect that Ava had had on him, and happy to have met Elsa—and to have shown her this wonderful city he'd loved so much.

There were times when Nico wondered, as he knew Ava

did too, what might have happened between her mother and his father had a fatal heart attack not claimed his life so cruelly.

"My father had the happiest time showing you Verona," he said, sitting up in his chair and putting the pen down. He knew he had to let go of the past so that he could embrace the future but it was always easier said than done. Ava tried to do her best to keep his mind from sinking too much into the sadness but he was aware that things weren't so easy for her. She was juggling far more on her plate than a six month pregnant bride—soon to be married in four days' time—ought to. "There is a lot to be done."

Elsa laughed. "There's not a lot to be done, but a lot of enjoyment to be had," she said. "It's time to get it all together. You're getting married! I don't understand why the pair of you find it so difficult to detach yourselves from your computers."

He couldn't wait for it to be over. For months he had been dealing with all the documentation and the religious paperwork required by the church where his parents were married. Despite his initial concerns, the priest had agreed to allow the ceremony with an obviously pregnant American woman. But until he had a ring on Ava's finger and until they walked away as husband and wife, Nico would not be able to rest.

It was the wedding reception, and the long honeymoon that he was looking forward to the most.

"I was checking a few things."

"That's what Ava keeps telling me. How many things do you both have to check? And why is this checking taking place constantly? What will go wrong? We were far luckier in my day than you are now. We didn't have these things." She pointed at his computer and at his cell phone which lay on the desk. "Nobody had a computer at home, or a phone they carried around with them all day long. We got by just fine."

"I'm sure you did." He got up and stretched out his shoulders. His body was stiff from sitting around for the past few hours without moving. He couldn't wait to take Ava away from all of this. Just having the time to themselves—that was what he wanted more than anything.

"Come with me." Elsa moved towards the door. "Help me to remove your fiancée from her desk and unplug her from her computer. It's going to take both of us to achieve that."

"You might be right."

CHAPTER TWO

"I'm sorry. I...I..." Ava stammered. "No. Mi dispiace," she apologized. "I don't speak Italian. Non capisco. I wanted information about your furniture...um...for the children. Bambino? Parla inglese?" She rested her forehead in her hands. "Nessun problema. Ciao." She couldn't put the phone down fast enough. "Impossible," she wailed, massaging her temples gently. "It is *so* hard trying to get through."

"You *are* in Italy," declared Rona. "It seems only fair that you speak the language."

"I thought English was universal."

"So what if it is? You're in Italy and you plan on living here. I'd say it's time you learned Italian."

Ava groaned again.

"Do you know you put on a false Italian accent when you're talking?"

"I do?" Ava was shocked.

"It's not going to make them understand you."

"I know," Ava mumbled to herself. "I didn't know I was doing it. Oh, god. I hope they don't think I'm being offensive."

"Your children will be fluent in Italian, Ava, so you might

want to think about taking some lessons." Rona pulled open the filing cabinet and rifled through it. Ava considered her sister's advice, not that she often took it, and groaned even louder, causing Rona to drop the file she was holding. "What's wrong?" Rona asked, looking worried.

"A new language, new places, new customs, a new life, new country, new husband and a new baby."

Rona's features relaxed. "I thought the baby had kicked or something. Your point?" Rona crossed her arms, waiting.

"I'm scared."

"About what?"

"Of everything happening so fast."

"You should have thought of that when you had unprotected sex."

"I don't mean about the baby," retorted Ava. "I..." She didn't know how to explain it. Her whole life had changed ever since she'd come to Italy and now she was taking the next step up, a real commitment, with a man who loved her. But the magnitude of the change still overwhelmed her.

"You have Nico. There's no reason to be scared. And they also drive on the same side of the road, so that's a bonus. One less thing to worry about."

"Some days I miss Starbucks. Sometimes I crave Dennys and IHOP."

"What for?" Rona shot her a confused look. "You get nicer, tastier, and classier coffees and pancakes here."

"But it feels strange to know that I am leaving it all behind —the places I grew up in."

"You miss Denver?" Rona picked up the file and slipped it back into the cabinet.

"I have, lately." This was what happened when she started to slow down at work in readiness for her wedding. Not being crazy busy gave her the time to sit and reminisce and to consider the life changing step she was about to embark on.

She wasn't only getting married, she was emigrating and bringing her children up in a new country. A country she had come to love, but a country that was still as new and as unfamiliar to her, as it was beautiful. It would be home to her children and her Italian husband, but would it ever feel like home to her? She'd thought so the whole time, had fallen in love with the place as deeply as she'd fallen in love with Nico. But now she was beginning to wonder, and the doubts had started to creep in. She would miss her mom, and Rona and Carlos and her niece, and her friends in Denver. She would see them, but perhaps once a year, maybe less?

"I've never seen you happier, Ava." Rona tried to assure her. "These are just last minute wedding jitters. It's natural."

"But what if I'm making a mistake?"

"Marrying Nico?" Rona stared at her in surprise.

"Not Nico," Ava replied. "He's the one constant in my life." She exhaled loudly. "Maybe you're right," Ava sighed. "Maybe I'm being nostalgic because it's getting so close to the wedding. I keep remembering the things I've left behind." She rested back in her chair and let her hands fall to her lap, as she stared down at the bump that now passed for her stomach. Being six months pregnant, it resembled the size of a small rounded watermelon. "I'm scared about the baby. I don't know *anything* about babies; I've only looked after Tori and I must have changed her diapers a handful of times. Mom isn't going to stay here forever. What'll I do if I'm stuck? Who will I call?"

"You can call me." Rona sat down at her small corner desk. "And as a mom, it's all second nature. I didn't have a clue but it kinda comes to you."

Ava listened to her sister but felt a strong urge to go for a walk in the gardens and to forget her troubles.

"Hey." Rona's voice turned soft. "What's going on? You're not having second thoughts about moving here, are you?" She walked over to Ava's side and placed a hand on her sister's shoulder. Ava reached up and put her hand over it.

"No second thoughts," she replied. "I'm happy. I really am," but she was beginning to well up. One lousy call to a supplier whose nursery furniture she'd seen online, and a few minutes of non-communication had left her almost in tears. Lately, she'd been mulling over things. In the early days she'd been caught up in her roller coaster romance with Nico, and then she'd fallen pregnant not long after they'd met, and with the news of her pregnancy, then the shocking news of Edmondo's passing—all of the months leading up to now had been filled with one drama after another. She'd never had time before to think about the change that had taken place in her life in the space of less than a year. But now that she was starting to slow down, with her wedding only days away, she found herself thinking too much about many things and it often left her feeling sad. She wasn't sure why.

"Hey," Rona kissed the top of her head.

A quick rap on the door commanded her attention as the door opened and Elsa and Nico walked in together. They both stared at her.

"What's wrong?" they both asked in unison, as two pairs of eyes descended on her. Ava smiled. "Nothing," she replied, staring back at Nico and feeling heat radiate through her chest. She loved the way his eyes shone full of love and concern each time he looked at her. That was all it took for her fear to disintegrate.

"Still working?" Nico asked her. She'd bet ten dollars he'd been at his desk until a minute ago.

"You told me you would stop today." Elsa looked at Ava's cluttered desk with disdain.

"It's no use," Rona appealed to both of them. "You're going to have to physically remove her."

"Ava, honey. Time to unplug and remove yourself." Elsa's voice was firm.

Nico stepped forward, the warmth emanating from his relaxed smile. "Come on, Ava. Time to go. We've got a few things to do yet and I've booked you into the spa tomorrow, once you've got your wedding dress fitting out of the way."

Ava looked horrified. "But I don't have the time—"

"And that's exactly why you need it."

"A bride with no time to unwind?" Elsa asked her, in that simple and effective way she had of dealing with her girls, with her usual healthy dose of common sense and kindness.

"Why don't you close the office for a few days?" Rona suggested.

"I can't," replied Ava, testily. "You're going to have to keep an eye on things until the wedding day." She wanted to knock that idea right out of her sister's head.

"I was hoping to go sight-seeing with Carlos and Tori." Rona stuck out her bottom lip.

"Lose the pout, honey," said Elsa. "Don't go giving Tori ideas."

With her attention still on Nico, Ava listened to the exchange between her mother and her sister. Rona going sight-seeing with her husband? This was news to her. Things between the couple had been icy lately but after Tori's temporary 'disappearance' a few days ago; she'd noticed that they seemed to be more attentive towards one another.

"If you could work a few hours between now and Thursday then sure, by all means, you and Carlos take some time together," Ava told her. She'd have to revisit her ideas about getting her sister to look after her business while she and Nico were away on honeymoon. It didn't seem fair to ask Rona to work and it was definitely not fair for Carlos, since he'd made the effort to come over for the wedding a few weeks earlier than planned.

It must have taken some heavy convincing to take so much time away from the busy family run restaurants he worked in with his father and brothers.

"Have you tried on your bridesmaid's dress? Does it need any adjustments?" Ava asked.

"I tried it on a couple of weeks ago—sure it fits. It was fine then, it'll be fine now. Remember, I'm not the one who's growing by the hour."

"And that kind of comment isn't going to get you any half days around here," said Ava, wanting to wipe that smug smile off her sister's face. At times she still had to remind her sister that she was the boss.

Rona's face turned somber. "I'm almost done with filing all the most recent orders and I updated the website this morning. If I finish what you gave me, could I take the afternoon off?" Rona never changed. But if it meant Carlos got to have some downtime, then who was Ava to stand in the way? "If you've done everything you needed to for today then you're free to go."

"How about *you* finishing *now*?" Nico asked her.

And do what? She still had more emails to go through, a call with Kim to schedule, and some statistics she wanted to check.

"How about you at least stop for lunch with me?" Nico suggested. "We can make a list of the things we need to do between now and Friday. That's our wedding day, in case you forgot."

"I haven't forgotten," she said quickly, not wanting this

wonderful man to think that she was treating their wedding day as a normal day of the week.

"Lunch would be a good thing for the baby," Elsa reminded her.

"Shouldn't you be resting, Mom? I don't want to hear about any more dizziness or falls from you."

"Your doctor has given me different medication and this one suits me better. I haven't felt dizzy in days."

"No more hospital visits or being taken out on a gurney, okay, Mom?" Rona insisted.

Elsa gave her daughters a haughty look and made a move towards the door. "I'll leave this to you, Nico," she said, nodding at him. "I'm going to check on that new gardener of yours and to make sure that he hasn't hacked my lemon trees." She addressed the girls. "Your Uncle Hugo and Aunty Camile arrive tomorrow, and I've been telling them about the gardens. I hope that man hasn't ruined them," she said before slipping out of the office.

"Since when did they become *her* lemon trees?" Ava wondered out aloud.

"Mom seems to think she has dominion over the gardens. Poor Salvatore," said Rona. She flitted back and forth between her desk and the filing cabinet, and put away a pile of recent order sheets. Ava watched her, not having seen Rona move so fast before.

Her sister's early arrival, almost a month and a half before the wedding, had been a gamble. Rona had helped and over time she had become more diligent and conscientious about her work. But, goodness, she took her sweet time doing it. Not for nothing did Kim have good reason to complain about her. Ava considered Kim to be a valuable addition to her business for it was Kim who held the fort over in Denver, dealing with customer queries and sending out orders. Together with Rona, the women worked out of Ava's old apartment but they seemed to clash more than they got on.

"I'm done," exclaimed, Rona, standing up and getting ready to leave.

"That was fast," Ava commented, drily. "Did you—"

"Yes, I've filed the recent orders, double-checked the new order for Andrea, and I've updated the product descriptions for the new high-chairs. You said I could go now. May I? Please, Miss?"

Ava tut-tutted with her mouth. "Go on," she said. "Be nice to Carlos." With only her and Nico left in her office, Ava sat back in her chair, resting her arm on the armrest. Nico smiled at her. "I swear, each day you get bigger and rounder —" He stopped abruptly as the scowl settled on her face. "You're going to look lovely," he told her. But she knew he liked her this way; softer, more curvy. Just as well there was no need for birth control anymore because Nico couldn't keep his hands off her. As her pregnancy had progressed, her sexual drive had shot through the roof and each night ended well. Happily.

"Rona and Carlos might have reached a truce," Ava commented, then shrugged away the tension that was beginning to build up in her shoulders.

"I agree," said Nico. "Maybe coming that close to losing Tori—"

"*Thinking* they lost her." Ava corrected him.

"Same thing. They didn't know she was safe with Lizzi. All the same, it must have been scary for them both. I think it brought them together—and it's a good thing. It's one less thing to worry about on the wedding day." He held out his hand to her.

"Are you worried about the wedding day?" she asked him. Because she wasn't. Her only concern was how she would look in her dress, and it wasn't the image of the svelte bride that she'd had in mind. She got up slowly and took his hand.

"I'm not worried, especially now that I've given the priest a sweetener to turn a blind eye to the fact that we've obviously gone beyond the kissing stage in our courtship." He ran his fingers over her belly.

"Don't say that." Sometimes she wasn't sure whether to believe him or not.

"You know I didn't. Thank goodness my father was held in such high esteem in Montagnano," he said, referring to the village he grew up in and the place where they would be married.

"I can't wait to marry you, Ava Ramirez."

"I can't wait to marry you, Mr. Cazale."

"You don't have to change your name, you know."

"So you keep telling me." Many women in Italy didn't take their husband's surname. "But I want to have the same name as our baby. And I don't like double-barreled names."

"No?" asked Nico, considering it. "Cazale-Ramirez doesn't hold much appeal?"

"*Ramirez-Cazale*," she insisted, changing the order, "is too much of a mouthful. It's the sort of thing Connor would have done."

"Must you mention him?"

"I store my products in his garage. Be nice to him." She wanted to tell him before the wedding.

Nico raised an eyebrow. "You haven't secretly invited him to the wedding have you?"

"No," she said slowly. She would never have. But his recent request for her to loan him some money had put her in an awkward position. She didn't want to hide this from Nico.

"Good. I'd rather you didn't mention his name to me, and I'm going to get your space issues resolved so you'll never have to feel obligated towards him." He kissed her lightly on the lips. "Lunch, and lists, and freedom. I've booked lunch in Verona, at that restaurant with a balcony view."

"How thoughtful of you." It would be better to leave news of Connor to the side, for now. As they walked out of the double glass doors and she carefully walked down the steps, she asked, "When do you plan to tell me where we're going on our honeymoon?"

"Not yet." He was obviously still sticking to his guns.

"I need to know so I know what to pack," she protested.

"Dresses and skirts for the day, nothing for the night." He slipped his hand around her bulging waist. "I can't wait to get away from here and to spend all day and night in bed with you."

CHAPTER THREE

"You'll have to deal with it, Bruno. I'm not planning on coming to Ravenna, not until we return from our honeymoon." Nico looked at his watch. Three days until he got married and the last thing he needed was his project manager to report back with more problems.

Taking on the building of a new spa center as well as refurbishing the old hotel was a completely new project for him. But when he'd bought this hotel, he'd assumed that he would have his father's good counsel throughout the entire project. It had never occurred to him that he'd have to deal with this alone.

With Edmondo gone, and the hotel his, he had no option but to move ahead. What spurred him on the most was that he'd shown his father this place shortly before his death and Edmondo had been so proud of him for coming up with a new initiative. It was now Nico's goal to open the best and most luxurious new spa hotel that Ravenna had seen. He'd sought out advice from others in the hotel business, people he trusted and who had the greatest respect for his father.

He'd worked the project plan diligently, along with

Bruno, the main project manager, as well as the construction manager, the interior designer and the hospitality management consultant. Together they had created a spa center that would have the treatment rooms and infinity pools he'd envisioned. He'd carried out several cost planning and engineering exercises to ensure the project would be on time and on budget, as best as possible. He'd made provisions for project completion dates with incentives for early completion and penalties for delays in the contracts.

Yet even though each day seemed to bring a new raft of problems, he knew that if he let it ride, they would soon be fixed. The completion date he had in mind—the end of November—was something he was striving towards. It was tight, but it was doable. With their baby arriving mid-November, he knew he was pushing things, but so far everything seemed to fall into place and was running according to plan.

Could he make one last trip to Ravenna before the wedding? He shook his head, annoyed with himself for even thinking this thought. How could he when his fiancée was at the Cipressi Salon having a facial and a head massage? She hadn't gone easily either.

"I don't want to worry about the hotel, Bruno. That's why I hired you. I'll check in later but I have a few other things I need to deal with right now."

After he had dropped Ava off, he'd rushed back to the office to finish off last minute things.

Lately, dealing with everything had become one gigantic pressure that continued to grow and there were always other issues occurring all around him. It was becoming increasingly impossible to leave work at night and to not think about things. There was always some problem to deal with, whether it was to do with the new hotel, or the spa center, or the existing hotels. At any given moment something or someone always required his attention.

He was going to have to ensure that nothing disturbed them while they were on honeymoon. There would have to be boundaries, perimeters of acceptable business practice which could not be broached. Ava needed this break more than he did. She'd worked crazy hours lately and he could see how tired she was by the evening. Lying by her side at night he could almost hear her mind churning over facts and figures and costs and expenses. Their foreplay consisted of talking more about their numbers, than about the things they wanted to do to one another.

That would have to change. And it would start to change on their honeymoon.

Bruno was a good project manager and Nico trusted his work implicitly, though he still found it difficult to let go and to hand things over completely. He would never let go. The spa hotel was his baby. Figuratively. He had two babies to think about this November and he knew that from then on his life would never be the same again.

He glanced at his watch. Damn it. He'd only been back a short while. Had it really been two hours since he'd been here feverishly working away? He was already late to pick Ava up.

Rushing out of his office, he almost flew across the checked marbled reception floor when Gina accosted him mid-flight. "We have a clash," she announced.

His eyebrows snapped together in reply.

"I'm scheduled to go on a training course next week but I don't think I can be away if you're away too."

He puffed out a short breath. He still needed to hire a few managers to take over the tasks that he'd been doing until recently. Managers who could work with Gina and help with the running of the Cazale empire. He should have had these people in place already but he'd been so caught up with the new hotel that time had flown through his fingers like caramel-colored sand. The new hotel sucked up his time like a hungry octopus and not only was the hiring of these crucial people being delayed, he knew that he was neglecting the other Cazale hotels too.

He didn't understand how his father had managed it all, relying on the services of accountants and other professionals as and when he'd needed them. The Cazale hotels were small, discreet and elegant hotels and not the huge, ugly, concrete ones with hundreds of rooms and staff to manage. But still, the family owned eight of them and soon there would be nine, when the new hotel was complete.

His father had left a lot to the individual hotel managers to deal with by themselves, and of course Nico had taken a lot on too. He wanted all hotels to perform as well as the Casa Adriana, the main flagship hotel where he and his father had been based, and which Nico had used for trialing his own ideas. The Casa Adriana had begun to show a marked increase in visitor numbers as well as a higher proportion of extremely satisfied customers.

Promoting Gina had been the smartest move he'd ever made. All he needed were a chief technology officer and a marketing manager. Gina took care of the overall running of this hotel and kept an eye on the others too. She was the one who handled the weekly conference calls with the managers of the other hotels and he sometimes felt guilty, knowing he had given her too much to handle.

"I'm sorry, Gina." He rumpled his fingers through his thick hair—which reminded him, he had a haircut and a proper barber's trim and shave booked for the morning of the wedding. He needed an assistant, that's what. But, thinking about it, Gina doubled up on that account as well, whether she knew it or not. She was always there whenever he needed her.

"I will cancel," she insisted.

"No, you won't. You will attend the course and we will make do." But he knew it wouldn't work.

"No, Nico. I insist on it." Gina was friendly and soft on the outside, but working closely with her over the years taught him that she was as strong as steel inside. Ever since the promotion she'd come on in leaps and bounds, soaking up every responsibility he'd given her.

"It's not fair to you. This is my fault. I should have hired more people by now." They were at the glass entrance doors and he rushed to get away.

"And seeing that you haven't, are you now going to cut your honeymoon short?" Her eyes blazed. "I didn't think so," she replied, not waiting for his answer. "It's not something I would allow you to do. I can postpone. These courses run every month. When are you back?"

"On the sixth of September."

"You and Ava need this time. I can manage here."

"I'm sorry I haven't made any progress with the new recruits." Each spare moment he had went on the spa hotel. Having a team in place would free him up no end and leave him to give all his attention to the spa hotel.

"Let me have a look at the résumés while you're away," Gina offered. "I know they have been coming in because I've been watching the pile grow."

"Could you?"

"Certainly. How about if I interview the promising candidates? I know what positions you're looking for. I might not be equipped to ask them relevant questions, but I'm sure I can get a feel for their personality and general experience level. I could hold the first round of interviews and with any luck we'll have a short list by the time you get back." He felt his shoulders loosen. Gina eased his life. She really did.

"That would be a big help. Thank you." He placed his hand on the cold glass door, ready to leave.

"Can I suggest one thing?" Gina stopped him from making his escape.

"Anything," he said quickly, thinking it was high time to give her another raise.

"Absolutely no working while on your honeymoon."

He chortled. "Ava's already been on at me about—"

"She's one to talk."

"I know. We've come to an agreement. We'll check what needs to be checked twice a day, morning and night and that will be all."

"As long as each of you stick to it. You're both as bad as each other."

"I know Gina. And thanks."

"You don't have to thank me, Nico. I'll postpone the course until late September." He smiled and paused as he fished out the car keys from his pocket. "Are you ready for the wedding? You are coming, aren't you?"

"Yes, of course. I wouldn't miss it for the world."

"We look forward to seeing you." He wondered whether she was coming alone or with a partner. It occurred to him that he didn't even know if Gina had a partner because she never disclosed anything about her personal life. Maybe Ava knew more. "Will you be bringing a guest?" he asked.

"No," she replied. Getting information out of her about her personal life was as tough as extracting a wisdom tooth. "Now I must phone the company who is doing the management training and get them to change my course dates."

"I'll leave you to it," he said, taking his dismissal easily as he rushed towards his car in the parking lot.

"Hey, Nico!" With the car keys inside the door, Nico turned to find Carlos walking towards him with Tori peacefully asleep in the stroller. Nico couldn't help but smile. He wanted a girl too; someone who looked just like Ava. They had no idea what they were having since they had both decided not to find out the gender, preferring to have a surprise when the baby came. But secretly, he wished for a girl.

"Carlos." He shook hands with his soon to be brother-in-law. Sometimes Nico didn't know whether to shake hands, which seemed too formal, or high five him, which seemed too juvenile, or to hug him—which still seemed not the thing to do. His relationship with Carlos bordered between that of a good family friend and a friend who was almost family, and the subtlety existed because he hadn't yet figured out which form of greeting would do.

"How're you doing, buddy?" Carlos asked, looking more relaxed than he had lately. Nico noted that the man was actually smiling.

"Counting down the days," Nico replied easily. "How're things with you all?"

"Better." Carlos's his eyes sparkled. "This angelic wildcat has been on a tight leash." He looked down at his sleeping daughter. "We're too scared to let her out of our sight."

"I can imagine," replied Nico. "Make sure you keep her on a tight rein at the wedding. The party will be huge and it's outside. Enclosed and on private grounds, but still..."

"You bet. Do you need a hand with anything?" Carlos was always eager to help. "Rona and I feel as though we should to be doing something."

"It's all taken care of. All you need to do is to turn up on the day and enjoy it. How're things with both of you?" Carlos hadn't looked so happy a few days ago, when he'd gotten into a fight with someone right here in the parking lot. "Everything okay now?" Nico asked.

"Couldn't be better."

"That's great," Nico replied. The last thing he wanted was family awkwardness around the time of the wedding.

"Nothing makes you appreciate what you have more than knowing that you came this close," Carlos gestured with his index finger and thumb, "to losing it."

Nico nodded in agreement.

"I came that close to it," continued Carlos. "It was the scariest thing in the world."

"Well, you look happier than I've seen you on this visit."

"Family," said Carlos, beaming, "is everything."

Nico nodded his head. "I'm glad that things worked out for you."

"It was nice of Ava to give my wife half a day from now until the wedding. We were going to take Tori to the Park in Molina."

"Ah," Nico nodded. "The Parco delle Cascate di Molina?"

Carlos nodded. "We went there last time."

"It's the perfect day for it. Enjoy yourselves."

"Nico..." Carlos appeared to hesitate. "We don't want to mess up your plans or anything but I want to run something by you first. Ava has plans for Rona to stay here until you guys return from your honeymoon."

Nico nodded. That had been his understanding. He glanced at his watch quickly, conscious that Ava would be waiting for him at the salon. "Ava mentioned something to that effect. Why, is there a problem?"

"Tori turns a year old on the thirtieth of August and we'd

like to return home. You and Ava aren't going to be here, I'm not sure how long Elsa is planning on staying. Rona and I don't really know anyone in Verona and as nice as it is to be here, we want to get back home and celebrate with my family and our friends."

"I completely understand. I don't think Ava will mind." But he knew she would worry, and he didn't want her to stress about the business or anything else, and especially not this close to the wedding.

"Maybe not, but we don't want to leave her at the last minute so that she'll worry about the business either. Problem is, we only decided a few days ago. I mean, before that, Rona and I..." Carlos looked away. "Things weren't so great back then, but now we want to mend things. Do you think it would be okay to leave the business unattended? Rona is worried that Ava will be logging in to check things every hour. I know that's not what you'd want."

"Don't worry about it. Ava can put plans into place. She has Kim and they already have the gardener's granddaughter, Lizzi, helping out."

Carlos nodded. "I wanted to check with you first."

"I'm sure things will be fine," Nico assured him. "It's good that you and Rona are working things out. Tori's going to be one already?" He wasn't sure whether Ava would remember with everything else that was going on.

"Seems like only yesterday that she was born." Carlos smiled from ear to ear. "It was a surreal moment and one I'll never forget."

Nico wondered how it would be for him, when their time came.

"Hey, no bachelor party, buddy?" Carlos asked.

Nico shook his head. "It's been the last thing on my mind. I don't think it's even occurred to Ava to do anything."

"Rona asked her but didn't want to push it. Ava said her idea of a good night was an early night in."

Nico laughed. "That is her idea of a good night."

"I'll let you go. I can see that you're eager to get away," said Carlos. "Let me know if you need anything."

As he started to walk away, Nico remembered that he *did* need something, and the closest person he could think of for being his best man was Carlos. He hesitated, knowing it sounded desperate, but other than Carlos there was nobody else he would rather have.

"There *is* something," Nico cleared his throat, not wanting to get all sentimental, but wanting to tell the truth. "My best man called to say he wouldn't be able to make it. I know this sounds like a desperate last attempt, but Carlos, you're the only one I would even *want* to consider having as my best man." He had cousins, lots of them and they were all coming for the wedding. He felt sure that any one of them would be honored to stand in as his best man but Nico didn't feel that kinship with them. Carlos watched him, lines appearing on his brow as he waited for Nico's words.

"I'd be honored if you would be my best man. And I understand if it sounds like a cop-out, as if I'm asking you because there is no-one else. I have cousins who would happily step in but I'd be honored, Carlos, if you would be."

"You sure, buddy?" Carlos asked.

"Completely."

A huge grin spread across Carlos's face as he considered the proposal. "Then I'd be honored, Nico. Sure. Sure, I would."

Nico held out his hand, but Carlos ignored it and gave him one of his legendary tight bear hugs instead.

CHAPTER FOUR

He rushed into the cool, white salon and found Ava waiting for him. She looked radiant, but then again, he thought: she always did.

She looked up from her magazine and her face lit up the moment she saw him. He hoped it would always be like that. "Sorry," he said, rushing to her side. "I got held up."

"Anything urgent?" she asked, as he kissed her on the lips.

"It's always urgent. But I do have a best man now."

She stared at him expectantly.

"Carlos."

"Carlos?"

"I couldn't think of anyone I would rather have," he explained. "How was your massage?"

"Heavenly. Don't I seem calmer to you?"

"You're always calm, and that's one of the things I love about you."

"I had a facial too." She moved her face from side to side with exaggeration. "You didn't notice my firmer, plumped up, iridescent skin?" He grabbed her hand, helping her to get up.

"You always look great to me. Though you look a little shiny right now." He observed, peering closer towards her.

"I believe it's called 'dewy'. See my tight pores?" She moved closer to him and he searched her face as though looking for forensic clues.

"Were they ever loose?" He traced his finger delicately over her cheek. She laughed as he squeezed her hand. "I think I look the same, too," she whispered, "but it feels cleaner. Maybe that's something you men don't understand. Maybe..." she turned to him wide-eyed with wonder. "We can have a couple of treatments together on our honeymoon. This secret place we're going to has a spa, I assume?"

Before he could answer her, an assistant rushed up to Ava with a bag in her hand. "You almost forgot the treatments you bought, Ava. I could give you a quick rundown of how to use them, if you have time. It's important to understand the five-step cleansing ritual." Ava gave him an apologetic smile as the young woman led her to the counter. He looked around the clinical white interior of the beauty salon while he waited, and then he felt a small pinch on his waist and turned around.

"Nico." Silvia stood almost in his face and the shock of her platinum blond curls, slightly longer than when he'd last seen her, dazzled his vision.

"Silvia." He forced the word out of his mouth.

"What a surprise to see you here," she stated. He was too shocked to reply.

"Pre-wedding nerves?" she asked.

"No," he replied calmly. "What, apart from wishful thinking, would make you say that?"

She ignored the question and turned to look at Ava. "I see she came in for a relaxing pregnancy massage. Perhaps, *she* has pre-wedding nerves. It can't be easy for her—especially after getting dumped the first time around. She's probably worried as to what might go wrong this time."

How she could say this to him with that plastic smile stretched across her lips? *What had he ever seen in her?*

"My fiancé is looking forward to the wedding as much as I am," Nico growled and slid his hands into his trouser pockets. "How is Alessa?"

"Growing older gracefully."

"She's five," said Nico tightly, crinkling his nose.

"I'm hoping to send her to a boarding school in Switzerland," Silvia announced as she examined her fingernails. Nico stared at her as if her dress had just fallen off. "She's a *child*. Why would you do such a thing?"

How could *anyone* do such a thing?

"The exclusive boarding schools there have very long waiting lists. She won't be starting yet."

"You're crazy." Nico felt sorry for the little girl he'd come to love as his own. But maybe getting away from Silvia would not be such a bad thing.

"You were crazy in love with me once." Silvia slid her hand slowly along his shoulder, making him recoil.

"I was in a dark place then," he told her, remembering that time, and removing Silvia's hand. His beloved mother had just died.

"If you ever change your mind..." she drawled. In the next moment he felt a familiar hand, warm and soft, slip around his waist.

"Silvia," said Ava, as though it was the answer to a quiz. "We meet again. Didn't your treatment end when I came in?"

"I remembered I had to buy an anti-aging serum," Silvia replied stiffly.

"I hear it's better to start using them as soon as possible.

You might already be too late." Nico sniped. Beside him, he heard Ava stifle a gasp.

"Good luck at the wedding. You'll both need it." Silvia sneered.

"Will we see you there?" Ava asked.

Silvia shook her head. "I'm going to Monaco for a few days."

"Then we're sure to have a great day," Nico retorted, slipping his hand into Ava's. "Shall we go?"

She nodded and he began to walk off, murmuring a bored 'Ciao' into thin air. He was disgusted with the woman he'd once been involved with so many years ago. Even now, merely running into her had already put a dampener on his mood.

"Why did you ask her if she'd be at the wedding?" he asked as they stepped outside onto the quiet side road. "I didn't invite her. You must know that I'd never have that witch at my wedding."

"I was being polite."

He turned and was about to walk when Ava pulled at him and refused to move. "What was that about?"

"What?" he cocked his head. A dart of sunshine pierced through the sky like a blade and he lifted his hand to his face to block out the light.

"You being so nasty to Silvia."

"The woman is a viper. She never has anything good to say, even after all this time and knowing that we've both moved on. I thought she might have changed as she got older."

"Maybe she just needs more time," Ava suggested, and moved toward him, placing her hand on his chest. Just by doing that she undid the tension that had built up in his body. "And she needs to accept that you're all mine now." She tilted her head up so that he could kiss her. The scent of fresh apple shampoo floated through his nostrils. He planted a kiss, as soft as velvet, on her lips.

"Thanks for rescuing me," he murmured, feeling better already. Things were piling up on him, and this latest run-in with Silvia had only made him more tense. He didn't want to be reminded of the vultures he'd associated with in his past, and especially not now, as he was trying to unwind and get ready for the wedding.

"She's set her sights higher." They held hands and walked down the street slowly.

"What do you mean?" Nico asked.

"She's dating a local politician, apparently. I heard the beauticians talking when she left. Then while I was waiting for you, I saw a picture of her and her new man in a magazine."

"A politician?" He scoffed at the idea. That woman was hungry for power and fame and one day she'd be in the news for all the wrong reasons. She'd only been a part of his life for a short while and he considered himself very lucky that he'd met his one true soul-mate.

Silvia really seemed to be scraping the barrel. Maybe it would be better for Alessa to be away from her mother. Nico shook his head, unable to understand what drove a parent to send their child away to school.

"According to what I read. I can't remember his name. Armando something. He looked like a silver tongued lizard." Ava made a face. "He looks old enough to be her father."

Nico wasn't surprised. "She was always hungry for power, or prestige, or fame, or something."

"What was she talking to you about?" Ava asked.

"Nothing of any importance. You're right, maybe I shouldn't have been so nasty." He wouldn't have been but

Silvia was such a manipulative and scheming woman. It was a good thing Ava hadn't heard what she'd said to him.

"Do you want to grab lunch?" he asked.

"I actually want to have a nap."

"I'll join you." He was starting to get into a relaxing mood himself.

Ava giggled. "That sounds exciting."

"My thoughts exactly." He was looking forward to it already. They walked down the cobbled street when Ava stopped walking again. "I need to call Kim about something."

"Can't it wait? Or do I have to lock your office and make it out of bounds to you?"

Ava made a grumbling noise. "I'm getting more and more complaints from my third supplier. I'm lucky I have Andrea and Geraldino and they're great, but I'm not so sure about this other company. Their products aren't so great; they break easily and we're getting more returns from them than anyone else."

"You need to stop doing business with them."

"I already did. I severed our agreement a few days ago. I want to check how many customers are still waiting on their products."

"Why? Give them refunds, or suggest an alternative product from someone else."

"That's what I'm doing. I *do* know my business Nico."

"I know you do." Of course she knew what she was doing, and it was one of the things he loved about her. She was independent and strong-minded enough to want to carry on working hard even though she had so much going on. He had to be careful and not tell her to slow down too much—in case she took his advice the wrong way. "Can't you call Kim from home?" That nap sounded tempting the more he thought about it.

"I can't. I have to go through my emails and make a list of things to pass over to Rona tomorrow. And my laptop is at work."

"Darling, can't it wait until tomorrow?"

"I won't be able to relax until I have the things I'm carrying about in my head, down on paper and handed over properly."

This was what he was most afraid of—her inability to let go of all things business related. She was worse than him. It made him wonder what sort of a child they would have; possibly a highly strung high achiever who could never relax. He cleared his throat and considered mentioning to her that Rona and Carlos would be returning to Denver soon after the wedding.

"How badly do you need Rona to look after things while we're away?" He tried to say it as ambiguously as he could but, as he suspected, Ava came to a stop and stared at him. The tug of her hand stopped him too.

"Why?"

"No reason. I was just wondering. I thought you'd trained Lizzi to help out?"

"Rona did. Why?" She stood directly opposite him and peered closely into his eyes. "What are you not telling me, Nico?"

He wasn't going to be able to hide it from her. "Carlos spoke to me earlier. He and Rona are thinking of returning to Denver a week after our wedding. They want to be back in the US for Tori's birthday."

"Tori!" Ava's eyes widened like big moons. "She's going to be one soon. We'll still be away."

"Carlos seems adamant on returning, and Rona feels the same way. They say it will seem odd celebrating her birthday here especially since we won't be around and they have lots of friends and family back home."

Ava frowned. "But what about the store? Who'll look after that while we're—"

He wasn't going to give her the chance of wallowing in worry. "Your store isn't going to fall to pieces if you neglect it for a few weeks."

"Don't be so patronizing."

"I'm not. I'm being honest."

"And if I told you to leave the new hotel, say if your building manager or that Bruno person you keep talking about suddenly disappeared for a few weeks, would you be okay with that?"

Of course he wouldn't.

But she had the ever efficient Kim—for that was how Ava always referred to her—looking after the store and Rona was still working part-time. Bruno abandoning him was completely different and had a bigger impact.

He could see that she was annoyed, and she was starting to look stressed again. "I'm sorry. Look, it doesn't matter. Let them return if that's what they want. Lizzi can help out and you still have Kim and Rona."

Ava made an agreeing sound. "I need to get back to the office," she said in a tight voice. The results of the relaxing massage were beginning to fade fast. But he knew, especially with his cousins and aunts and uncles beginning to arrive, with most of them staying at the Casa Adriana, that she wouldn't find much peace and quiet there either. It almost made him reconsider his suggestion for them to sleep separately on the eve of their wedding day.

"Are you sure you want to go back to the hotel? Most of my family has arrived and they will accost you and ask you a million questions." They'd started arriving this morning, which was one of the reasons Nico had considered taking Ava away for a beauty treatment. They meant well, of course, but she already seemed worried about her online store and Rona's return to Denver, and he didn't want to risk her getting more upset.

Her face crinkled with disappointment. Just as he suspected, she wasn't too keen on the idea any more.

"I've got an idea," he suggested. "I'll drive us back and then I'll get your laptop," he offered. "Then we can go home and you can work from there." He'd also give Bruno a quick call and check to see that things were okay with Gina before he abandoned her altogether.

"Okay," she said, reluctantly.

CHAPTER FIVE

"Eet is spec-tacular," drooled Zanobi, the half-French, half-Italian designer of her wedding dress. When he sucked his breath in sharply, it had the effect of making his thinly painted eyebrows lift upwards.

Ava looked at her reflection in the mirror and had to agree. The cream full length intricate lace and silk wedding dress did look spectacular and suited her dark hair and light eyes. It was fitted around the bodice with cream lace covering the silk fabric. Intricate lace, decorated with a few sequins and pearls, covered her arms just past her elbows, as well as her shoulders and above her bosom giving her the appearance of stylish modesty. Her veil was as silky and as thin as gossamer and she'd given up her childhood dream of having a long, flowing train.

As a six-month pregnant bride she'd opted for a dress that would be more practical, and less the fairytale dress she'd had in mind. With the bodice tight and fitted, the rest of the dress was loose and flowing from her baby bump downwards. The column dress emphasized her height, even though she'd filled out all over, and now had fuller breasts, fuller hips and a huge stomach. The overall effect was one of elegant grandeur and she was secretly pleased she hadn't opted for the free-flowing Grecian dress she'd been drawn to initially. Though it had been comfortable, she'd felt as though she was floating around in a white United Nations tent. She'd put her comfort aside in order to present Nico with an image of her that he would never forget.

And of course Zanobi wouldn't have let her opt for comfort. "Non! Zeez is your wedding day. You must look like an angel—a pregnant angel, oui—but you have height, you have slim arms and a long neck, you only have zee bump." He'd insisted on the dress she now wore.

"It is...it is...it is..." He put his fingers to his lips, kissed them and twiddled them around in that effeminate manner she'd become accustomed to, as if he was flicking germs off them. "Trolley, de-vanely, an-sanly, beyotiful."

Truly, divinely, insanely beautiful, assumed Ava, amused by his choice and pronunciation of words.

"Zeez is perfect." He kissed his fingers again, making that 'mwah' sucking noise and she looked on helplessly at Mia, his dutiful seamstress, who hovered around in the background. "You are getting bigger, no? We only see you a week before?" His light brown brows pinched together. "Baby slow down." He stared at her baby bump and she thought he was going to reach out and stroke her belly; instead he waggled a finger at her stomach. She breathed out a sigh of relief because she didn't like anyone, apart from Nico, touching her stomach.

"I'm growing. I *am* pregnant. It happens," she protested.

"Mia! Mia!" Zanobi's voice pitched to high level and the thin, rake-like girl flitted closer. The way Mia looked at her convinced Ava that she looked like a million dollars.

"We will have to let out a leetle material on zee sides..." Zanobi stood in front of Ava and pinched the material on either side of her bodice, just under her armpits. He bobbed his head around like one of those dancing dogs she'd seen at the back of cars as he scribbled some things down and spurted off to Mia in Italian, and occasionally breaking out into French as well. They 'Si'd' and 'Oui'd' and tsk'd, or rather he did, while Mia merely bobbed her head and agreed to everything, jotting down notes in her tiny notebook as he pinched material, and measured her all over again.

Had she really grown in just a week? She was aware that her body felt squishier, and softer and more loose all over. Nico loved it; he couldn't get enough of her naked— but she missed her taut muscles and her lean build.

Zanobi tutted and tsk-ed, and wiped the back of his brow with his hand.

"We adjust again a lee-tle bit?" His painted brows snaked together.

Ava groaned. "I can't come back here again for another fitting. I get married in two days' time." She wasn't going to allow him to make more adjustments. It didn't feel *that* tight.

He pulled a stern face. "Zen you must not eat anyzink for days," he told Ava, and she wasn't sure that he wasn't being serious. "I can't help it. It's the baby."

Mia gave her a roll of her eyes. "Of course you must eat. It will be fine." Ava sighed. It was all well and good having a fitted bodice that made her look slim and not like a snow beast but it had its disadvantages. If she'd gone for the tent-like Grecian wedding dress that she had considered, if only for comfort, then she wouldn't be having any of these problems.

"Perhaps a lee-tle?" Zanobi asked, twisting his face in ways that would have filled Jim Carrey with envy.

"It's fine like this," Ava countered. Heck, it was only two days away. "I'm changing into another dress for the evening. It will be fine. I can survive in this for a few hours."

"Non adjoostments?" Zanobi winced, screwing his face up tightly as though the very idea pained him. He pinched the material between his fingers again.

"No. This is fine. Really." She didn't want to come back—she had so many things to do tomorrow, and she had yet to pack for the honeymoon. Not only that but Nico had told her she'd be staying in the room at the top of the Casa Adriana. When he told her it was because of tradition—because the bride and groom shouldn't see one another the night before the wedding—she'd been taken aback. Until she found out that he had asked a domestic company to come in and give their home a good clean. Especially now that the refurbishment to their bedroom and the nursery was complete. They had been sleeping on another floor in the house while the renovations had been going on and Nico hadn't let her take a look as the work was being done. She knew he now wanted to surprise her when they went home for the first time after they were married.

"Eef you insist." Zanobi made a sulky face. Ava found his mild tantrums a little off-putting at times, but there was no denying the fact that he had designed her an exquisite dress that made her look and feel like a million dollars. "Now we will see your party dress."

"I'll try it on," she said, wearily, "but first I must go to the ladies room, once I've taken this off."

CHAPTER SIX

"I wish you'd let me know sooner." Ava was mildly irritated. Her feet were beginning to swell up and she already felt over exhausted.

The hotel was starting to fill up with so many of Nico's extended family, and she hadn't been able to spend much time with her own family; not even Uncle Hugo and Aunty Camile who had arrived earlier.

She was anxious to get back to the room where she was staying tonight without being stopped by yet another one of Nico's relatives and being asked how she and Nico had met and what she did for a living, and how her pregnancy was going and what was her dress like or of being told how lucky she was to have gotten her hands on someone as handsome and as wealthy and as wonderful as Nico.

The rehearsal dinner, which ended up being a huge affair because so many of Nico's family had turned up, was held in the marquee that had been erected in the gardens. Extra staff had been drafted in to help out at the Casa Adriana tonight.

She was thankful that it was all over, but where was Rona? She'd been wanting to speak to that sister of hers all evening, but she'd been more slippery than an eel. Finally, she found her trying to make her getaway from one of Nico's elderly aunts. She grabbed Rona's hand as Carlos and Elsa walked back towards the cars with Tori asleep in a stroller.

"When were you going to tell me you were leaving?" Ava asked.

"Oh, that," Rona replied, looking guilty.

"Yes, that."

"I'm sorry, I should have come and spoken to you directly, but you've hardly been around, and I've been taking half days."

"You could have let me know."

"Carlos and I didn't work things out until very recently. It was a spur of the moment decision but we'd like to celebrate Tori's birthday at home."

Ava waited patiently. She'd been worrying about this all day and had compiled a list of everything that she needed to pass onto Lizzi. Luckily she'd managed to speak to Lizzi and the girl was able to come in and keep an eye on her store while she was on honeymoon.

"Why are you worrying about it? Shouldn't you go and get some rest so that you wake up nice and happy on your wedding day?" Irritation crept into Rona's voice. "It's unfair to Carlos if I'm working the whole time, or even half days. And I have to think of Tori as well. Not everything is always about you."

"I know it's not," said Ava quickly. "I'm sorry. I didn't mean it to sound like that." Sometimes, lately it seemed that she and her sister were swapping roles. She's always strived to put others before her, and here she was getting all uptight because she was so worried about her business. She ought to have been happier that Rona and Carlos had patched things up. "I obviously need to get away and I so badly want this all over with. Everything's getting on top of me."

Rona put her arm around her shoulder. "It's only natural. I'm sorry—I should have told you the moment Carlos and I decided. I went over everything with Lizzi; your business is in safe hands."

"You did?" asked Ava weakly.

"I did. Everything. The A-Z of the daily tasks that need to be done in order for your store to continue to run smoothly. We're here for about a week after the wedding but if it's okay with you I'd like to take that time off and show Carlos the sights around here. Maybe even visit Venice."

Ava's heart melted. "You should. Show him as much as you want. Don't even do the half days, Rona. Have a good time."

"When we get back to Denver, and after Tori's birthday, I'll be working two days a week for you. Or maybe four half days. If that's okay?"

"What about your college job?" She knew Rona's year off for her maternity leave was almost up and her sister hadn't yet decided what she was going to do. Rona's decision would have an impact on her.

"I still haven't made up my mind."

"Don't you think you need to?"

"Don't rush me," Rona said. "Now go and get some sleep. I'll be over tomorrow morning with Uncle Hugo. Nico said the car would be here by ten."

Ava looked over to where Carlos was standing. "Don't be late."

"I won't." Rona kissed her cheek and hugged her tightly before she rushed off. She'd been left alone for no more than a few seconds before Nico came up behind her.

"Come on." He grabbed her arm gently. "I want to make

sure you're properly settled into the room upstairs and that you have everything you need for tomorrow."

"Do we *have* to do this?" Ava felt a little anxious and unsettled and didn't want to be alone on the eve of her wedding. "It's a tradition. You don't really believe in it, do you, Nico?"

"I'd like to follow this one."

They maneuvered their way around the lobby which was occupied by many of Nico's family members. The sofas had been commandeered by a group of his aunts who seemed to be permanently glued to them while other relatives took residence in the conservatory.

Her own uncle and aunt were staying in a pensione around the corner from where Elsa was staying. Ava was secretly pleased to see Uncle Hugo and his wife turn up. Not only because Uncle Hugo was Elsa's only sibling, but because they didn't see their uncle often enough. And he'd come to give her away on her wedding day.

When they at last walked into the room, Ava was reminded of the time not so many months ago, when she'd stayed here before. "Are you leaving already?" She started to get anxious when Nico set her luggage down. She'd hoped he'd stay a while. Actually, she hoped he would never leave.

"I'm going back to see some of my uncles. And besides," he answered the door the moment there was a knock. "There's someone here to see you." He smiled as Elsa walked in.

"Mom? What are *you* doing here?" Ava was surprised to see Elsa again, thinking she'd returned to her pensione.

"Hugo and Camile are sitting downstairs getting to know Nico's family. I wanted to see how you were."

"I'll be back." Nico kissed her on the lips before he left.

"How are you feeling, Mom?" Ava sat down on the bed

and removed her shoes. Her ankles were all puffy and swollen again.

"It's the eve of your wedding day, honey, and you're worrying about *me*? Typical."

"I want to make sure you're going to be alright."

"Of course I'm going to be alright. And I'll be even better if I know you're not worrying about me. Time to stop worrying, Ava. Time to think about yourself, for once. I know you put Nico and your baby first, but you have to make sure you're not at the bottom of the list."

"It's easier said than done, Mom."

"I know, honey. I know." Elsa sat on the side of the bed as Ava edged over to the middle to make more room. "It was like that for me when your father died." Ava looked at her mother's heavily lined face and noted the way Elsa's face always seemed softer whenever she spoke about her husband.

"That was harder, Mom. Much harder," said Ava gently. "You were alone and you worked hard to keep it all together. You didn't have much help either, did you?"

"I had some help. Uncle Hugo and my parents weren't close by but they would make an effort to come and see us more after your father passed away. But in the end, it was only the three of us. The three musketeers, you, me and Rona and we had to carry on."

"You worked real hard for us and I bet you were always at the bottom of the list."

"I wanted to make it up to you girls. My heart broke each time I looked at you. You were so young, you and Rona and I was fighting to keep it all together. Your father...he was such a big influence, such a warm and lovable person, he spread light and happiness wherever he went. When he left us, the light was extinguished and it left me in a dark place. I know you girls were hurting, but I never wanted you to go to that dark place where I was. I had to do my best to keep it all together."

"You did do your best, Mom." She reached out and leaned in towards her mom. "You more than kept it together and our family, too."

"But it took a toll. I got ill. Friends rallied around to help me but I couldn't expect them to neglect their own families."

"What about Vernon? Was it Uncle Vernon?" She suddenly remembered. "He was around a lot wasn't he?"

"Yes."

"How come?" It had been a while since she'd thought about that time. "Was he your friend?" Ava asked, frowning as she recalled that he was over so much.

"He was your father's friend first. He was a lovely man," her mother answered, adjusting the collar of Ava's dress. She smoothed it down, just as she'd often done when they were children. "The point of this isn't to get you and me feeling sad again. It's to tell you that in wanting to do your best to care for others, you run the risk of running yourself to the ground. And you can't. You mustn't. They say men are the breadwinners, or at least they did in my day, but it's the women who are the backbone of the family. If you fall ill, your children will suffer. Nico will suffer. It's important to take care of yourself so that you can take care of others. It's not selfish, it's not even that we're the weaker sex—because we're not the weaker sex, men often like to think we are—it's quite the opposite. We have great power, and we must use it carefully, especially when it comes to bringing up our children, and creating a tight knit family unit. If a woman leaves or becomes ill, the unit falls apart quicker."

"I'm feeling fine so far, but I'm sure the time will come when I'll be forced to slow down." Her pregnancy had been fine for the most part, except for the recent headaches she'd been suffering from and the swollen ankles. She put it down to the flurry of activity in recent weeks and now the worry over leaving her business. And she was still concerned about Nico—that he overworked himself, trying to keep himself so insanely busy so that he wouldn't have time to dwell on the father he'd lost. "I'm worried about Nico, he's trying to be strong for me, for us, but he's drowning underneath all that work."

"You have to look after him, and I know you do and he does the same for you. That's what marriage is all about but remember that there will be good times and bad times. It won't always be plain sailing. A good marriage is about riding out the bad times, not just enjoying the good times."

"I know Mom. And I know I don't need to say it, but what you did, bringing up the two of us, when it must have been so difficult for you," she stared at her mom and her eyes filled with tears.

"No tears, Ava." Elsa wiped them away gently with her fingers.

"If I'm half the mother you were, I'll be happy." She found the tears falling, fast and furious, and didn't know where the well of emotions had come from.

"Ava, Ava." Elsa looked visibly alarmed before leaning in and hugging Ava to her chest. "Shhhh."

"I'm sorry. I don't know what it is. Lately I'm all over the place. I didn't even want Nico to leave tonight. I feel...scared, and I have no reason to."

Elsa stroked her hair and listened.

"I'm scared that I'll mess up."

"You're allowed to mess up."

"But what if I mess up bad?"

"What if you do? Go ahead and mess up bad. If you're lucky you'll learn from it."

"You won't even be around so that I can come over and see you."

"I'm going to make a trip here every so often and I'll stay for a few months each time I come. I promise. But you won't need me for bringing up your baby. You're going to do fine. Do you know why? Because you won't wait around for me to help you, you'll get on with it. Rona came to rely on me a little too much than was good for her. If I hadn't been so easily accessible, she'd have had to learn to cope. And of course, she had Carlos."

"Poor Carlos," said Ava, fondly.

"Even his long hours at the restaurant didn't excuse him from baby chores when he got back home," Elsa said, with a smile. "And that's how it should be, too. Because being home all day with a baby isn't easy, either. Don't worry. You'll be a pro at this without realizing the exact moment you became one."

"So make one thing easier for me, Mom," implored Ava, shifting her head back so that she could watch her mother's face. "Make me not worry about you and make sure you take your meds on time, and eat well and have plenty of exercise."

"I'll miss your constant reminders, but I know you'll call me daily to remind me." Her mother looked away. "I never thought that when you decided to go on that trip to Italy, the supposed honeymoon without Connor, that you would never come back home again." Ava sensed a tightness in her mother's voice.

"I came back a few times," recalled Ava, remembering how she'd fled Italy, without telling Nico that she was pregnant with his child.

"Your heart belongs here, with Nico. *This* is your home now."

Ava nodded. This was home, and she was going to have to

get used to it. "You have to promise me that you'll come more often, Mom."

"You can bet I will. I have to make sure that gardener doesn't undo all of Edmondo's good work."

"Salvatore is a good gardener, Mom. He knows what he's doing."

Elsa snorted disapproval.

"I think he knows best, Mom." Elsa was a homemaker, a wonderful cook, a good friend but when it came to gardening, she wasn't green fingered at all.

"We'll see about that," said Elsa. "Do you need anything from me? Are you all set for tomorrow?"

Ava nodded. As set as she was ever going to be. It still felt odd sleeping alone tonight and she wished she could have spent the night with Nico. "Make sure that Uncle Hugo is here in time for the car at ten."

"In that case, I'll get going and spend some time with Nico's family. They're a lovely bunch, aren't they?" They embraced, and held each other tightly, understanding already that a shift had taken place, that this was a moment that would be savored and remembered now, and committed to memory forever.

"My daughter's getting married tomorrow," whispered Elsa softly, her words tied up in a ribbon of pride.

CHAPTER SEVEN

Nico knocked on her door and waited as his heart threatened to rattle inside his chest. It didn't make sense because he would be marrying his soulmate tomorrow and yet he felt strangely nervous all the same.

When Ava opened the door they fell into each other's arms. The way she clung to him, tight, and for a long time, made him think that he wasn't the only one feeling anxious.

He'd been almost tempted to go back on his idea of them both spending the night apart. It wasn't so much that he believed in the tradition, but he'd asked someone to come and give the place a final clean from top to bottom. He also didn't want to risk Ava accidentally seeing anything: not the nursery or the new bedroom—which he'd had refurbished completely.

"I'm nervous," she whispered, running her hands slowly over his face. "I am loving this dangerously sexy look." He hadn't shaved for a few days.

"I'm excited."

"Maybe I'm excited too," she confessed. "My stomach keeps doing cartwheels."

He placed his hand over her stomach and felt their baby

kick. "She's excited." He took her hand and walked over to the window where they stood silently, arms entwined around one another as they stared out into the gardens below.

"Is that Uncle Hugo with your uncles?" A group of elderly men stood around with glasses in their hands.

"It is. I've just left them—they're having a good time, drinking whisky and cracking jokes."

"Where's Aunty Camile?"

"Sitting in the pergola with my aunts and your mom." He hugged her close to him, knowing that she would be here alone tonight and that he wouldn't be able to sleep without her warm body to curl up against.

"We call it a gazebo."

"You can call it what you want," murmured Nico, not wanting to let go of her.

"I'm thinking of taking Italian language lessons."

"Or I could just speak nothing but Italian to you and you'd soon pick it up."

"That would drive me insane," she giggled. "You jabbering away and me not having a clue what you were talking about."

"Does this mean we'll be celebrating Thanksgiving from now on?"

"Not this year, but from next year onwards, most definitely." They were quiet, thinking over the future and what it held.

"What if I come back home with you now?" she suggested, turning to look at him with those large liquid eyes of hers that had held him captivated ever since she'd come barreling into his life that day when she'd bumped into him at the airport. He turned to face her and couldn't help but graze her earlobe with his lips. She smelled good—of honeysuckle and lavender—and he was tempted to take her back with him but he held fast in his resolve. "As much as it kills me to be apart from you tonight, know that tomorrow we'll be together, forever."

She didn't look convinced. "I can't get you to change your mind, can I?" Not waiting for him to answer. "I need a good night's sleep tonight anyway."

"You and me both, because we're *not* sleeping tomorrow night," he told her, feeling the stirrings in his loins already. He rubbed his hand over the roughness of his face. Tomorrow he'd be spruced up and clean-shaved and ready for his bride.

"Here," he said, handing her the Flamentagostini bracelet he'd given her in Venice. "I thought you might want to wear this tomorrow."

"Where did you find it?" she gasped in surprise. Though she would never own up to it, he had a feeling she'd misplaced it.

"In one of the shoe boxes in my cupboard."

"So that's where it—" She stopped and his smile widened.

"Did you lose it, darling?"

"I put it away in a really safe place. We were rushing to leave the house one weekend and the cleaners were coming ... so I hid it."

"We have a safe, Ava."

"I know that now. But, thank you." She held the bracelet in her hands as though it was silk, then ran her fingers over it gently. "I love this, I wanted to wear this tomorrow and I've been looking for it for weeks." She clasped it to her chest. "It will always remind me of the first time we got together." She sounded choked up and he felt his heart dip and hurtle towards his feet.

"I love you, now and forever." He leaned in and kissed her deeply, then held onto her as though it was the last time he'd see her again. They stayed like that for a while, and when he tried to pull apart, she wouldn't let him. So he kissed her again, this time sinking into a deeper kiss, the taste and the feel of her causing little shivers of delight to spring up all over his body. They finally came up for air and he knew he would have to leave otherwise one thing would lead to another and he wanted to save himself for tomorrow night, when she walked back into their home as his wife.

"Zanobi is coming here at eight, with the dress and a hair stylist and a makeup person," he announced.

"I wish I hadn't agreed to all of that." Ava looked pensive.

"I know you don't want those people. But, unfortunately, he sees this as an opportunity to have his dress advertised in the papers." Her horrified expression told him she hadn't even considered that possibility. Nico had deliberately not mentioned the paparazzi who were interested in getting photos of the couple. It wasn't major, international press interest but all the same, he knew she hated any invasion into her private life.

"There are going to be photographers there?"

"They'll see you walking into the church and coming back out of it. I can't stop them. They'll be there." His contacts in Montagnano had already told him that there had been a few paparazzi floating around there this evening.

She closed her eyes and the color drained from her face. "Don't worry." He rushed to reassure her, not wanting to leave her with the idea of evil, faceless photographers looming everywhere. "Our reception will be private." He'd arranged for a large open area near a converted barn overlooking fields. It was large and private, and owned by one of their friends and it would be perfect for the wedding reception and the all-night party. "It will be alright. I'll see to it that you are always going to be alright." He put his arms around her.

"I know," she said. "You'll be with me. So it *will* be alright."

He kissed her again just as he left the door, and the last impression he had was of her holding the bracelet to her chest and trying to put on a brave face.

CHAPTER EIGHT

"I s a leetle tight?" Zanobi warbled his disapproval, as he held his chin in his hands. He shook his head, then his narrowed eyes flitted up to meet her gaze. He winced. "But I think you will be okay. You have the party dress for later, oui?"

Ava looked at herself in the full length mirror. It felt a little tight around the side of the bodice but it wasn't *too* tight. She could manage for the few hours that she'd be wearing it. "It's fine." She didn't want to leave him feeling as deflated as he looked. "Zanobi, don't worry."

Thank goodness she'd had the sense to have another dress made for her reception—though she was tempted to change into it straight after the ceremony. As she looked at her reflection in the mirror, Ava couldn't help but smile. It was beautiful. She looked beautiful. And Nico would love it.

Zanobi clapped his hands together and his minions scurried into view, as he sang out orders for them to finish doing her make-up and hair.

At a quarter to ten, Ava stepped carefully down the stairs of the Casa Adriana to find Rona and Uncle Hugo standing around in the deserted lobby waiting for her. They didn't see her at first, but then Uncle Hugo looked up, soft spoken and shy, he shook his head and his eyes lit up as Ava walked down the stairs regally. When she walked up to him, he shook his head, a huge smile on his lips. "My, Ava. You look so beautiful. Your father would have been so proud."

Beside him, Rona stood uncharacteristically speechless. Ava felt her sister's gaze pass over her, taking in her face, her hair, her dress, and her bracelet. Rona's eyes welled up. "You look, you look ..." She fanned her chest and her glossy pink lips, lined to perfection, almost crumbled. "Beautiful, Ava. So beautiful."

"Zeez is what I like to see, the family in tears," exclaimed Zanobi, as he air-kissed her. "I 'ave to leave. But my dear, I wish you zee best of luck and zee best of 'appiness for you and Nico."

"Thank you, Zanobi."

"You look like a Hollywood princess." His words rattled in the air as he flounced out with his assistants on either side of him. Ava pulled a face. She didn't want to look like a Hollywood princess—whatever Hollywood princesses looked like—and she was certain that she didn't. She wanted to look like herself, and thankfully, the makeup artist had managed to make her look perfectly glowing and healthy. And even though the man had slathered plenty of goo onto her face, looking in the mirror Ava didn't feel she looked like a painted rag-doll. Her hair was worn loose but pinned back at the sides, high at the top, backcombed to give it lift, and curled into ringlets that tumbled around her back and shoulders.

"Here." Rona handed her the bridal bouquet as she dabbed the corners of her eyes with a tissue.

"What's the matter with you?" Ava was surprised to see Rona's face crinkling. She herself felt calm this morning.

"It's so … emotional." Rona whispered.

"Nervous?" Uncle Hugo asked her.

"No, Uncle Hugo." Ava smiled at him. "I'm not nervous at all. I can't wait to walk down that aisle." They waited for the wedding car to turn up and Ava looked around and smiled at the sparse hotel staff who kept flitting in and out, stealing glances at her and occasionally feeling brave enough to come out and wish her well. A few asked if they could take a photo of her and Ava didn't want to refuse. They seemed so excited and happy for her big day.

"It's ten past ten." Rona paced around, looking at her watch.

"Shouldn't the car have been here?" Uncle Hugo looked nervous. Ava fingered her bracelet, fidgeting around with the feel of the metal and the beads. She'd worn no watch today, no earrings, no tiara or necklace. Just the bracelet. "It'll be here any moment," she said confidently.

Uncle Hugo looked concerned. "How long does it take to get to the church?"

"Around half an hour."

"He'd better get here soon otherwise you're going to be more than fashionably late for your own wedding," Rona added.

But twenty minutes later, they were still waiting for the wedding car.

"Call Nico," urged Ava. She'd left her own cell phone upstairs. Today was a day she planned to enjoy fully without the need to connect to the rest of the world; no internet, no cell phone, no laptop. Her heart fluttered wildly and the baby started to dance around in her belly. She tried to listen in on Rona's conversation but the thought of running to the washroom suddenly preyed heavily on her mind.

"It won't be long now," Uncle Hugo assured her, giving her another one of his shy smiles.

I know, she thought to herself, and tried not to think of a visit to the washroom. She'd purposely avoided drinking too much water this morning, or having a big breakfast. The dress was comfortable—but she had to admit she could feel a slight pinch along her sides. If she had to begrudgingly admit it, she should have agreed when Zanobi had suggested letting the bodice out *just a leetle*. She was beginning to feel constrained below her ribs. Still, the dress hung softly over her stomach and hips and she felt free and unburdened for the most part.

Rona rushed towards her. "Carlos says the car was stuck on a narrow road where there'd been a minor accident. The traffic's built up but its slowly moving again. He says the car should be here soon."

Ava heard her words and debated in her mind whether she should go to the washroom now that she had the chance. She decided it would be better to go than to risk the journey to Montagnano with an active baby in her stomach pushing down further on her bladder.

"I need to go to the washroom. Now!" She shoved her bouquet at Uncle Hugo. "I'll need your help," she told Rona as she walked away in her low-heeled wedges. Once inside, Ava started to bend over to lift up the bottom of the dress.

"Shouldn't you unbutton it and pull it down?" asked Rona, staring. "It's going to crease a lot if you roll it up."

"Nah-Uh," Ava shook her head. "Have you seen how many buttons this has?" Zanobi, being the dramatic designer that he was, had opted for a long row of tiny buttons along the back and they had taken forever to do up this morning. When she'd asked why he couldn't put a zipper there instead, he'd looked mortally offended and told her that he believed zippers on wedding dresses should be illegal.

"I'll help you," offered Rona, as they both stood face to face in the tiny cubicle with the door open.

"It's not necessary," began Ava, bending down. The other reason she didn't want to undo the buttons was because she knew that once she undid them she'd get used to the few moments of relief. Undoing the dress completely would give her the kind of relief she usually felt when she undid her bra at the end of the day, which, these days, she took off faster than Nico did his tie as soon as they both reached home.

Right now, she was more desperate than ever for bladder relief.

"I don't think you should bend—"

Criiickkkk. The subtle sound of silk tearing apart filled the silence. "Is that—?" Ava stood upright instantly, dropping the end of the dress she'd been trying to hoist up.

"Was that your dress?" Rona's face looked deathly. Ava felt her heart thrash and was too scared to look. She felt with her fingers instead, and when she touched and felt her skin instead of lace and silk, she knew the damage was bad.

"Oh, no! No! No! No!"

"Ugggh." Rona's gasp sounded worse.

Ava dared to look down, and lifted her arm. A two inch long gash exposed the pale pink fabric of her strapless satin bra as well as her skin. She groaned loudly, sounding like a wounded animal.

"Okay ... we can fix this." Rona leapt into action. She fingered the gap. "It's not as bad as it looks. Okay, okay," she said, breathing fast and looking around.

Ava stood speechless for a few seconds before announcing, "I still have to pee." Priorities first.

"Don't bend over again!" Rona shrieked. "Don't move! Let me."

Ava breathed out slowly. "Need to pee," she said, as

calmly as she could with her heartbeat galloping. Rona bent down and lifted up the dress carefully with both hands. She told Ava to hold the edges while she pulled down her panties. "I can do this because I'm your older sister." Ava was too shocked to argue. "Pee," Rona ordered.

"Can I at least sit down?"

"Don't bend," threatened Rona, as Ava gingerly lifted herself onto the toilet seat. She sighed with huge relief as she emptied her bladder, and was grateful that her sister had looked the other way.

"Tissue," whispered Ava, as Rona then held onto the dress edges and placed the tissue on Ava's lap. "I can pull my panties up myself," insisted Ava.

Slowly, they moved towards the sink and Rona smoothed down the heavily creased silk. "Silk is supposed to have creases. There ..." She frantically ran her hands over the dress. "You can hardly notice."

But Ava didn't believe her. She washed her hands while standing as far from the basin as she could and surveyed the damage. Where her dress had ripped, a couple of sequins and pearls hung off the delicate lace that covered the silk. "Go to Gina's drawer, underneath the computer. You should find some glue in there."

Rona ran out of the washroom, while Ava looked glumly at her ripped dress. Her sister walked back in a few seconds, breathless, with a sewing kit, a tube of glue and a stapling gun. "I found half of Wal-Mart in there," announced Rona and came at her with the stapling gun first.

"You can't *staple* my dress together," gasped Ava, as Rona quickly unbuttoned her from behind. "Take your arm out," she ordered, clearly intending to put things right.

"Great," moaned Ava looking at herself in the mirror as

Rona examined the damage from the inside and picked up the stapling gun.

"You can't staple the seam together!" shrieked Ava.

"We don't have much time—the car is here."

"It won't hold," Ava raised her voice. "The fabric's too delicate." She didn't want to know what Zanobi would have to say about this. Without waiting further, Rona pulled off the twist-off cap on the tube of glue and smeared the inside of the dress with it before Ava could stop her.

"It's..." Rona gaped at the fabric as Ava craned her neck to see what was going on. "It's..." Rona gasped.

"What?"

"It's not sticking ... and it's ... it's melting the fabric ..." Rona's face looked like a tomato. She wiped her hands and picked up the sewing kit.

"I told you!" Ava's heart lurched violently, and she felt nauseous again. "What have you done?"

"I'm going to fix it." Rona tried to sound calm but Ava could still hear the worry in it.

"Stand up, don't move!" Rona commanded.

Uncle Hugo knocked on the door. "Girls, the car's here. We're running *very* late."

"Five minutes, Uncle Hugo!" Rona shouted and set to work. Ava stared at her miserable face and dared not look at the frayed mess that had once been her dress. "It's working," Rona murmured. "It's a bit wet, but," she pulled out some toilet paper and quickly dabbed the soggy patch. "But ... I ... think ... it will ...hold." She continued sewing in the painful silence that fell for a few moments. Ava stared miserably at her reflection in the mirror. Disbelief shadowing her carefully made up face as she watched her sister put her dress back together again.

"There, slip your arm back in," Rona ordered. Ava did as

she was told, she'd have done anything at this point. Even when Rona tugged at her bra, she said nothing. "Lift." Rona ordered. "This will keep the sucker in place." Ava closed her eyes and tried to think of tomorrow, when this would all be over and she and Nico would be on their honeymoon. "There," chirped Rona proudly and started to do up her buttons. "All fixed." She stood behind Ava and showed her the seam. "Fixed. See?"

Ava lifted her arm slightly. "It feels...*stuck*." Ava lightly touched the place where the hole had been. She lifted her arm up slowly. "What did you—"

But Rona pushed her out of the door where Uncle Hugo was waiting with a tight face. The car driver rushed out, apologizing profusely as they all bundled quickly into the car.

"Don't worry," Rona told her proudly. "That sucker's not coming undone anytime soon."

CHAPTER NINE

"Calm down, Nico. They'll be here. The bride *is* allowed to be late."

But Nico stormed out impatiently. He was having difficulty being calm today. It was only morning and things had already started to go wrong. He stood at the doors of the fifteenth century church, peering out for signs of the wedding car which should have brought his wife-to-be here almost an hour ago.

In the distance, parasitic photographers bayed around the walls that encased the church grounds. He'd been relieved to see that there weren't hordes of them, but there were still enough of them to ratchet up Ava's tension. Nico bared his teeth as he watched them roaming around the walls like cockroaches.

He sensed that Ava would already be stressed out from the car being so late and had tried calling her but she hadn't answered. When Rona had called, Ava had been busy in the washroom. Unable to hear her voice, or to determine her mood, he was already on tenterhooks. He shook his head, his neck muscles tight. This wasn't the start to his wedding day that he had envisioned.

Footsteps sounded behind him and in the next moment he felt a firm hand on his shoulder. "Relax, Nico and smile, buddy. People get married every day. Stuff like this *always* happens. It wouldn't be a proper wedding if you didn't have any dramas on the day."

"Everyone's here." Nico looked back at the packed church where roughly two hundred people were waiting. He knew most of them, some of them very well, most of them in passing. Many had known his parents and Edmondo had kept his links with Montagnano and its people through the years.

"Most of those people aren't clock watching like you are," Carlos told him. "They're here to enjoy themselves, they haven't even noticed the time. Listen to them; they're catching up with friends and laughing. They're *enjoying* the wait. It's only *you* who's getting worked up."

"The car should have been here by now. Rona said they left half an hour ago." Nico pulled at the collar of his shirt, feeling constricted by his tie. "You've got the ring?"

"I've got the ring and Elsa's got Tori. Breathe, Nico. Try to enjoy the moment—it'll be over before you know it."

It was good advice. *For someone else to give.* His insides were spinning around like Catherine wheels and he knew he would relax only when he saw Ava's face. He'd never been so anxious before; not even when he'd been negotiating to buy the spa hotel. This moment now—the tortured waiting for Ava, moments before he married her, made it hard for him to stand still. His hands felt clammy as he held his breath, waiting for the first glimpse of her.

If *he* was feeling like this, how was *she* feeling? Thinking of her calmed him, and when Carlos announced that the car was in sight, Nico let out an involuntary gasp and straightened his cravat before smoothing back his hair.

Flashes of light ricocheted off the glistening car windows as the Fiat Balilla, a vintage car reminiscent of the 1930s and oozing pure Italian charm, swept majestically along the long path, cruising slowly down the driveway towards the church courtyard. His heart thundered, and he was desperate to see her.

"Time to get to the front," Carlos told him. But Nico wanted to stop and stare; wanted to see what she looked like, wanted to treasure the first glimpse of her in her wedding dress.

"You can't stand here, Nico. At the front, buddy. You can stare all you like later." Slowly, he walked away, having one final look over his shoulder where he saw the driver get out and walk over to one of the passenger doors. Nico looked away and walked to the front with Carlos beside him.

He smiled at the congregation as they turned and looked at him, their happy faces and beaming smiles illuminating his walk to the altar. Pure love from the faces of all who had gathered showered him as he slowly made his way to the front. He saw them all, Elsa, and little Tori, Ava's aunt, his own aunts and uncles and cousins, and Gina, too.

But no Edmondo.

Nico swallowed as a lump threatened to settle in his throat, and focused his attention to the front, where the priest waited with a tight face. Slowly, the priest smiled. It was the smile of a relieved man, and Nico returned it.

They stood quietly at the front, waiting patiently as the wedding march played. And then a hush descended for a few seconds before the bridal march started. He was momentarily paralyzed as the hairs on the back of his neck stood up. His skin tingled, and his stomach felt completely empty.

She was coming.

It was hard not to turn around and stare, hard not to imagine her walking slowly towards him, hard for him not to see her face, bright-eyed and anxious but happy. Hard not to question why it was taking forever for her to get to him while his heart was ready to shoot up out of his throat and mouth; it was beating so wildly he was afraid that he'd barely be able to contain it.

When she finally came and stood alongside him, he turned to her and his heart almost exploded. She was a vision in cream lace and silk, with the brightly colored bridal bouquet that he'd had delivered to the hotel this morning.

She was smiling, and his eyes moistened as he stared at the curve of her lips as they spread into a gentle, shy smile. Their gazes locked and her eyes were so soothing, so hypnotic that he instantly found himself calming. And he began to breathe easy again.

For in that moment, it was him and her, and everything and everyone else in the church was forgotten.

CHAPTER TEN

Less than an hour later, Nico walked out proudly with his wife on his arm.

Rice showered upon them as they looked around at the outpouring of goodwill from their assembled guests.

Carlos had been right. The ceremony had been over before he'd had time to enjoy it. As they left the congregation behind them and stood near the doors of the church, Nico wanted to share a private moment alone with Ava before they were hounded by everyone.

"Congratulations, Mrs. Cazale," he whispered, his lips close to her ear. To his surprise she turned her face and kissed him. Sparks flashed not only in his stomach, but in the distance, like darts of lightning in the sky. They both turned and stared straight into the direction of the photographers who snapped away with their tele-photo lens cameras.

Ava smiled at them, pure joy radiating from her as she waved to them, much to his surprise. He wanted this moment to freeze forever, the vision of her in cream lace and silk. An image he would take to the grave with him. How proud

Edmondo would have been. He knew just how much his father had adored Ava.

"Darling, you don't have to do that." Nico gave the photographers a look that showed his displeasure. They were the bane of this life and he had no time for these rabid people, for he knew how quickly they could turn. "They're not your friends."

"But I feel so happy," she replied, smiling at him. He could see it clearly. She wore a glow, as if happiness itself was painted on her face.

"Seeing you in your wedding dress knocked the air right out of my lungs." Ava's eyes widened with surprise. "Seriously, Ava. You were too beautiful for words."

"You looked handsome, too. We make an okay couple, don't you?"

He nodded, and was almost about to make a quip about the photographers but held it in check. "I was so worried, about you, the car, the delay, and the photographers."

"It wasn't so bad." She moved closer to him. They pressed their faces close together, noses touching, and sharing a tender moment that was soon interrupted by another flash of light from the distance. "We're giving them too many good pictures. Don't be surprised to see yourself on the covers of the papers or magazines tomorrow morning."

"Today, I don't care what they do." She gazed up at him with adoration and he could do nothing but stare back at her with love. He was filled with happiness now that the ceremony was over and that things were going well despite the earlier car troubles.

Pressing his hand on her stomach, he asked, "Did our baby behave?"

"Our baby was fine," she replied, happily.

"I'm sorry about the car."

"The car was the least of my worries."

"Oh?" He bowed his head down, waiting to hear her words but their solitary moment was soon punctured by the wedding guests as they poured out of the church towards them. "Did you know that I'm supposed to tear your veil?"

"Tear my veil?" Ava looked horrified.

"For good luck."

"Please don't. I don't think this dress can take much more damage."

His ears perked up in alarm. "More damage?" But before she could answer him, he heard the drone of voices behind them as people began to leave their pews. "We should go out," Nico advised, otherwise he feared being surrounded by them in such an enclosed space. He looked outside and surveyed the cameramen, ready to snap at them again. Once out there, it was fine to be surrounded by everyone, at least it would shield them from the paparazzi.

He took her hand, gripping it firmly as he led Ava out. They'd only started to move in the direction of the doors when the lights blinded them. He wondered whether he should have hired a security firm for today. He'd decided not to but he'd clearly underestimated the level of interest in their wedding.

Soon, family and friends surrounded them and provided protection and they were momentarily lost to one another as they accepted everyone's good wishes. One of the church attendants brought out a cage containing a pair of doves. "We release them," Nico told her. "It's supposed to signify love and happiness. Are you ready?"

Ava pulled open the door to the cage and the doves flew into the air. Their guests cheered and cries of "Auguri!" filled the air.

In time and slowly, the crowd began to disperse as guests

began to make their way, he presumed to the wedding reception.

Nico placed a hand on the small of her back. "We should make a move. We have a wedding reception to attend."

"But I need to get changed," she said, as he began to walk with her towards the waiting wedding car.

"So soon?"

"I have a dress for the reception."

He remembered, she'd wanted something more comfortable to slip into for later. But the more he looked at her, the more he realized he wanted to treasure her in her wedding dress for as long as possible. "Could you maybe wear the wedding dress for the first dance and the cake cutting? I'll never see you in it again."

She broke out into another smile. "For you, anything," she whispered, running her hand down one side of her dress. He'd noticed her do that a few times. "I love the lace, and this," he said, letting his fingers graze the bodice of her dress.

"Hmmm," she said when someone tapped him on the shoulder.

"Nico." The voice was familiar. Whenever Corso Pelosa spoke to him, Nico was immediately reminded of his father. "Auguri!" The old gentleman congratulated the happy couple.

"It's wonderful to see you, Corso." Nico shook the old man's hand. His father and this man had been friends a long time before Edmondo had appointed Pelosa to become his lawyer.

"I wish you both the very best of luck for the future. It was a beautiful ceremony."

"Thank you," said Ava, smiling up at him. "You're coming to the reception, aren't you?"

"I certainly am. Where is my daughter?" The elderly man

peered around. "Gianna wanted to congratulate you both. Ah. There she is." He pointed over to the corner. Nico looked over and saw Gianna. He knew Pelosa's daughter well enough and recalled attending her wedding many years ago. But he couldn't as easily recall Gianna's husband, even as he stared at the two men she was with.

"Is that—?" Nico began, curiously.

"Her fiancé."

"I could have sworn I attended her wedding."

"Her *new* fiancé." Corso Pelosa exhaled a sigh.

"Really?" Ava stared over, intrigued. One of the men looked over in their direction as the other couple got into their car.

"That's Leo, Gianna's ex-husband. A wonderful man. It is such a shame that they are no longer together..." The old man's words trailed to silence as Leo walked towards them. The closer he came into view the more Nico remembered him. Corso Pelosa introduced them.

"We should get going, I'm sure the bride and groom need to get to their reception," Leo said, amiably.

"We have plenty of time," replied Nico, not wanting to rush anything today.

Leo turned to Ava. "We've spoken so many times on the phone," he said warmly.

"We have?"

"You're Andrea's friend, aren't you?"

"Andrea?" Ava replied, and looked as though she was trying to make a connection.

"Andrea Brunelli. I'm the Leo who works alongside her."

"Leo?" *The* Leo?" Ava replied, suddenly enthusiastic, as though she'd discovered a long lost friend.

"*Just* Leo," the man replied, looking slightly uncomfortable at the accolade.

"I feel I already know you, Leo!" Ava exclaimed. "We've spoken on the phone so many times," Ava explained, gazing at Nico. Then to Leo, "It's so lovely to finally meet you."

"The pleasure is mine," Leo returned. "Andrea always speaks very highly of you both. But, I haven't seen her around." He looked around at the crowd as if she might magically appear.

"I haven't seen her either," agreed Ava. She turned to Nico. "Have you?" He frowned. He'd been too busy with the morning's sagas but thinking about it, he hadn't seen Andrea either, and she was one of those people, like close family and friends, who would have come up to them if she was here. "No. I haven't."

"That's odd." Ava looked worried. "She was definitely going to come. She was bringing her new partner, at least she promised me she would. I wonder why she's so late."

"I'm sure she's on her way. I'll call her and find out," Leo assured them as Gina rushed up suddenly. "The photographer is looking for you."

"Shall we go?" Nico asked Ava. "Would you excuse us, please?" he said, to the two men.

"Certainly. And Nico," the old man laid his hand on Nico's shoulder. "Your father was already proud of you before he passed away. He already was. Never forget that." The man nodded at him and Nico nodded, silently acknowledging his words.

Beside him, he felt the squeeze of Ava's hand, felt its softness and warmth, and knew that he would be fine. They both would be.

"Let's go make some memories," he said, watching the photographer he'd hired, coming towards them.

CHAPTER ELEVEN

Ava stared at Nico's side profile. He was trying so hard to be brave and strong for them both and yet she knew this day could not be easy for him.

He'd looked so worried the moment she'd set eyes on him in church, but a smile from her had soon turned it around. While she knew that his father's absence pricked as sharply as the sting of barbed wire, today of all days, she didn't want him to be surrounded by sadness.

They'd taken their time having photographs at the church and were now having more photos taken in the private grounds where their wedding reception was being held.

Because she'd already promised Nico, she tried to get used to the fact that she would have to wear her wedding dress until after their first dance. Rona had done a stellar job of sewing the hole but the dress tugged even more at the sides than it had before.

But she put her own discomfort behind her. The photographer finished taking photographs and they were taking a moment alone. A waiter had brought over platters of the smallest and most picturesque looking canapes she had ever seen and she had listened spellbound as he'd told her of the assortment of tantalizing treats that had been put so lovingly and carefully together. Parmigiano cheese flakes with toasted almonds, Zucchini flowers, rice balls with cheese and truffle, spiced cheese in various flavors and textures, and beef rolls filled with rocket and ricotta. There were others too, but she felt full just looking at them.

At this rate, not only would her bodice explode, but her stomach would become even fuller and it would be too uncomfortable to sit down.

"Happy?" she asked Nico as they looked down from one of the rooftop verandahs and watched their guests milling around happily in the courtyard below.

"Never happier," he told her. "I have everything I want today. Except..." She watched a touch of sadness eclipse his happy demeanor.

"I miss him too." She touched his cheek tenderly.

"I feel him here." Nico placed his fisted hand over his chest.

"I know." She leaned forward and kissed him. They ate a little and then returned to the courtyard where they walked through the pathway that guests had formed for them. She felt the buzz of energy in the air. Smiling faces greeted her wherever she looked and they were soon lost in the exuberance and gaiety of the afternoon.

They danced their first dance and were followed by other couples after it had ended. Every so often, Nico would introduce her to new people and she soon lost count of who she had met. She recalled seeing her family among the crowd, but they too were quickly lost in the sea of faces that surrounded them.

Later she sat down to catch her breath and smiled as she greeted one guest after another as they came up to her and Nico to pass on their congratulations. She looked at the tables before them, dressed in white silk with bright pink organza bows and watched as people, flowers, food and candles formed a kaleidoscope of beautiful colors and textures all fusing together before her like one dizzy, euphoric dream.

Soon it was time for speeches and they laughed when Carlos spoke, and listened with sad minds and hearts when Elsa got up to make her speech. At first Ava had been surprised to see her mom speaking, but in the absence of her father, and of Edmondo, she understood that it was the right thing to do. Turning to watch him, she saw Nico swallow a couple of times when Elsa spoke with gentle fondness of Edmondo. Her mother revealed that in their emails to one another, shortly before his death, Edmondo had believed that his son and her daughter were perfect for one another. It was at this point that Ava reached out and took Nico's hand.

They settled down against their dark red velvet covered seats and watched the party unravel before them. The first course arrived and then the second and third and fourth. She quickly lost count and her appetite soon after her first course of Lobster salad with citrus sauce.

Music and laughter rang through the air as easily as happiness flowed through her veins. She wanted to freeze this day, to hold onto it forever, but knew it was already flying by at breakneck speed. Already her dress disaster from this morning seemed hours ago, almost like another day. Rona had done well, she thought, glancing down quickly at her side. The tear had kept together well.

What she wanted was to slip away and change out of her dress into something more comfortable.

"I'd like to go and change," she whispered into Nico's ear. He wiped his mouth with his napkin and took her hand. "Let's go."

They slowly made their way to one of the rooms Nico had reserved for them.

CHAPTER TWELVE

Nico stood behind his wife, grazing the sides of her neck with his lips. He blew soft kisses along her delicate skin before he turned her around to face him.

They stared at one another for the longest time.

"We did it." Her voice sounded raspy.

"We did." He leaned in and covered her mouth with his lips, seeking out her tongue feverishly. Their moans and groans broke the silence in the room and he knew that he could not take this further, not unless he had time to relieve himself. And he wanted to save himself for tonight. "Stop, stop," he moaned, finding it hard to pull away from her.

"I've missed you." She cupped his cheeks as his hands wandered freely around the lace of her bodice. "Make love to me here, Nico..." She pleaded as she slid her tongue over his lower lip. Her veiled suggestion poked at his consciousness, and he tried to react with logic.

"We don't have enough time," he replied, except that it wouldn't take long, the way he wanted to thrust himself inside her. The way she wanted it; he could plainly see from that wanton look in her eyes. He stiffened further, and forced himself to shut down that tantalizing avenue of thought.

"We won't need long," she whispered.

"I can't," he said, in a voice loaded with excruciating pain. "I want to. But I can't. We shouldn't. We have all night ... and three weeks of doing nothing but this." He stood behind her and started to slowly unbutton her dress.

She moaned loudly in disappointment as if she was unable to contain her desire for him. Her long drawn out moans made him even harder, as did the sight of her bare back, slowly revealing itself as his fingers slipped the dainty white pearl buttons out of the thin silk hooped loops. This would not do, he thought, knowing he could hardly walk back into his own reception with a rocket ready to shoot out of his trousers.

"That feels so good." Her voice was ragged, teasing him to throw caution away. It was going to be a long wait until they got home.

"You look good," he breathed, bending over to kiss the bare skin.

She arched her back slowly, releasing an animal purr. "Are you sure you can't ... just ..."

"Ava, we have people waiting for us." Reason sounded strange, and his words were strangled as he was overcome by the heat of his desire. She exhaled a loud sigh and he wondered if she was signaling her defeat.

"It was so tight."

"What was?" he asked, slowly lifting his mind from the haze of desire. He wondered who had had the patience to do up so many buttons.

"The bodice."

"How many buttons do you have?"

"Thirty."

"They're so close together and so fiddly. Why so many loops?" This slow undoing of her dress was tortured foreplay.

"Zanobi refused to put on a zipper."

"But why was it still tight when you'd been for so many fittings recently?"

"He wanted to let it out at the last fitting, but I convinced him not to. And I suffered for it all day." He spun her around, pleased with himself for having achieved a mighty feat.

"What do you mean?" His insides prickled with anticipation as he slipped off her dress but instead of it falling to the floor, it stuck at her side.

For one magical moment his gaze fell upon her half naked body, and he grunted his approval before peering closer. "It's stuck." His voice sounded odd. He examined the fabric as well as he could, but his senses were going wild and all he could do was think of the things he wanted to do with her. One side of her dress had slipped to her waist, baring the satin pink fabric of her bra cup. He couldn't wait to tear it off and to feel her breasts against his lips and tongue.

Perhaps they could share a few stolen moments, after all?

She looked down. "Oh, Jesus," Ava wailed, and tugged at the fabric. "Rona sewed the dress to my bra!"

Nico's eyelids flew wide open. "She did what?" On closer examination he saw that the fabric was indeed sewn to the side of her bra. He listened as Ava recounted the events of the morning. "And I thought my morning was bad." A smile lit up his face as he looked at her. In the next moment he unhooked her bra with one hand and stared at her topless body hungrily as the bra and the dress slid to her feet. Heavy, and pregnant, she stood in front of him only in her satin pink panties. "I want to kiss you all over," he murmured hungrily.

The devil danced in her eyes. "I won't stop you," she said, silkily.

"Aren't you supposed to wear a garter or something?"

"Are you serious?" She threw him a surprised look. "In my condition?"

"Look at *my* condition," Nico rasped, waiting for her eyes to hook down at his crotch.

"Baby, we're going to have to do something about that." Hope rang from her voice.

"As hard as it is—"

"You don't say." Ava reached out for him, and her touch sent him into a tailspin.

"I want to wait until we get home tonight." Nico inhaled slowly, watching the temptress as she brazenly posed in front of him with her hands on her hips. He shook his head, a man in a deep dilemma. "Are you relieved to be out of your dress, or are you just teasing me into submission for the hell of it?"

"What do you think?" she murmured, parting her lips provocatively.

"Ava," he groaned. He wanted to thrust into her right at this very moment and only the patience of a saint would stop him. "I want to spend all night with you. I don't want to rush this. Can't you wait until tonight?" He hoped she could because it was getting near impossible with every passing second.

"I *could* wait, if I really had to," she said slowly. "But I don't think you can." She licked her lips.

A knock at the door interrupted their verbal foreplay.

"Nico?" It was Carlos.

Ava crossed her arms over her breasts.

"It's locked," he whispered. Then in a louder voice. "We won't be long. Ava's getting changed."

"They're waiting for you. Everyone's asking for the bride and groom."

"We're coming!" Ava shouted.

Nico winced. How he wished they were ...

Thankful for the intrusion, he moved over to where Ava's dress was hanging and he slowly unzipped the suit carrier bearing Zanobi's infamous logo. He let out a gasp as he carefully took out the silver beaded cocktail dress.

"I can't wait to slip into that."

"And I can't wait to slip it off you again," he replied, trying hard not to look at her. He tried to think about the spa hotel instead, about Bruno, and the infinity pool, and the mold problem that had started to rear its ugly head, and the old wiring that was giving him nightmares. But none of it helped.

"Oh no!" she cried, making him spin around to face her nakedness again. *Oh god*, he thought, and closed his eyes. "What is it?"

"I didn't bring another bra. I didn't think I needed to."

He opened his eyes and they both stared at the dress and the bra that was stuck to it. "Can't you do without?" His words were strangled. It was hard to not look at her, standing topless in his direct line of vision.

"And look as though I have two watermelons suspended above my stomach?"

He looked away. Having her go bra-less wouldn't do either. He bent down and picked up the wedding dress then quickly ripped the bra from it. A shriek from her almost perforated his ear drums.

"Nooooooo! Zanobi will go berserk if he sees the state the dress is in." But she seized the bra from him and slipped it on.

He turned away again, not caring much for what Zanobi thought and tried instead to focus on the brickwork of the old walls.

"Nico, are you listening?" Ava's voice pricked his concentration.

"I'm trying to distract myself ... things are a little stiff at my end."

"Oh. Okay." He heard her snicker as he continued to focus on the dull grey bricks before him. "I wonder why he came."

"Who?" His gaze was still pinned on the brickwork.

"Leo."

"Why wouldn't he?"

"Because they're divorced."

She was right. He'd invited Pelosa and his family so why had Leo come if they were divorced? It didn't matter. The guy seemed pleasant enough. Right now, Nico was relieved to have another more exciting topic to take his mind off his current state.

"He said he was going to call Andrea and find out why she missed the wedding."

"Let's ask him when we see him," suggested Nico. Ava had told him that Andrea had been looking forward to the wedding and apparently had a new man of her own.

"I'm ready." Ava announced. He turned around and his jaw dropped for the second time that day as his eyes trailed down the length of her dress. She'd pulled the pins out of her hair and thick curls hung around her shoulders, giving her face a softer appearance. She hooked her arm in his. "Let's go and enjoy our reception."

CHAPTER THIRTEEN

Ava felt so much freer now that she had changed into her party dress.

The silver beaded knee length cocktail dress shimmered as she moved. Worries about the torn wedding dress still lingered on her mind but she told herself that it could easily be mended.

She didn't relish the thought of seeing Zanobi's face when she handed it back to him for fixing. He'd told her that he considered his 'creations' to be as precious as his lovers.

One day she hoped to hand the dress over to her daughter, if she was ever lucky enough to have one.

She and Nico wandered around hand in hand, feeling relaxed and happy as they mingled with their guests. Ava glittered and shone in her dress and almost everyone complimented her on her outfits. She briefly recognized some faces from the time of Edmondo's funeral but many of them she was meeting for the first time. She was awash with a deep happiness and an inner security and contentment. Being with Nico had given her that feeling slowly over time, but now it felt as if their being together had been cemented and set in stone.

"They're serving dessert," Nico observed, as they walked back to their seats.

"I can't eat anything else, except for our cake."

"They won't serve it until later on. I can ask the waiter to get you some."

She shook her head as they sat down. "I can wait. I'm feeling pretty full but it's such a relief to be out of that dress." She stared at a shiny metallic silver-gray bead in her hands and watched the way the light sparkled off its shiny surface.

Nico gave her an apologetic look. "I'm sorry I asked you to wear it for longer than you wanted to."

"I'm glad I did." She stopped fingering the beads and leaned toward him with interest. "My mom was right, you only get to wear your wedding dress once."

"You seem more at ease," he commented.

"Taking it off feels as freeing as taking off my bra."

Nico groaned. "Don't put that image back into my head again." Her attention drifted to the couple in the far corner of the dance floor.

"What is it?" Nico asked, but she didn't reply. Tension spread along her face as she watched Salvatore and Elsa walking over to the dance floor. The music slowed down and they looked to be getting ready to dance. Ava tried to decipher the look on her mom's face but even from where she sat, a distance away, Elsa didn't look as angry or as irritated as Ava had expected she might. "Ah, Elsa and Salvatore," Nico commented with amusement. In the next moment she watched Carlos lead Rona to the dance floor and she waited, anticipating the moment that Rona would discover her mother with Salvatore.

And then it happened. Rona looked their way then turned

to face Carlos, only to snap her head back sharply towards her mother again. It was comical, Ava thought, as she watched her. And yet she wasn't sure how she felt about seeing her mother with Salvatore.

Was her mother smiling?

"I didn't think she liked Salvatore much," remarked Ava.

"He's being polite by asking her. It's only a dance, Ava."

"It's a little too early," commented Ava, thinking how Edmondo had only passed away a few months ago.

"Early, for what?"

"She adored your father."

"My father isn't here anymore."

"I know but that's not what I—" She turned to Nico but he waved his hand dismissively. "Your mother is only having a dance, Ava. It's interesting to see, in light of past events." Nico's voice trailed away. The music became louder and she leaned towards him, straining to hear him.

"What past events?"

"I'll have to tell you another time," said Nico, raising his voice and speaking directly into her ear. "But that's Salvatore's son over there with his wife, sitting at that table behind the ice sculpture."

Ava looked over to see Lizzi sitting with an older couple. "How come you and Lizzi's dad were friends? His daughter is almost nineteen and your first baby hasn't even been born yet."

"He's a few years older than me and married very young. I only know of him because Salvatore and Edmondo go back a long way."

"Who's Gina talking to?" Ava asked, "near the ice sculpture." They watched as she appeared to be in deep conversation with someone. "Who is he?" Ava asked, turning to Nico.

"I have no idea. Is that her 'plus one?'"

"She doesn't have a 'plus one'," Ava replied. "I made a point of asking her and she firmly put me straight."

They both squinted and looked harder.

"Care to dance?" he asked, holding out his hand. "This next one's a slow song as well."

She could do slow, she decided. Slow was good. She followed her new husband to the dance floor where everyone cleared the floor to make way for them. Nico put his arms around her waist as her hands climbed up to his shoulders and they stared into each other's eyes.

The evening sky was bedecked with a crocheted shawl of shell-pink and oyster blue. Night would fall soon but it wouldn't matter. The August evening was warm and sultry. Nico's forehead dipped down and fit snugly against hers until they were nose to nose, lip to lip and heart to heart with one another. She moved slowly with him, more in tune with his body than with the music.

"Tired?" he asked.

"Happy," she murmured. "I could stay like this all night."

"Then stay like this all night."

She tilted her head up and kissed him.

"We can leave whenever you get tired." His lips brushed her ear, and his hot breath tickle her face.

"We shouldn't leave until the final guests have left."

"True," Nico replied. "But I was thinking more of you."

"You always think of me." She was grateful to have finally met a man who cared so deeply about her. How different love felt when shared with a man who treated her with such love. He'd shown her that it was safe to trust again, to fall in love again, to believe again.

Nico had done this for her and she considered herself to be the luckiest woman alive. She'd been given a second chance at love, and she knew it could have turned out so differently. She could have returned to Denver and immersed herself in her business and she might even have succumbed to blind dates and dating agencies later on when she had healed.

She might have met the wrong man all over again.

But instead she'd met Nico and her whole life had changed.

It hadn't been easy for them. In the beginning they'd had their dark moments, but now she couldn't imagine a world in which he didn't exist.

"What are you thinking?" He stared into her eyes, ever mindful, and always so in sync with her thoughts and feelings.

"I don't want to leave," she replied, dreamily and closed her eyes, knowing that he would take good care of her forever and that she would do her best to do the same for him.

Like a bolt out of nowhere, she remembered. "Have you seen Leo?" She was still concerned about her friend and the new man Andrea had been telling her about.

"I haven't." Nico looked around. "But they're still here. I saw Corso earlier."

"I'm worried." She tried not to think that the absence of any calls or messages from Andrea suggested something terrible might have happened.

"I'm sure there's a perfectly good reason she hasn't turned up."

"Maybe." But she doubted it. She knew Andrea was busy with her business and perhaps something more urgent had come up last minute. "I'll call her tomorrow."

"Don't forget, we're leaving at mid-day," Nico reminded her.

"I haven't forgotten. When will you tell me where we're going?"

"Do you really want to know?"

She widened her eyes at him and nodded. "Of course I want to know!"

"Amalfi."

"Amalfi?"

"You don't like it?" He looked anxious.

How had he known? She had dreamt of going to Amalfi ever since college. "Sometimes I swear you can read my mind." She rested her hand on her chest, overcome by his choice of the honeymoon destination.

"That's because sometimes I can." Nico's expression was serious. "I wish I could read your thoughts right now. How does Amalfi sound? Do you want to go there?"

"Oh, god, yes," she replied quickly. He'd asked her to pick a honeymoon destination but since she didn't want to travel abroad, she had left it to Nico to pick the perfect honeymoon spot in Italy, knowing that wherever they went, would be wonderful. That he had come back with a place that had been so dear to her heart, was as frightening as it was magical.

"Many years ago I saw a picture of Amalfi in a magazine. I was in college at the time and it was the first I'd ever heard of the place. The ad was for a perfume and the photo shot was taken from a woman's back as she stood outside on a balcony overlooking the sea. I remember seeing the hotels and white houses with their terracotta roofs all nestled higgledy-piggledy on the steep hills. I knew then that I wanted to go to that place and—" She stopped short. She'd considered it for her honeymoon when she'd been with Connor, but he'd wanted to go to Verona and Venice instead, and because she didn't mind either way, she'd agreed with him. But secretly, she had continued to look at pictures of Amalfi in the travel magazines that she and Connor had lying around.

Somehow it didn't feel right telling Nico that. But he was smiling at what she had told him. "I did well, then?"

"You did well. I can't wait to see it for real."

"It's even more stunning in real life, you'll see. The photos don't do it justice."

"I'm sure they don't."

"And you will fall in love with the place we're staying at."

She knew she would. She didn't need to ask him to describe it because Nico had great taste, and she knew he would want to take her somewhere that would leave her breathless. She could barely contain herself. "This time tomorrow night we'll be there."

"This time tomorrow night, I'll have you screaming out my name," he assured her.

This time tomorrow night, she could hardly wait.

CHAPTER FOURTEEN

The dark, inky night closed around them as Nico carried Ava to the front door. Wall lights on either side illuminated them as she fumbled around in the pockets of his jacket for the keys to the house.

"I'm heavy, Nico. Put me down," she giggled, her dress shimmering like silverfish under the wall lights.

"I will once we're inside."

She unlocked the door, and he slowly pushed it open with a gentle push of his foot. "Careful," she squealed. "Don't trip. The last thing we want is for me to break my waters before we leave for our honeymoon."

He clasped her even tighter. "It's a tradition," he whispered and she clung to his neck as he slowly walked in. She'd started to fall asleep in the car on the way over but she was wide awake again, and way too excited for three o'clock in the morning. The prospect of going to bed with this man, now her husband, excited her further.

Nothing had technically changed. He was still Nico and she was still the same woman. But something had shifted; something small, imperceptible, invisible and it was beautiful.

"Mrs. Cazale, welcome."

"Why, Mr. Cazale. Thank you." He walked into their home and closed the door with his back as glittering beads of her dress jingled and jangled like crazy. "Nico, I insist you put me down before we both collapse in a heap on the floor."

"Hold on," he breathed, and kissed her. She tightened her arms around his neck and moaned softly feeling his mouth on hers. Placing her down gently, he undid his tie, slipping it off easily. She couldn't wait to get out of her clothes either, and to snuggle up alongside him. The moment seemed surreal, them being back home again with their long and beautiful wedding day behind them, ready to start the next chapter in their lives. "Ready?"

"For you? Always."

Her words brought a smile to his face. "Are you ready to see the room?"

She nodded eagerly. "But you can't carry me up the stairs."

"I wouldn't. It would be too dangerous and I've had a little too much to drink."

As sober as she was, not having touched a drop of alcohol, she brazenly reached out for his manhood. "I hope you haven't drunk too much that you won't be able to rise to the occasion."

"Not with you." He grabbed her around her waist and kissed her deeply until she couldn't breathe any more. She melted into his mouth and felt heat coil around her body as his hands reached down and claimed her bottom, pressing her hips against him even more.

"Let's not waste any time," she whispered into his lips as her body loosened and became heat and liquid. Her heartbeat hammered under her chest as he grabbed her hand and they walked carefully, and urgently, up the stairs.

"I hope you like it." His face filled with pride and he seemed eager for her reaction. He pushed the door wide open and she gasped as she walked in and looked around. It was completely changed, and unrecognizable from the room they'd shared before. It was still the same size and shape, with its high ceilings and two walls with large windows that let in so much light during the day, yet the room had been transformed.

"These are the colors you picked. Do you like them?" He sounded anxious. They'd picked the palest mint green and white luxury damask curtains and a chaise lounge of the same color. There were also matching covers for the largest bed she'd ever seen.

"It could sleep a family of five," she quipped, eyeing it as she walked around the room eyeing the antique table and lamp that stood next to the chaise lounge. Their bedroom was soft and sensuous, and the perfect sanctuary to retreat to. "It looks completely different. Completely transformed. I love it, Nico. I really, really, really love it. Thank you."

"You don't have to thank me, Ava. This is your home." His eyebrows pushed together. "It doesn't sound right you thanking me."

She kissed him instead. "The crib will go there?" She moved to the side of the bed. The crib hadn't arrived yet. She'd ordered it from one of Andrea's suppliers and she and Nico had both agreed to have the baby in their room until he or she was a year old. Then they would move the toddler into the nursery next door—there was a connecting door between the two rooms.

"Wherever you want."

"It's beautiful." She gazed around the room happily, surveying the huge bed once more. It was dressed up with soft, velvety chocolate colored cushions which looked so soft that she wanted to hug them to her chest. She walked up to him, enraptured.

"You like it?" he asked, slipping his arms around her waist.

"I love it." She kissed him, then eyed the bed again. "We need to break in the bed."

"Hmmm." He kissed her again, this time softly, as if she was delicate and might break if he pushed too hard. "We do, Mrs. Cazale. Did you want to see the walk-in wardrobe first?"

"No. I was thinking we could do something more exciting instead." She splayed her hands across his lower back. Her body was tired, her mind was woozy but she wanted to christen that bed this first night with her new husband.

"There are better things to do," he agreed, stroking the skin across her wrists. Her lips curved into a smile when his hands slid over to her bottom and cupped it tightly, pulling her hips into his.

CHAPTER FIFTEEN

He kissed her hard, then held her face between his hands and felt the softness of her hair as he moved his fingers through them. He eyed her lips for a few seconds before feeling the urge to taste them again.

They hadn't even been together a year and yet it seemed as though he'd known her a lifetime. It was as if she'd been predestined to be his from the start, from before they'd even met and that their getting together was just a formality.

His connection to her was something he had never experienced with anyone before.

He dipped his head and kissed her once more, loving the familiar, finding comfort and peace in her touch. Sliding his hands up along her back, he unzipped her slowly. "Thank goodness," he murmured, still joined at the mouth as he finished kissing her long enough to concentrate on removing her dress. He imagined that this one would be easier to take off than her wedding dress had been.

"Thank goodness for what?"

"For this zipper." His voice was raspy as he pulled it down.

"Wedding dresses are sacred, according to Zanobi," she told him. Just pulling her dress down to reveal her flesh had him harden even more. The desire and feeling that had been building up during the day—and which had been fueled further by seeing her half-dressed as she'd changed into her party dress—was at breaking point. All the heat and sizzle that had zing'ed around his body as he'd danced with her and held her throughout the evening, had concentrated into a ball of sexual tension that now needed release.

Undoing her dress had tipped him over and he wanted nothing more than to slide into her and to make her moan until they both exploded together.

"Do you mind if I slip into the shower quickly? I'm all hot and sticky..." She teased him in her pink bra and panties. His restraint reached new heights, that even he wasn't aware of until this moment and he was left unable to voice an answer. He briefly considered taking a shower with her, but he knew where that would end and how long that would take. Besides, taking her in the shower wouldn't be safe.

"Go ahead," he managed to say.

"Wait for me." She suggestively removed her bra and slid down her panties. Nico swallowed, his lips half-parted. He just about managed a "Not going anywhere" and tried to hold himself together as she slipped out of view and into the bathroom. He ripped his suit off until he wore nothing but happy excitement.

When she reappeared moments later, wearing a new sheer black lace nightie, he couldn't control himself and reached out for her, his hands roaming freely over her lush body, his lips kissing her face, her lips and her neck. His fingers dipped lower and sank into the heat and silk of her, and she moaned in response, arching her back, slippery against him.

"Give me two minutes," he begged.

"Not going anywhere," she murmured, and sank onto the bed, waiting for him. He dragged himself away and rushed to shower. Fresh and clean he emerged, moments later, eager and excited, only to find Ava peacefully asleep, in the same position, but hugging a cushion.

He sighed and his excitement dropped quicker than his mood. Breathing loudly, he went over to the cupboards to take out another duvet, not wanting to wake her up. Staring at the sheer lace fabric of her outfit, which revealed her naked body completely, he was tempted to awaken her but when he saw how peaceful she looked, he knew he would wait until tomorrow.

Spreading the duvet over her, he climbed into bed alongside her. No sooner had he lain down on his back, than she turned towards him and slipped her hand over his chest, snuggling into him.

It wasn't long before sleep came to him, either.

CHAPTER SIXTEEN

He stared at her lips, parted and crimson stained, as her soft moans—the sounds that made him shudder—fell from her mouth with easy abandon.

Nico was entranced, as well as in heaven, as he lay on his back watching Ava writhe as she straddled him; the position she loved and the one he felt most comfortable with, especially in this late stage of her pregnancy. Her ripe, rounded breasts bounced wildly and sweat licked her skin as sheer rapture painted her face. With eyes half-closed she mewled and murmured his name, as sighs fell from lips wet and wanton with hungry desire.

Watching her ride him, he considered himself to be the luckiest man alive because she was his. She leaned back slightly with her hands resting behind her on his thighs and he watched her face, felt her quiver as he painted gentle strokes between her legs with his thumb. An involuntary growl escaped his mouth as her movements sped up. She mewled, this time louder, and he knew he wouldn't be able to hold back for much longer. Her muscles clenched around him and he heard her animalistic cry of release.

"Nico..." she uttered, and a sigh fell from her lips, a half-breath hitched, as her hips bucked against him and she shuddered and spluttered, reaching her own release as he exploded inside her. Quivering, and spent, she fell forward slowly and rested against his chest.

He was worried about the baby because of the way Ava lay pressed into his stomach, lost in her own euphoria, quivering and breathing heavily as they lay in the soft wetness that bound them together.

"The baby ... " he said softly.

"Is ... fine," she whimpered, pushing herself up a little, so that her breasts were no more than a few inches from his face. He reached out and cupped one in his hand, felt the stirrings in his loins once more. "Nico," she murmured, satisfied and spent, her hair falling over her, over him and her hands resting on either side of the bed, alongside his face. It wouldn't be long before he entered this state of nirvana all over again.

"Don't move," he warned, wanting to suckle her while their bodies were warm and silken and fused together.

This woman was his for eternity.

"He's kicking again," she cried, wincing.

"Told you, *she* doesn't like this position." He raised himself on his forearms. She pushed back and lifted herself from him before lying down beside him.

"I love our honeymoon suite," she murmured, still breathless.

"I love our honeymoon and all that it promises," he replied, turning to his side.

He moved her hair away from her face and watched her heaving chest slow down. "That was amazing," she cooed, and he knew they would barely get to leave the room today. Unable to christen the bed this morning when they'd woken up late in Verona, he'd been desperate for release ever since, as had Ava.

And the release had been as sweet as the wait had been torturous.

"Ava ..." He gasped in a voice that sounded strangled, as her fingers reached down for him again.

"Ready when you are."

"I need a few moments." He tilted head towards her and dipped his tongue into her collarbone. Days and nights of doing nothing but this. This had to be heaven.

"We didn't get to say goodbye to Rona and Carlos," she remarked.

"We didn't get to christen the bed either."

"Are you glad you kept that sexual energy simmering?"

"Let me catch my breath again, woman."

"I'm waiting," she whispered, biting his lower lip. "You were going to tell me about Salvatore." "

"*Now?* You want to know about Salvatore, *now?*" He had better things he wanted to do to her.

"Now." She raked her nails lightly across his naked back.

"Did you know that Salvatore was in love with my mother?"

She stopped clawing him. "What?"

"It's true. Many years ago when they were teenagers. This is what my mother told me. I never heard it from my father. But back then, Salvatore and my mother liked one another, I'm not even sure if they dated. She said he was fond of her, but he was very shy and never made a move. Then later, she met my father, and after meeting him there was never anyone else for her. Edmondo had captured her heart forever, she told me. She said Salvatore held a grudge against my father from that moment on. But later, he met someone and they settled down. They were happy enough. But Salvatore and my father weren't really the best of friends." He teased her nipple with his tongue.

"That's so sad."

"Is it?" asked Nico, begrudgingly taking his mouth off her breast.

"It is for Salvatore."

"Why? He met and fell in love with someone else. My mother and my father hit it off from the beginning—just like you and I did."

"I didn't hit it off with you in the beginning."

"Maybe for you it was different." Nico entwined his fingers with hers. "For me, you were all I could think of. It was a miracle I could even drive you back to the hotel and concentrate, what with you in the car, and me trying to order your clothes in order to make up for your lost luggage."

She laughed. "You were the best thing to happen to me, Nico. Sometimes I feel as if Connor did me a huge favor."

"Connor," sighed Nico. "Let's not dwell on Connor. In fact ..." He kissed her nipple. "Can we make our honeymoon a Connor free zone? I don't want to even hear his name."

She looked at him. "He means nothing to me, you know that, don't you?"

"I know that, and I don't see why we still end up talking about him." He wanted no part of Connor on their honeymoon. Slipping his hand over her stomach, he felt the gentle butterfly kicks their baby was making.

"She's doesn't like it when we argue."

"We're not arguing." She playfully swatted him across his chest. "She?" Ava questioned again, like she always did. "You still think we're having a girl?"

"I hope so. I want a mini you."

"And I want a mini *you*," she retorted.

"And since we're not having twins, one of us is going to be disappointed."

"I'll never be disappointed."

He kissed her other breast before trailing his tongue around it, getting even more turned on by the way her nipples stood to attention.

"I don't care what we have. As long as you and the baby are fine. We can always have another one if you want. Whenever you want. In case you hadn't noticed, I love the process of making them."

"Hmmmmm," she murmured, as he sucked her breast for the longest time, knowing he was ready for her again. This was sheer bliss, no work, no employees, no Bruno, no work and no spa hotel to worry about. Just bed and Ava and making love all day long. Even though they had only checked in a few hours ago, arriving late in the afternoon, they'd been in bed for hours, making up for lost time.

"Are you sure that's not a directive—to have another baby?" Ava asked.

"I'll never give you a directive, darling. You should know that by now."

"I do," she breathed, huskily, raking her fingers through his hair. "Let's get this one out first and see how things are."

"We have all the time in the world." He lifted his head and looked at her.

"Make love to me forever," she begged, staring up at him with those blue-gray eyes; eyes he would grow old with, and he felt a comfort at the thought. Her voice dropped lower as her fingers moved beyond his stomach. He almost whistled when she curled her fingers around him, stroking him to perfect stiffness in the blink of an eye.

He licked his lips, unable to speak, but content to lay on his side, with her lush, swollen body close to his, and her hands, like a wand, performing their own magic. Nico marveled at how his life had turned around the moment he'd picked this woman up from the airport. Today she lay naked beside him as his wife. He dipped down and kissed her, because he could. And she looked about ready for the next round.

"I called Andrea today." She announced calmly, exercising her restraint, as she often did when she drove him crazy with her touch. It amazed him that she was capable of continuing a conversation as if they were sitting at a table drinking coffee.

"I don't want to think of Andrea right now." He wasn't going to give her the chance to talk, he decided, and rolled carefully on top of her, covering her body with his and supporting his weight on his arms. He left small kisses along her neck and shoulders, then sucked the skin above her breast, hearing her moan with satisfaction. He was once again addicted to the sound of her sighs and felt himself harden some more; she only had to breathe or emit a note in that husky voice and he was as stiff as a steel rod.

He dipped his head and took her mouth with his, making love to it as though his life depended on it. Eliciting another moan from her his whole body was flush against hers and he was ready to thrust into her again.

"You don't want to think of Andrea?" she asked, slipping her finger into his mouth. The minx. He ran his tongue over it, sucked it, then grabbed her hand and pulled it away gently.

"How is she?" he asked, not really caring about Andrea, not in this instant, but wanting to show Ava that he had restraint too. Or the semblance of restraint. He gazed down into her liquid eyes. Beads of perspiration glistened beneath her nose.

"She didn't pick up so I called—aaaaah," She let out a

drawn out sigh as he shifted into position, poised and ready against her wetness. The feel of her hard nipple across his tongue drove him insane, just as it did her. He stopped sucking and lifted his head. "You didn't speak to her?" he asked, through gritted teeth, knowing that he could no longer keep up this farce. That all he wanted to do was to bury himself inside her.

Her eyes were shiny, her body slowly beginning to move with his. Thankfully, small talk was over. She moaned and stretched out her hands, holding onto the thin black bed rails above her head. He couldn't help but stare at her, arms outstretched, breasts peaking and rising as her breathing deepened. "Don't stop," she cried, as the color spread across her face and neck, turning them a flushed shade of red.

"I ... don't ... plan to ..." he managed to say, as he moved gently to her rhythm.

CHAPTER SEVENTEEN

She stretched out lazily, unaware of what time it was and not caring either.

They hadn't left the honeymoon suite ever since they had arrived at the Palazzo Acacia, which—judging by the plum-colored sky from the window—told her had been many hours ago.

Nico had surpassed himself and she'd been speechless, her jaw open as she'd surveyed the luxurious hotel. It was without a doubt one of the most beautiful places she'd ever had the privilege to stay in. The hotel, a late 19th century Liberty style villa, was surrounded by enchanting scenery as well as the perennial blue of the Mediterranean sky and the aquamarine sea. When viewed from their terrace the ocean spread out like a watercolor painting sprinkled with glitter.

Shocking-pink look-at-me bougainvillea cascaded across the landscape like bunches of pink Christmas lights and the fragrant scents of orange and lemon groves infused the air. She was momentarily dazzled by the hotel and the spectacular panoramic views of the Amalfi Coast held her in awe.

It was breathtaking.

And when she'd stepped into their honeymoon suite Nico had looked perplexed, mistaking her long silence for quiet disappointment.

"Is it too much?" he'd asked, hastily. In their early days she'd often told him that she didn't need ostentatious displays of affection for him to win her over. But this place he'd chosen for their honeymoon was better than anything she'd imagined about Amalfi during the years. "This is heaven," she'd whispered.

"You like it?" He sounded anxious and she wanted him to know her real feelings.

"It's the most beautiful place I've ever seen." She'd been awestruck as she followed the hotel staff to their honeymoon suite and once their luggage had been left, she'd continued to stare in quiet amazement as Nico showed her around the place that was to be their home for the next three weeks.

Their suite, the most opulent and largest in the discreet hotel was housed away in its own grounds. On two levels, the uppermost level had a living room and a steam room, as well as a Jacuzzi bathtub on a large private terrace with a breathtaking view of Amalfi spread out before it. The floor below boasted one of the largest bedrooms that she'd ever seen in a hotel. It was even bigger than their room at home. This floor also had a lounge, a second bathroom and another terrace which led out onto an enclosed private garden with its own heated infinity pool and a decked area for two sun loungers facing the sea.

It was jaw-dropping awesomeness. Nico had initially suggested that they go to two different places but she'd been desperate for rest and had told him she wanted to stay in one place. On the way here he'd told her that he had considered spending ten days in Amalfi followed by ten more in Positano.

Now that she was here, she knew she'd made the right decision. Three weeks didn't seem long enough.

She turned and watched him sleeping, contentment flowing through her. Unable to stop herself she leaned over and traced a line along his brows. He shifted, scrunched up his nose when she dipped her fingers lower and tickled under his nose. He pushed her hand away while still asleep.

Deciding to let him sleep, she reached over for her cell phone to check for messages. She dialed Andrea's number and prayed for her friend to pick up but Andrea didn't answer. Ava contemplated sending her a text message but decided it would be better to call again tomorrow. She was still curious to find out why her friend had missed the wedding. Slipping the cell phone back onto the bedside cabinet, she slid under the duvet to find Nico beginning to stir. He put his arm over her stomach protectively and she entwined her fingers with his.

"Good morning," he mumbled, trying to open his eyes.

"It's still evening, Nico," she giggled. They hadn't even made it out of the door. He'd given her an unforgettable start to their honeymoon. Rubbing his hands over his face, he blinked a few times and shook himself wide awake. "Evening?"

"Yes," she laughed. "Your performance seemed to have worn you out."

"I haven't finished yet," he murmured, sounding sexier than ever.

"Good, because I'm not done either."

"There's no real reason to leave the bed, is there?" He turned to his side and propped himself up an elbow.

"None whatsoever." She splayed her hand against his chest. "We have everything we need right here, the infinity pool. Food, TV, books, you, me."

Mischief twinkled in his eyes. "You calm me. I haven't slept so well in days. I couldn't sleep the night before the wedding."

"Nerves?"

He shook his head. "I wasn't nervous—until I had real reason to be when the car was late. I couldn't sleep because you weren't there."

"That was your fault. You're the one who insisted on sleeping apart."

"Aren't you glad I did." His voice dropped to a whisper. "Could you tell how much I missed you?"

"Three times? Not that I was counting. Is that a record for you?"

"No, but I'm in the mood for setting a new one."

She smiled widely. "Connor couldn't go more than twice in one night. And that was on a good and very rare night."

"I thought we had a rule about not mentioning Connor?" His face turned hard and she immediately regretted her words, wishing she had told him about the money before. This had been her attempt of slipping in her news. "Sorry," she whispered. It would have to wait until they returned. She changed the subject, not wanting to cause him stress. "I called Andrea but she didn't answer."

"Don't worry about Andrea. I'm sure Leo would have called us if something had happened to her."

"He doesn't have our number."

"No, but if something had happened, he'd have found a way of contacting us. The fact that he hasn't should put your mind at rest."

"I'll rest easy once I've spoken to her. Admit it, Nico. Andrea was so excited about our wedding." She mulled it over but Nico did have a point. If Andrea was in trouble—and that thought had crossed her mind—then Leo would have found a way of letting them know.

"How long have you known Leo's father-in-law?" she asked as Nico slipped his hand under the covers and traced his fingers along her hip.

"For years. He and my father were close."

"Imagine," she murmured, enjoying the way his hands roamed over her skin. "Leo turned out to be *Andrea's* Leo. What a small world."

"I thought she was with someone called Ray?"

"Riley. I was looking forward to meeting him," she mused, and shuddered as Nico left wet kisses along her chest. She arched her back in happy acceptance.

"I'm sure we'll get to meet Riley another time."

"I'd like to meet up with them both. The last time I spoke to Andrea she was crazy about him."

"I'm crazy about you."

"Then show me all over again," she said sinfully, settling into his soft, wet kiss, the kind of kiss that made her melt into him as she savored the taste of his mouth. She slipped her hand down past his stomach and circled her thumb around the tip of his most sensitive part, drawing out a deep moan from him.

This. Him. Her. All night long. She parted her legs, sighing deeply as he filled her completely.

CHAPTER EIGHTEEN

They managed to venture out the next day even though she could have happily retreated into their honeymoon suite for days without the need to leave.

Between the two terraces, the private, enclosed garden and the infinity pool, Ava could have quite happily stayed inside with nothing more enticing to do than make long, lazy, love with Nico.

Yet it would have been a waste not to go out and visit the charming little town. Even the drive here along the Amalfi coastline, with its sprinkling of piazzas and beaches and crumpled wedding-cake-towns, left her agape with its picture-postcard prettiness.

Nico was most eager to show her Amalfi, a place he knew intimately. She considered this to be one of the perks of being married to this sexy Italian. There would be no more reliance on tourist guide books anymore. And indeed he left no stone unturned in his desire to show her the dazzling sights and smells of the beauty that was Amalfi.

A couple of days they went on gentle walks to get a feel for the place. Many of the hikes and trails weren't ideal being so high up but Nico had found a few gentle ones that they were able to enjoy and they spent many hours walking throughout the picturesque scenery, admiring the stunning views of the sea and mountains. During one of their walks they saw breathtaking waterfalls from the safety and distance of bridges. She snapped away on her camera wanting to capture and treasure these beautiful moments and to keep them forever.

It wasn't that she forgot about her online business, or that Nico had temporarily ceased to think about the new hotel or the existing hotels, but for the first time ever in their relationship, they were able to stop and put themselves before their usual daily business dealings. They allowed themselves an hour to check their emails and business statistics in the morning and then again in the evening before they headed out to dinner.

The Palazzo Acacia boasted the finest world-class cuisine its three restaurants and they ate here a few times. The rest of the days they walked along the charming streets of Amalfi and picked whatever restaurant caught their eye along the sea edge.

One evening they chanced along the enchanting town of Atrani, a pretty little fishing village littered with pavement cafes and a small smattering of restaurants in its scenic little piazetta, the open public square. Another evening he took her to Ravello, a stunning cliff top town where she almost stopped breathing as she inhaled and absorbed the panoramic view from high up.

They went out on excursions or walks in the morning, and during the afternoons they would go for a swim or visit the hotel spa where they both enjoyed a few treatments. She'd convinced Nico to have some though she usually ended up having one while he waited for her. She sometimes wondered if he was secretly using her treatment time to go over his allotted one hour of business time. She was certain that he was secretly catching up on his correspondence while she was being pampered. Though she wasn't completely blameless either and was sneakily doing more than her share as well and often managed to reply to and send out her own emails from the safety of the ladies room.

Nico never suspected a thing.

They quickly reached their first week anniversary and celebrated the day by visiting Sorrento, another coastal town perched atop cliffs and a ninety minute drive away. There, sitting high up in a fish restaurant, enjoying a lobster bisque and freshly made artisan bread, they toasted their first week as a married couple with a glass of champagne from which she only took a sip, ever mindful of their baby.

These were romantic, magical, sublime evenings and she was all too aware that this time together would soon be over. There would still be future vacations, and the thrill and joy of getting away, but it would be with the children and it would be a different type of vacation, one that they would enjoy and love and cherish forever, but for different reasons.

This, with just the two of them, was something they would not experience again until their children had grown up. Already she felt sad thinking that far ahead in their future, knowing, as Elsa had often told her, that time flew by, that life was short, and that it was important to savor every moment.

"Happy anniversary," she said, happiness flowing freely through her veins.

"Happy anniversary, to us, and forever." Nico raised his glass to hers.

CHAPTER NINETEEN

"Won't find out what?" Ava asked him.

Who was he talking to?

She'd had the most relaxing massage—something she knew she would miss badly when they returned to Verona—and had tip-tiptoed up behind Nico as he sat in the spa reception, huddled in a corner. She was almost certain he was doing what she was doing in the washroom: business related tasks but as she approached, she'd heard his words. *"I'm hoping she won't find out."*

And it had sent chills along her spine.

He hung up hastily and spun around, looking as though he'd seen a ghost. The peaceful feeling of wellness she'd attained after her massage crashed violently to the floor like a chunk of iron. He turned to her, his mouth pressed into a hard line. It was the first time she'd seen this expression on their honeymoon for he usually wore it during his normal working day back in Verona.

"What is it?" she asked, probing, but he offered her a false smile, and she instinctively knew he was covering something up. He'd never once had to force a smile with her. "Is it Elsa?"

She was suddenly worried as this new thought punctured the cushioned bubble of her days.

"No, no." He took her hand and lead her towards the soft, bouncy sofas that lined the spa reception.

"Rona? Carlos? Tori?" She was becoming more worried by the second, especially when he remained silent. His refusal to say anything only told her that this was serious. She sat down stiffly on the sofa, even though she didn't want to, and watched as he sat beside her, still not letting go of her hand. She felt more anxious than ever. "Tell me, Nico. No secrets, remember?"

He pulled back his hand and she could see his eyes narrow to a slit. "It's not your family."

"Then?"

"It's ..." He paused, and the pause made her even more nervous. She placed a protective hand over her stomach.

"It's Gina."

"Gina?" She jerked her head in surprise at the unexpected name that fell from his lips.

"She's had ... a ... problem with ..." Nico appeared lost for words.

She craned her neck forward. "With?"

"There's a—"

"A?" She watched his Adam's apple rise and fall and still nothing from him.

"There's been a slight problem with the ... interviews she's carrying out."

"Interviews?"

Nico cleared his throat. "She's carrying out some interviews for me, for the management team." He coughed again and it made her suspicious.

"And?" Now she was doubly intrigued.

"She used your office."

"So?" Why would that be a problem?

"She knocked over your lamp and broke it."

"Was that all?" She wasn't convinced he was telling the truth.

He nodded. "She felt bad."

"She shouldn't. It's not my lamp anyway. It's yours, Nico. That was your old office."

"All the same."

"So she damaged the lamp?"

Nico watched her carefully. "You know how anxious she can get sometimes, looking after the hotel and keeping an eye on everything."

"It doesn't make sense for her to get so worked up about something so small."

He swiped a hand across the back of his neck. "She uh— she also spilled coffee, accidentally, over your desk and it went on some of your papers."

"It did?"

"She sounds overwrought and overwhelmed. I need to make it up to her when we return."

"You have to give her a pay raise at least," suggested Ava, thinking how clumsy Gina had become.

"That's the first thing. She even postponed her training course until we got back."

"The woman is a savior."

"You don't need to tell me. How was the massage?"

"Wonderful." She had been feeling relaxed until he'd suddenly scared her just now. "I'm going to find it hard adjusting to not having them when we return."

"There's no reason why you can't continue in Verona. If it relaxes you and helps, then you should have them regularly."

"It would mean an increased chance of running into Silvia. She uses the same beauty salon."

"I'm sure we can arrange for the masseuse to visit you at the hotel, or at home," he suggested. "We have a lunch date. I booked the restaurant by the sea again. You liked that last time, didn't you?"

"I like all the restaurants in Amalfi."

He smiled at her. "Hungry?"

No, she wasn't. Not really. More than anything she was feeling sleepy, like a tight coil that had been unwound, she felt suddenly loose and full of light and not in the mood for having a big lunch. But Nico seemed eager, so she went along with it.

"Let's go," she offered. "Let's have lunch."

He got up, but she noticed he seemed quieter. "Is something wrong?" She reached for his hand again. He looked as though he suddenly had the worries of the world on his shoulders and she wondered if he'd heard from Bruno.

"No. Why?"

"I thought for a moment you might have heard from Bruno."

"Bruno?"

She examined his face carefully and noticed that he was miles away. "From the guys working on the spa hotel."

"Bruno. Right. He said there was a problem with the infinity pool, but nothing that he can't fix."

"Nothing to worry about, then?"

Nico gave her a pinched expression which he smoothed over quickly. "Nothing to worry about at all."

"Good." She kissed him on the lips. "Do you mind if I rush off to the washroom?"

"No. Go ahead, I'll wait here."

No sooner had she gone than Nico knew he needed to stop the news from reaching Ava.

A fire had spread inside Andrea's warehouse and everything had burned down. Not only that, but the huge shipment that Ava had been relying on to reach Denver, had gone up in flames too.

He called Gina first and reiterated to her the news he'd just heard from Andrea and told her to keep all news of the fire from Ava. Then he spoke to Rona but she and Carlos were sight-seeing in Venice and Rona was barely paying attention. He asked to speak to Carlos instead.

"Thanks for telling us, buddy. We didn't know," said Carlos, "but don't worry. We won't say a word."

"When are you flying out?"

"In a couple of days. I'm sorry we won't be able to meet up with you when you both return from your honeymoon."

"I'm sure there will be other opportunities. You're always welcome to our house and the Casa Adriana whenever you want."

"Thanks Nico. That means a lot to me."

"We're family now," Nico replied., then huffed out a loud breath. "Can I ask you one more thing? It will be early morning in Denver and I don't know when I'll be able to get the message across to Kim, but can you get Rona to call and tell her about the fire and the shipment? I'll try to call her when I get a chance. I don't know exactly how much the business is going to be impacted but it's difficult for me to speak about this with Ava hovering around."

"Sure. Don't you worry about a thing," Carlos said. Nico saw Ava making her way back towards him.

"She's back," he told Carlos and quickly hung up.

"Who were you talking to?" He flinched a little at Ava's hard stare and frantically tried to think of a credible reply.

"Bruno," Nico blurted out.

"Bruno?"

"I'm sorry." Nico stood up slowly. "I know we have this policy of limited business time."

"Relax, Nico," Ava laughed. "What did he want?"

"Uh—he wanted to tell me about the issues with the infinity pool."

"Again? I thought the problem was under control. What's happened now?"

"Some of the fixes weren't really working out. He was giving me an update."

"That hardly sounds urgent." Ava looped her arm through his.

"Sorry, darling. It's been a crazy morning. What can I say?" He hated lying to her through his teeth, especially when they'd just taken their vows. He'd taken a long and windy path to finding the woman of his dreams and he didn't want anything to mess things up. Least of all, he didn't want to start their married days with secrets and lies.

As they left the spa and ambled through the picture perfect gardens of the Palazzo Acacia, Nico convinced himself that keeping this news from Ava was for her own good.

He would achieve nothing by telling her what had happened in Montova. How would it help—especially if the rumors about arson were also true?

CHAPTER TWENTY

She swam a few lengths in the pool and had braved wearing a bikini—only because Nico had wanted to see her in one. Otherwise, she'd brought along a robust swimming suit which, although not sexy in any way, made her feel more together.

But when she'd pulled out her army regulation ensemble and was about to put it on, Nico had snatched it from her. "Our baby is nothing to be ashamed of," he'd told her.

"I'm not ashamed of our baby." She'd tried to yank it back from him. "I'm sure our baby will be cute enough. All babies are. It's this humungous bump I don't feel comfortable parading everywhere."

"I love you, bump and all."

How could she resist when he looked at her with charm dripping so effortlessly from his smile—and with that look of pure love pouring out of him?

So, she'd worn the bikini. Yet despite her bravery, she was relieved to find that it was only the two of them in the pool. She now looked over at Nico who was at the other end of the pool and swam back to him, doing a butterfly stroke which made her glide calmly through the water. She could feel her baby rolling and jumping as she swam.

She sometimes still found it amazing to think that she carried a living creature inside her. All too soon their baby would come into the world and it would happen regardless of whether she felt ready or not. Sometimes she wondered if she would be able to cope with this new change in her life.

With no family around to help out, except for Nico, she didn't think it would be easy. He was all that she needed for now, but what about when the baby came? Nico was a busy man. Ava would miss the reassurance of having Elsa around, or her annoying sister to bounce ideas off.

You're going to be fine, she kept telling herself.

By the time she came to a gentle stop in front of Nico, she felt his arms around her, and then they slipped down her waist and rested along her hips.

"Just watching you swim to me has me all excited." He leaned in to kiss her wet face as she fell against his chest. She could already feel the evidence of his excitement.

"I can tell," she murmured, pulling away and watching his dark brown eyes staring at her hungrily. Surely those enviably long lashes were wasted on a man?

She snaked her hands across his chest and could almost feel the heat of his raw passion just by standing so close to him, even in the warm water of the swimming pool. He ran his hands over her stomach, stroking it softly, his thumbs resting above her navel and his fingers sliding along her bloated waist.

"I feel so blessed," she murmured, as his hands slid higher up and across her body so that his thumbs rested on her bikini. She threw her head back softly, her body familiar with his touch, already knowing what would follow next. "I wish we could go on a honeymoon every year."

"We *will* go on a honeymoon every year," he whispered, rubbing his thumbs over her nipples until they peaked and made her desperate for him again. Even in the water a fire slowly sparked all over her skin, spreading like lightning to all corners of her body.

"But it won't be the same."

"Why not?"

"Because with time we'll get used to one another. We'll start to take one another for granted and then we'll become angry and jaded with old age. And the children will take up all of our time. It won't always be like this. Like the first time."

"You've already decided how we're going to be?" His fingers skimmed over her skin and she could tell he was restraining himself. "Each time will be its own first time. We'll take it in our stride, Ava. Just like we've taken everything else in our stride. This hasn't always been plain sailing for us, has it?"

She shook her head. It hadn't been an easy romance, but they had coasted the waters and survived. She shivered as she thought how close she'd come to losing him, of not telling him about the baby and returning to Denver. But she also knew that he would have come looking for her eventually.

His gaze held as he stared at her. "I love being with you, I love you, I love every moment we have together."

His words soothed her. "I love that I have you."

Soft lips fell together and tongues meshed and tasted as their hands roamed over wet skin, eager to explore. Nico's hands cupped her breasts once more and a gasp fell from her lips as he freed one breast from her bikini and rolled his thumb around the peak. Her eyes widened, first in sheer enjoyment and then with fear at the idea that someone might walk in and catch them. Scenes as sexy as sin flew through her mind as intense flames of liquid heat seared her skin, drenching her in desire and fearful anticipation. Nico bent his head and sucked her breast hard, eliciting another whisper from her parted lips. "Nico ..." She wanted him now, here, but knew they could not.

He slipped his hand between her legs and rubbed her. "Not here," she moaned, caught between the heat of wanting him and the pain of fighting it.

"You drive me insane, Ava. I feel like a teenager all over again when I'm with you." She closed her eyes and settled against his hand; hot, yearning and overcome by the rapture of the moment.

"I want to take you here, in this pool," he murmured, his breath hot and full of promises.

"We ... can't. Think of the others..."

"I don't care about the others. I care about what you want and what I need. And what I need is to lick you and suck you and take you every which way." An animalistic mewl fell from her throat at the idea of him doing those very things to her. For hours, she hoped.

"God, yes, please. I want you to ...," she begged, giving in easily.

CHAPTER TWENTY-ONE

It was with great difficulty that they slipped on their robes and made it back to their honeymoon suite. It was difficult for him especially, to hide the obviously large tent pole that shot out from his swim shorts.

The desire to take Ava became even stronger when she leaned against him, pushing her hips into his and kissing him like a woman possessed. Unable to control her ardor, she reached out for him in the elevator, and stroked him until he whimpered. The woman drove him to the edge of despair—not that he was complaining.

Being pregnant seemed to have set her hormones on fire. Taut and wound up with frustrated lust, he was overcome with the need to possess her completely and to sink inside her. It was instant release that he sought, and only this woman could satisfy his animal need. She stared back at him with eyes dark and hooded, and he knew that she was as hungry for him.

He wasted precious seconds fumbling around with the keycard to their suite, and once inside, he pinned her against the wall, tugging at the front of her robe. But the sound of Ava's cell phone ringing stopped them cold. She started to move away from him, ruining the moment.

"It can wait," he cried, grabbing her wrist and pulling her back to him just as he slipped the robe off her shoulders.

"But ..." Her denial was overturned by his kisses and he hungered for the softness of her body as she melted against him. His tongue fought with hers for dominance as they tasted and kissed freely in the privacy of their own suite. He stripped off his swim shorts, desperate to feel her naked body against his.

"Nico, let me answer—"

But he wasn't having any of it and knelt to remove her bikini bottoms. It was at that moment that the cell phone stopped ringing. He kissed her there, below her baby bump as she raked her fingers through his hair. She gently thrust her hips towards him and he got up quickly, untying the string of her bikini until it fell to the floor like petals in the wind. He gaped at her, stiffening even more as the image of her naked body, swollen and ripe before him, imprinted on his mind forever.

Sweet Jesus.

Privacy, peace and Ava—it was all he wanted. Perfect bliss for hours.

Just as he took her face between his hands, the cell phone rang again. *Damn these blasted things.* He kissed her hard and hungrily, hoping he could erase the sound of the offending device by the ferocity of his kisses. For a moment she yielded, her mouth soft and wet against his.

"It sounds urgent," she groaned, and made to answer it.

He growled as she slipped away from him, the sight of her rounded bottom and the loss of unfulfilled promises driving him to insanity and beyond. He followed her impatiently, like an addict desperate for a fix, waiting for her to take the call. But the cell phone stopped as she answered it.

Damn. That. Device.

Raking his hands through his hair, more out of frustration than anything else, he waited for her to come back to him but she stared at the screen with a curious look on her face.

Ava frowned. "It's Kim, and she's called me four times."

Why? He sucked in a breath. She'd been instructed to call only in the case of extreme emergency.

The fire.

Did she know? Had Carlos told Rona to call Kim and tell her? He had no idea and knew then that he should have taken care of it himself. He had no way of knowing whether Kim knew or not, and this made him wary.

"We're on our honeymoon, darling." He moved towards her and tried to take the cell phone from her but she held onto it.

"Let me get it, Nico. It must be urgent. Kim doesn't usually bother me."

"This can't wait." He pointed to his manhood.

"Trust me," she smiled, tapping on her screen. "I'll make it worth the wait."

But he didn't dare to risk it. "I need you *now*." Before she could utter another word, he kissed her. She moaned again, as the phone slipped from her hand and he led her, with their mouths still entwined, towards the bed. He was going to explode if he didn't get immediate release.

Ava lay back onto the bed, as if admitting defeat and inviting him in, then at the last minute she snatched the cell phone off him. She smiled up at him, legs parted, willing and wet for him.

The cell phone rang again.

This last intrusion tested his patience, making him grit his teeth together. *"Don't—"* He warned as she stared at the screen.

"Geraldino?" Ava sat up, her ample breasts hanging freely like fruit from a tree. Forcing himself to focus on her face, he ran his fingers across his creased brow and backed away a little, both curious and anxious.

Geraldino? What did he want? Nico's irritation grew. He was only concerned in this moment with what *he* wanted. And he was hungry for Ava. It was impossible for him to be this close to her and do nothing. Impossible to stay sane in the face of such temptation. Once again, the cell phone stopped ringing.

Maybe he could slip out and call Kim? Find out why she'd called so many times—and stem that potential problem at source.

"I need to call him, Nico. I'd ordered some wooden toys from him—maybe he's calling about that. I'm all yours after. I promise."

Forget the blasted wooden toys, he wanted to scream but he also knew this would be his only chance to call Kim and see what she wanted. He got off the bed. His excitement had all but died down as he watched Ava sitting naked, getting ready to make a phone call. "Don't be too long," he told her, then grabbed his shorts and his cell phone and headed for the washroom.

He called Kim.

"Nico?" Kim sounded surprised. "Aren't you guys meant to be on—"

He didn't have time for pleasantries. "Do you know about the fire?"

"Uh—yes, Rona told me." *So the message had gotten through.*

"I don't want Ava to know." He spoke in hushed tones.

"I know. Rona impressed that point upon me."

"We need to discuss the impact of this but I can't talk yet. It's hard with Ava around."

"Why are you calling?"

"To find out why you called her today."

"Sorry. It was an emergency. Connor wants us to empty his garage."

"He does?" More problems than he wanted to handle, especially on their honeymoon. Nico rubbed his temples. He really had to go to Denver and find a warehouse that they could use.

"Don't worry," Kim assured him. "I'll have a word with him tomorrow. Is it true about the shipment we were expecting? That it's been destroyed?"

"Unfortunately, yes."

"That's a shame. I guess it means we won't have the hassle of storing all of that stuff now but the customers aren't going to be happy."

"Will you deal with them as best as you can? I don't know how fast Andrea can restock and send over another shipment again. I imagine it can take weeks."

"Don't worry about the customers. I know how to handle them."

"I appreciate that you're doing what you can."

"We need to fix the storage problem for next time, Nico."

"I know. I'm coming over soon," he promised her. "But, please. Do whatever it takes to make sure that Ava doesn't find out the shipment was destroyed."

"Don't worry. She's not going to find out from me."

He relaxed. If only he could take on extra Kims and Ginas in his team. "I'm doing my best here to keep the news from her, but in case she finds out, and if she asks you, please could you downplay the incident?"

"You mean lie?" Kim asked.

Nico let out a groan. "Be creative. If you could see how happy and stress free she is these days, you'd understand why I want to avoid her finding out the truth."

Their days here reminded him of their first days together in Venice when they lived in a happy, cozy bubble, isolated from the world. It was like that for them once again and he wanted to keep it that way. The world would still be as hectic and as busy, and the paparazzi would still lurk everywhere when they returned to normal life soon enough.

"She won't hear a thing from me."

"Thanks Kim. I appreciate it. And be sure to call and let her know that Connor wants his garage emptied. I can't tell her, otherwise she'll get suspicious as to why we were talking."

"I'll call her now."

"No," said Nico quickly. "Maybe wait a few hours." Cell phones were both a lifesaver and a pain in the butt.

He hung up, feeling relieved. There was no way he could tell Ava what he knew—not only of the fire but of the shipment that had been destroyed. It pained him to lie to her but the alternative, to tell her the truth—that he'd known all along, and that he knew of the extent of the damage—wouldn't make things better.

He walked back to the bedroom and found her sitting on the edge of the bed, She'd slipped her robe back on, and looked ashen. "There's been a fire in Andrea's warehouse," she said slowly. "Geraldino found out from some friends. He said her warehouse is completely burned out."

Nico didn't need to try to look shocked. Her words stopped him dead. *Geraldino had told her?*

"No," he answered slowly, more in response to the news he'd been trying to keep secret being revealed from a source he'd never considered. "That's terrible." He tried to mask the anger he felt for Ava's supplier. "What else did he say?"

She looked crestfallen, as though her world had imploded and the sizzling atmosphere in the room deflated faster than his excitement. He sat beside her. "Just that ..." She looked away and he could tell that she was already thinking about it, churning the ramifications of this event over in her head, worrying about her customers.

"Just what?" he asked, rubbing her hands in his. "Did he know anything else?"

She shook her head. "He said that he'd heard about it. I should call Andrea and see how she is."

"It will be alright, Ava. Perhaps it's not so bad after all. Andrea would have called us if it was. She has insurance, don't forget. She's a savvy business woman and believe me, she'll want to get her business up and running as soon as possible. From what she tells me about Leo, he seems pretty sharp too. There's no way he's going to sit around and not get things moving fast. Don't you worry about it, Ava." He kissed the back of her hand, hoping to pull her away from the dark despair of her thoughts.

"I feel so bad for Andrea. I wasn't thinking so much of my business. I still have a huge shipment that's due to reach Denver any day now."

"There you go, see?" He kissed her cheek. "Promise me you won't think about it too much?"

"It happened a few days ago. I'm surprised we didn't hear about it." She got up and walked towards the living room. Nico followed her, and saw her reach out for the TV control.

"It's hardly national news. A fire in a warehouse in an industrial unit in Montova isn't going to make headlines here." He grabbed the remote from her. "So, ..." He cupped her cheek softly. "Where were we?" But he could already see that he'd lost her.

"Maybe that's why we haven't heard from her? She missed the wedding—"

"The fire only happened a few days ago."

"How do you know?"

"You just told me."

Her face relaxed. "I need to call Andrea, I need to know if my shipment went out. I mean, after I find out that she's alright. This must be a devastating blow to her. She'd only just started to scale up, so that she could keep up with my demand. I need to speak to her." She tried to wriggle out of his arms but he bent forward and brushed his lips gently across hers. "Nico, wait!" she admonished, trying to escape again. He paused, moving his lips away so that they barely touched hers. "I need you ..." he whispered, inhaling her breath, getting high just from being around her.

She stopped wriggling, and ran her tongue over his lips and her hands through his hair, and moaned as he undid her belt. The robe fell to the floor. The caress of naked skin on skin instantly revived his sagging arousal and this recent and intrusive turn of events added fuel to his fire. He pulled her towards the bed, then pushed her gently back down on it. Staring into her eyes, he lost himself in the heat of her gaze, before thrusting into her, deep and hard. Sighs escaped from somewhere deep in her soul; he heard the mewls and the soft, guttural sounds fall from her lips, and knew that she felt what he felt.

The fire—their fire—not only re-ignited, it quickly spiraled out of control. Her soft arms closed around him, her sharp nails pierced his skin as she clawed into his back. She opened up to him, with her ankles around his waist, rooting him to her as he plunged deeply and buried himself in her softness.

"Harder!" she cried, digging her nails in deeper.

And all the little white lies quickly evaporated away.

CHAPTER TWENTY-TWO

They'd ordered room service again and stayed in for the rest of the evening. The next morning, Ava lay lazily in bed, thinking of Andrea and feeling guilty that she hadn't called her friend.

The air in the room was old and stale as she slowly stretched out on the bed, her body well used and worshipped by Nico for hours. Last night their love making had been infused with a new urgency; Nico had been passionate, commanding and hungry for her—as if the buildup from the swimming pool had wound him up to a new level.

Their release had been long and slow, and she was left feeling a little sore, yet happy and satisfied.

She got up, slipped on her robe and opened the doors to the terrace then stepped out into the warm sunshine. It was another glorious day in paradise. Holding onto the iron railings, she stared out at the sparkling blue of the Mediterranean ocean. It struck her then that this scene now playing out before her was almost identical to the very image she'd seen in that magazine during her college years. She smiled at the thought of it.

How strange that she'd come full circle. She felt deliriously happy and despite her present state of euphoria, she remembered Andrea again.

As she wandered back inside, her attention was stolen by the sound of Nico's phone ringing. She looked over. The display name showed that it was Bruno. Undecided whether to answer it or not, she finally picked it up, hoping to take a message, but the call ended. Without thinking, and with curiosity getting the better of her, she hit the call logs button, wanting to find out if, like her, Nico had also been conducting his business dealings out of their usual one hour slot.

She had expected to see lots of calls to and from Bruno but her eyes stilled when she saw something else.

He'd recently called Kim. Yesterday in fact.

Thumbing down the list of contacts, she saw that Nico had also called Gina and Rona recently.

And Andrea had called him, too.

What the hell was going on?

She swallowed again. There was only one way to find out. As calmly as she could, she called Andrea.

"Hello. Ava?" Andrea's voice sounded unnaturally high-pitched.

"Hey," Ava replied, anxiety also making her voice sound odd. "How are you?"

"I'm ... good. Great. You caught me at a bad time."

"Did I? Sorry. We've been worried about you."

"Worried?" Andrea let out a nervous giggle. "Why? How's the honeymoon?"

"It's been wonderful. Very relaxing." *Or it had been, until now,* Ava thought, bitterly.

"That's what it should be. Leo told me you'd called the other day."

"We were worried when you didn't show up for the wedding."

She heard Andrea let out a deep sigh. "I'm so sorry about that. I meant to call and explain but it never seemed a good time and I didn't want to worry you on your honeymoon."

Yet you called Nico. "Don't worry about the wedding." *That* could wait. "What's going on with you?" she asked, better to be direct than to beat around the bush.

"What do you mean?" Andrea still sounded nervous.

"Did you call Nico?"

"I ... I might have dialed his number by mistake."

And you spoke to him for a few minutes. "Oh?"

"Uh-huh. Hey, Ava, sorry. A new shipment has arrived and I'd better take care of it. We have to meet up once you return."

Ava got the feeling that not only was Andrea not thrilled to hear from her but that she couldn't wait to get off the phone.

"I'll let you go, seeing as you're really busy." Ava's tone almost bordered on icy. "Oh, one more thing," she said, seeing that Andrea wasn't going to mention it. "I heard about the fire."

"The fire?"

"In your warehouse. I heard about it from Geraldino. He said the whole place had burned down. Is that true?"

"No!" Andrea laughed. "Of course not! We had a fire, yes, but apart from a few things ... the office is fine."

"It's not so bad, then?" Ava asked, her hopes lifting.

"No," replied Andrea, in an I'd-have-told-you-if-it-was voice.

"How bad *is* it?"

"Not bad at all. It's nothing to worry about, Ava."

"Geraldino made out that it had wiped you out of business."

"Geraldino should know better than to bother you on your honeymoon. Crazy man."

Andrea laughed and her cheerful mood now prompted Ava to ask her, "Any idea when that shipment should be hitting Denver?"

"Uh ... maybe a couple more weeks?"

A couple more weeks would be fine. "Thanks," said Ava, feeling relieved that things were going smoothly for them both.

"We'll catch up properly when you're back."

"I can't wait." Ava hung up and waited for Nico to come out of the shower. He appeared moments later with a towel draped around his middle and his skin looking freshly scrubbed and dewy. "I called Andrea," she announced.

"Andrea?" He looked puzzled. "We're only allowed to make our business calls—"

"Morning and evening, I know," she parroted. "But this was more of a social call and because I wanted to find out about the fire."

And because she also wanted to know why one of her closest friends had called her husband and why her husband had failed to mention it to her.

Nico let out a laugh, but kept his gaze on her. "What did she say?"

"She said it wasn't so bad. Knowing Geraldino, he probably caught the tail end of the rumors.

Nico's smile widened. "Probably."

"Why did you call Kim?"

He scratched his chin. "Kim?"

"Yes, Kim. Yesterday. What did you call her about and why didn't you mention it to me?"

"You were on the phone, darling, talking to Geraldino."

"So you snuck away to call Kim?" She almost laughed at the idea of it.

"Is that a crime?" Nico raked his hands through his wet hair.

"No, but now you're beginning to sound cagey and I'm beginning to get worried."

"What's this about?"

"I don't know," she said slowly, puzzled by his refusal to give her a straight answer.

"Don't you want to know why I called Kim?" he asked.

"Sure I do. And I also want to know why you never thought to mention it to me."

"Because we got busy doing something that was much more fun." He came over and sat by her. Everything she said he refuted and he had a perfectly good answer to her questions.

Then why did she sense that he was holding something back? She knew this man, knew him like she knew herself, and her inner radar told her something wasn't right. She'd meant it when she'd told him she didn't want any lies between them, or secrets. "So, why did you call her?"

He winced. "I was worried. She'd called you a few times and I was worried it might be something to do with the store, something that would prey on your mind. You called Geraldino and so I thought I would call Kim. It turns out it was related to what I suspected. I told her I'd deal with it."

"Deal with what?" *What had she missed?*

"Your storage issues," he replied, calmly.

"What about them?"

Nico was speaking in riddles again, and either she'd had too much sex and her brain was now addled, or she was missing the connection here.

"Connor wants them to remove the stock from his garage. Says he needs to empty it completely. That's why Kim rang you. She didn't know what to do."

"Connor?" She let out an angry gasp. All that money she'd lent him and he was doing *this*?

"See, that's *exactly* why I didn't want you to worry. You're angry and upset already."

"We have a new shipment going out and it's huge. Where are the girls going to store the new products?"

"I know," Nico answered. "Obviously you can't continue to put your stock in a variety of residential homes and garages." His voice was soft and full of concern, and she melted against him as he put her arm around her.

"I know. It was only meant to be a short term fix." But with getting pregnant and then Nico proposing to her, the decision had been made for her to live and settle in Italy. She'd only just about managed to hire Kim to work for her full-time instead of being her virtual assistant. Storage issues had been the last thing on her mind.

"When I go to Denver I'm going to fix this for good. Kim and Rona will never have space issues again."

"Don't bet on Rona working for me for too long," said Ava, snuggling up against Nico.

"No?"

"She's good at what she does, when closely supervised, but she's not cut out for working hard. She's my sister and I love her but she's no Kim ..."

"Is Kim really that good?"

"Kim is to me what Gina is to you," explained Ava. "She's exactly what I need to hold the fort over there."

"Every business should have a Kim and a Gina. I'm going to take care of your space issues I promise and you will never have to rely on Connor again. He can go to hell."

"Nico."

"He can. You don't need any help from him anymore."

"But ..." She considered telling him about the money but seeing that he was already slightly wound up, she quickly decided against it. "Thank you," she said as he hugged her tight.

He kissed the tip of her nose. "You're welcome."

There was still something else. "The other day, Bruno didn't call you. He only called this morning."

He turned pale. "Bruno called?"

"While you were in the shower. You lied, Nico, the other day in the spa when you said Bruno called you."

"I'm sorry." He squeezed her hand. "It's silly of me."

"What's silly of you?"

"I spoke to Rona and Carlos. I wanted to check when they were leaving so that I could let my agent know that the pensione was being vacated."

"Why lie about it?" she asked, wondering why the color had drained from his face.

"Because ... because I know how much you hate me meddling in your business—"

She frowned, not understanding.

Nico continued. "I wanted to check that things were in order, and that Lizzi was going to come in to keep an eye on your business once Rona left."

She almost choked out a laugh because she felt so guilty. "You made these calls behind my back because you were concerned for my business?" She felt ashamed for suspecting he'd been up to something. "Oh, Nico ... baby. You're *so* good to me."

"I'm not always that good," he murmured. "And now, tell me. What were *you* doing going through my phone? What were you looking for? Signs of an affair or some other nonsense?"

She laughed at the absurdity of it. "No." She'd crossed that bridge a while ago and now, carrying his child and understanding this man on a deeper level than she had any of her previous lovers, gave her a reassurance she'd never had before. With Nico, as naive as she might be, she felt secure. No longer did she have that same fear she'd had earlier in their relationship when she'd discovered that he'd been a player in his younger years. Her insecurities had mounted as she found out, at each turn, that almost every woman she came across claimed to have had a relationship or a one-night-stand with him.

If anything, she was coming to realize that she wouldn't lose him to a woman. She was more scared of losing him to his driving ambition to succeed in his father's footsteps. Her fear was that she would lose him to his work and his obsession with the new hotel, to prove himself to a man who was no longer here.

"What was it?" he asked.

"I was checking to see if you were making business calls while I was having my beauty treatments."

"I see. And you slipping into the washroom with your cell phone at every available opportunity wouldn't have made me suspicious?" He'd obviously noticed. Amusement danced in his eyes as he started to loosen the belt of her robe.

"We're as bad as each other," she replied, getting up and slipping off her robe so that she was naked before him again. "I'm having a long soak in the bathtub," she declared, reveling at the effect she had on him, and the way his mouth fell open. "I'll make it up to you, if you want to come and join me."

CHAPTER TWENTY-THREE

In all of this Nico juggled to keep an eye on Ava and the calls she got, hoping to keep her from discovering the real extent of the damage to Andrea's business, and therefore hers too. And he was also trying to weather his own problems back in Ravenna.

No sooner were the issues with the infinity pool resolved than he learned that there might be a problem with the elevators. Bruno had also told him that the final inspection for the hotel safety was scheduled for the start of November.

"But we're opening at the end of November," Nico protested.

"It's fine. There's nothing to worry about. You've got some of the best consultants and architects on this. They know what they're doing. Everyone is confident that they'll pass this hotel with flying colors."

What he really wished for was to suspend time, to stay here for longer, but with the last week of their honeymoon beginning, Nico lamented the fact that the days had slipped by so quickly. Still, he had the rest of his life with this woman.

And that sobering and happy thought lifted his spirits once more.

Confident that Bruno was on the case, Nico was reminded that he needed a full-time marketing manager as soon as possible, and someone who could help with the advertising for the new hotel as well. Until his father had passed away, Nico had carried out these kinds of tasks but heading the Cazale empire left no time for him to do this anymore.

He called Gina one day, when they'd returned from a trip to the Bay of Naples and was amused by the way she greeted him. "Why are you calling?" she barked, if it were possible for the polite and ever smiling Gina to bark at anything. But her voice sounded strained and less cheerful, and he understood the pressure she was under. Three weeks of being on guard, on his watch, would have exhausted anyone. He made a note to give her some time off as well as a pay raise.

"I was curious to find out how the recruitment drive was going."

"You don't have anything better to do?" Gina shot back.

He sure did. He'd done most of them, and he would continue to do them again and again with his wife. But a man needed to rest every so often.

"How's Ava?" Gina asked.

"She's happy."

"She still doesn't know about the fire?"

Nico's jaw tightened. "She knows. She found out from one of her suppliers."

"No!"

"Yes, and then she called Andrea to ask about it. Luckily Andrea made out it wasn't a big deal."

"That was lucky."

"It hasn't been easy lying to her. I seem to need more white lies as the days go on."

"That's a shame," commented Gina. "Hopefully Ava will understand when you tell her the truth."

"I hope so."

"You're both in the papers and the magazines over here. Are they hounding you there?" Gina asked.

He shook his head. "A few times, not much. Thankfully." He'd taken care of that. It was one of the reasons he'd picked the most exclusive and private of places. But a few times he'd noticed a couple of photographers skulking in the shadows, and snapping them as they walked around the sea front. Ava had noticed too, but had chosen to ignore it. By not talking about it he knew she was dealing with it in her own way and as long as the photos were of them in public places, and very infrequent, he had to turn a blind eye.

"It must be difficult for Ava to get used to," remarked Gina.

"It is."

He wasn't famous for anything in particular. It had been his reputation as the playboy son of a wealthy businessman that had first made the Italian press sit up and take notice. But in this day and age of fifteen second slots of fame, he hoped his time in the limelight was coming to a close. But, with Edmondo's death, and the business passing to him, not to mention him taking on a beautiful American wife, the attention seemed to have been revived.

It would take patience, but he would wait for the interest to die down again until someone younger and wealthier replaced him. He was old news, he knew it and relished it, and he didn't understand why he would still sometimes find his face on the cover of some of the magazines.

He continued. "It looks like the spa hotel is on course to

open for the end of November. We have less than two months for the publicity drive." In fact, here was one case where his fame would help—in the opening of the new hotel. He had to use the press as much as they used him.

"That's not long at all, Nico."

"That's why I was wondering how you were doing with the resumes and interviewing."

"You're in luck," Gina chirped. "I have three people who are interested in the marketing manager's position and I like them all. You'll have to decide which one to take on."

Relief flooded his body. "Excellent!" He needed someone in that role fast so that he could have this new person get started on the marketing campaign for the new hotel.

"But you'll need to interview them and see for yourself."

"Of course. Can you also please book a meeting for me with Bruno for the first day back?"

"Don't you want to ease back to work gently?" Gina asked.

"I don't want to take it easy. There's a lot to do." He had to somehow manifest a trip to Denver, too.

"I'll deal with it. It's not your problem. Now, go and enjoy the rest of your break," she ordered.

CHAPTER TWENTY-FOUR

"Yes, Mom. It's amazing. If you thought Verona was beautiful then the Amalfi Coast will leave you spellbound."

"You sound so relaxed, honey. I can actually see you smiling. It was about time you both got away from your hectic lifestyles. Please tell me that you're not both still working away on your computers?"

"We're not. We're having an amazing time."

"That's how it should be, Ava. You'll never have this time again, with just the two of you at the start of your journey. Treasure it."

She didn't need her mom to remind her.

"I was hoping that maybe Salvatore might have convinced you to stay," Ava joked then waited for the fallout.

"That man? Never!"

"It looked like you enjoyed that dance with him."

"I was being polite!" Elsa cried indignantly.

Ava played devil's advocate. "Since when have you ever been polite to that poor man?"

"You're making me out to be a monster. He was being

polite and I had to oblige. Did you *have* to put us at two tables close by to each other?"

"Would you rather I had seated you both at the same table?" She smiled mischievously, wishing she could see the look on her mother's face.

"I would rather you had put us as far apart as possible. Everywhere I turned he was there. You wanted us close by just because he's a widower and I'm a widow."

Ava had thought they would make for good company. "I was only saying that the two of you seemed to be enjoying the waltz."

"To change the subject," commented Elsa drily, "I'm happy that you and Nico are both taking time to relax, for a change, instead of worrying about work. That's all I want to hear. How're you feeling?"

"Fine, mostly."

"Fine, mostly?"

"I'm getting a few headaches. Did you suffer from them?" She wanted to mention that she'd seen double once or twice, nothing much to worry about. But she decided not to say a word to Elsa. She didn't want her mother to worry, or to say anything to Nico. She would visit the doctor once they returned home.

"I didn't suffer at all," replied Elsa. "I didn't even get morning sickness. Most of the time I didn't really feel pregnant. It was the labor that killed me. Rona had such a big head, she almost ripped me to shreds. It's a miracle your father convinced me to have another one. And I'm so glad I did. I had you, honey."

Her pregnancy had been mostly fine this second trimester until the last month, and she put it down to overworking and stress over the wedding. She had assumed that being away on her honeymoon might help, but her double vision had occurred a couple of times even here in Amalfi. Luckily she'd been able to hide it well and Nico had been none the wiser. "I can't wait to see you again, Mom. I wish you'd stayed longer in Verona."

"With both of you away, it made more sense to return with Rona and Carlos. How could I miss Tori's birthday?"

"How is my little angel?"

"She tries to walk, then gets excited when she stands up and gets her balance, shoots forward, wobbles then falls and gets back up again—like you used to."

Ava laughed.

"I'll be over when your baby arrives," her mother assured her.

"That would be wonderful, Mom." Having Elsa around during the early weeks would be a great help. "Is Rona around?"

"She's got her hands full."

"Tell her I called and wish my niece a very happy birthday, would you?" She could hear the noise of what sounded like a gaggle of excited children running around in the background.

"I'll tell her. Be good to one another," said Elsa.

CHAPTER TWENTY-FIVE

During their last week in paradise Nico booked a few more excursions though they really didn't need to do anything.

Sometimes they just lounged around in the infinity pool or sat out on the comfortable chairs in their private garden and gazed out at the sea or read books, or talked.

One day they went on a lemon tour at a local farm where they walked around the lemon groves and were shown how limoncello was made. On another day they cruised from Amalfi to the charming town of Capri, stopping off at many wonderful grottos along the way. Only Nico jumped in for a swim before they ate homemade crab ravioli at a tiny, bustling restaurant with amazing views of the harbor.

They spent a few days visiting other islands around the Bay of Naples and enjoyed many happy hours wandering aimlessly through the small villages where purple and pink bougainvillea rolled and tumbled over the gates and walls of pretty, white houses, splashing wild color among the lush green landscape. Nico was used to bougainvillea but he could tell that Ava was still enchanted by their beauty, even now, despite having seen these blooms everywhere. She often marveled that the sight of the shocking pink and purple flowers took her breath away, and he was reminded to ask Salvatore to plant these flowers in their garden at home.

They returned to Sorrento one day and after dinner they walked around the Chiostro di San Francesco, a cloister near the public gardens. It was a place of beauty, a paradise haven fringed with palm trees and overlooking the sea.

"This would have been an amazing place to get married in," sighed Ava.

"We can come back here and renew our vows again some day," he told her in amusement. "If once wasn't enough for you."

She smiled at him. "I love that I married you once, and I'll treasure that memory forever. But look at this place, Nico. Don't you think it's beautiful?"

He had to admit, it was. He'd heard that many weddings were conducted here and looking around, it seemed the ideal place. "It's peaceful," he agreed as they walked to the terrace that overlooked the shimmering blue ocean.

They gazed at it quietly, saying nothing as the dusk settled. This view of the ocean was much like the one from their honeymoon suite, but they were barely there in the evenings, and so, enjoying it in this calm setting was like seeing it again with fresh eyes, especially as the sun was starting to steal away, leaving only a flamingo-pink veil across the sky.

He watched Ava as she looked around, taking her fill of the scenery, and waited until she was ready to go. She turned to him. "Shall we go?" He nodded, and took her hand.

They walked quietly, strolling along in happy contentment, along the narrow and winding maze-like alleyways of Sorrento. As they ambled along she suddenly missed her step and fell forward. Luckily he caught her and placed both his hands on either side of her arms, looking at her with concern as she shook her head.

"What is it?" he asked, suddenly fearful as the color drained from his face.

"I lost my footing." Ava shook her head and blinked a few times.

"Let's go back so you can rest up," he suggested, and slipped his hand into hers.

"Nico, I'm fine," she insisted. "Let's stroll by the sea and look at the views again. Please?"

"We can come back another time." Had she tripped? He wasn't sure but he'd noticed that her ankles looked slightly swollen. "Are you feeling alright?"

"I'm fine. It's just a walk."

He was forced to relent, knowing how much she loved walking along the seashore. He loved seeing the breeze combing through her hair. Looping his arm around her shoulder, he kissed the side of her face. "If that's what you want," he whispered, and headed off in the direction of the sea, feeling sad that this time had drawn to a close.

If only he could have this all over again with her.

But time moved forward, not backwards, nor did it freeze. He pushed all thoughts of the hotel and the recruitment drive and the problems in Ravenna behind him, and tried to live for the present.

He grabbed her hand and kissed it absent-mindedly, knowing that tomorrow he would have to tell her the real truth about the fire.

CHAPTER TWENTY-SIX

Nico walked around their home opening the windows on a lazy and warm September evening.

It pleased him to see that although they hadn't been here for a few weeks, the air wasn't musty or stale. Not only had Helena given the house a good cleaning, but she'd aired it regularly as well.

They'd only arrived home less than an hour ago and already he was getting anxious thinking about the workload that would smack him to reality on his return to work tomorrow. There was so much to think about and being away had enabled him to unwind, properly, for the first time in a long time. Now he had only memories to sustain him. Memories and the knowledge that he had a lifetime with Ava. He was suffering from the end of honeymoon blues and in time this would pass.

"Helena did a good job, don't you think?" He watched Ava as she examined the kitchen.

"She's even stocked the fridge," Ava commented, with surprise. "Did you ask her to? I see she's bought my favorite ham and yogurt."

"She must be telepathic," said, Nico, coming up behind her.

"A telepathic housekeeper? Even better." He knew she was still getting used to the idea of having someone around to help with housekeeping. Nico had also talked about having someone come in to cook for them once the baby was born but he hadn't been able to win her over on that idea just yet.

"I like it being only the two of us, in our home," she'd countered when he'd first raised the idea.

"But, darling, you've taken a lot on. When the baby's here, you said you have no intention of slowing down with your business." Although he hoped she might slow down a little. "It might be too much for you."

"Let me try to balance my baby and my business. You'll help too, won't you?" Of course he would, as much as he could but he already knew that the demands of his business were excessive. Even though he had every intention of pulling his weight around the house and helping with the baby, he knew the business also pulled him in many directions.

He was going to make a concerted effort to concentrate on Ava and the new baby when he or she arrived, and hopefully by then the hotel would be up and running and it would be an enormous pressure off his shoulders. He hadn't pushed any more housekeeping help on her just yet. For now, Helena was doing cleaning and light duties and that was some help.

"I feel sad to be back home," she said in a somber voice as they walked up the stairs. Nico carried their cases. "Me, too," he replied, feeling even more gloomy. He wasn't looking forward to telling her. He heard her gasp as she opened the door to their bedroom.

"I forgot about the room!" she exclaimed, happiness spreading out from the corners of her lips as she walked in. "Scratch that," she said, and walked around the room slowly, as if she'd never seen it before. "It's not so bad being back." She gurgled with pure delight and sank onto the bed, stretching her arms out on either side with glee. "The Acacia was to die for, but nothing beats coming home again."

He placed the luggage at one end of the large room and watched her, feeling a little less downcast.

"Don't unpack any of this yet. We'll do it later," he told her. "Enjoying the bed?" He stopped and stared at her before fetching the remaining suitcases.

"I'd forgotten how sumptuous it was," she purred. He knew she'd love the new super large bed he'd had specially made. Which reminded him ... Pausing at the door he asked her, "We never got around to christening it, did we?" She had fallen asleep on their wedding night and the next morning they'd both overslept and had rushed to catch their honeymoon flight.

"Isn't that a tradition which needs to be actioned immediately?" she asked in a voice that dripped of honey.

"Yes, Ma'am."

"Hurry back," she shouted after him.

He walked out feeling anxious again. He had to tell her without further delay, otherwise hiding the news any longer would only add to his gloom. When he had brought the last of their suitcases up, he sat down beside her on the bed, his mood suddenly sour.

"Why so sad?" Ava asked. He could feel her fingers stroking his back. "Are you also missing our terrace, and our suite, and the walks along the sea ...?"

"There's something I need to tell you."

"What is it?" She sat up slowly and he moved so that he could sit facing her and watched her eyes fill with apprehension. Taking her hands in both of his, he considered how best to break the news. "Nico? What's the matter?" she repeated, and he knew she feared the worst. Whatever her worst fears were, he felt some solace in knowing that *this* wasn't that bad.

"It's about the fire."

"The fire?"

Nico nodded, his jaw tight again. Clearly, she hadn't given it much thought since Geraldino had told her.

"You mean in Andrea's warehouse?"

He nodded.

"What about it?"

"It was bad." He watched the surprise on her face give way to shock. "The whole place burned down, apart from the office. It's damaged but they still have their—"

"*Everything?*" Creases decorated her forehead.

"Everything. The goods on display, and their entire stock. All destroyed." He could see her thinking it over and he could easily sense her worry.

"Why, how do you know all of this?" she asked him in a voice that was cold. He looked at her and took a deep breath. "I've known from the moment Andrea called me."

"When?"

"Soon after it happened, I don't know exactly when."

"When did she tell you—before I heard from Geraldino?"

"Yes."

"So you already knew when I told you?"

He nodded his head sheepishly.

"You *lied* to me?"

He closed his eyes and squeezed them tight.

"You kept this from me the whole time and then you lied when I found out anyway?"

"I am so sorry, Ava. I didn't want to worry you." He defended his stance.

"But you lied, Nico. And on our honeymoon too. What

does that say for our relationship?" She shook her hands free from his and got up.

"It's nothing to do with our relationship. Don't make it out to be about that. It's because I care for you—because I didn't want you to worry and because I knew you'd react like *this*." He waved his hands at her as she paced around the room, her face growing more contorted by the second. He could tell she needed to vent and to think it all through and he knew his deception had hurt her.

"You lied to me."

"I lied because I love you and I didn't want you to worry," he protested.

"Except that you have me more worried than ever now."

"I was thinking of your health, you'd only just started to unwind. What could you have done if you'd found out back then?"

"I could have handled telling my customers instead of saying nothing. Whether it matters to you or not, Nico, this is my business, it's what I love to do and this fire is going to hit me bigtime. When I spoke to Andrea she made out that it wasn't so bad." She seemed to be mulling something over. "She barely mentioned it." Ava stared at him as the realization hit; her breathing heavy, her shoulders stooped. Her earlier exuberance had vanished with his confession. "Did you tell Andrea to lie to me?"

"Andrea called and asked me whether she ought to tell you. She was worried about you, too."

"Thank you both for your concern, but in the meanwhile, my whole business is probably a mess, or will be soon. I've been in the dark the whole time."

"Two weeks."

"A day is a lifetime in business and you know that, Nico."

Damn. He'd envisaged an easy night settling back home

and taking things easy, getting ready to face the world tomorrow. Not a full blown counter attack. "I'm sorry, Ava. I thought I was doing the right thing."

"I'm sorry too. You didn't do the right thing. You should have told me the moment you found out."

"You'd have done nothing but worry."

"And rightly so!" She raised her voice, something she didn't do very often. "You told me it wasn't that bad. And how come none of the girls mentioned anything to me either? Rona or Kim—do they know?"

"Yes," he replied, wearily. "They know. I spoke to them. I told them to keep the news from you."

"You told them to lie, too?"

"I told them to be creative with the truth, that to tell you about the fire and the stock would only worry you needlessly."

"Needlessly?"

"If you must know, they happened to share my view." It sounded worse the way she repeated his good intentions back to him with malice. As much as she had every right to be angry, he felt that he had every right to protect her. "I told them not to tell you the truth because I didn't want to spoil our honeymoon." A ball of tension squeezed the muscles behind his neck. He'd been apprehensive enough about coming back and diving headfirst into dealing with the usual hotel problems, but he hadn't considered that he'd have to deal with personal problems, too.

Ava fiddled around with her engagement ring; her expression tight and knotted. "They would have received the last shipment by now. Maybe that's why things haven't seemed so bad," she murmured, her eyebrows inched closer together at the tip. "Otherwise they would have told me. I was starting to get momentum and my sales were starting to snowball." She let out a deep exhalation. "Maybe I still have some leeway. That was a huge shipment this recent one."

Nico shook his head, hating to tell her more bad news. "Your shipment didn't go."

She stared at him, wide-eyed. "What do you mean it didn't go?"

He closed his eyes and pushed the balls of his fingertips into the soft cushy part of his eye socket, below the eyebrows. He couldn't bring himself to repeat the words.

"Andrea told me it was on its way!"

He opened his eyes and stared back at her as calmly as he could. "It didn't go, Ava." He watched her face crumple like tissue paper. She was silent, her mouth open. "Andrea had meant to send it off, but she got busy. The fire happened when she was away on business for a few days and your shipment got waylaid. She was going to dispatch it when she returned."

"You knew that too?" Ava's nostrils flared and the depth of her anger took him by surprise. "You lied about that knowing I was worried about my business, knowing I had people waiting on me?" She flexed her fingers and let out an anguished sound. "I don't know what to think. I don't know what to feel." She looked up at him as if a new thought had come to her. "The broken table lamp and the coffee stains ...that was all lies too?"

Little white lies.

Nico looked down at the floor. The glow from recent honeymoon memories vanished swiftly. "Ava," he reached out for her hand.

"No," she cried, pushing his hand away. "All those beautiful days we spent together, walking and talking and making plans for our future and underneath it all you were lying to me."

He struggled to put it into perspective. "Don't make this out to be something it's not. This isn't about our relationship, it's got nothing to do with what you mean to me. This is purely about wanting you to enjoy our honeymoon, knowing that you could not have done anything had I told you the bad news."

"Why, Nico? You meant well, I get that. But it also tells me that you don't seem to think this is important to me. Maybe you still think I'm doing this for a hobby?" The look in her eyes made him feel guilty.

"That's not true. I know how important your business is to you."

"Do you? Do you even care what happens if my orders stall?"

He swallowed. "I spoke to Rona and Kim and told them to deal with the customers ... I mean, I didn't have to tell them to do anything. They knew what to do."

"It's my business, Nico. I've spent so much time trying to build it up. Surely you understand that? I was starting to get my momentum and now that will most likely be affected. In fact, it *will* be affected, since I now know that the shipment we'd all been waiting on got destroyed. I know it wasn't your fault the fire happened. It wasn't anyone's fault. But can't you see how wrong it was of you to keep that news from me?"

When she put it like that he started to see it a different way, but still, what he'd done, he'd done out of love for her. Why couldn't she see that? "I'm sorry I cared enough to want to protect you."

"If your spa hotel burned to the ground and I kept that from you, would *you* be okay about it?"

His mouth twisted. No, if the circumstances were reversed he wouldn't. "I'm not pregnant, Ava. So it's slightly different. You were so relaxed and enjoying our vacation.

You'd forgotten all about work, as had I, as much as was possible. I didn't want you to be in that same stressed out state again."

She looked mortified, and it made him wonder if he'd done the right thing.

"No secrets, remember what I said on our honeymoon? No secrets or lies between us." She got up and walked away from him.

"Where are you going?"

"To call Kim and Rona."

Nico hung his head and stared at the floor. So much for a memorable return home from their honeymoon.

CHAPTER TWENTY-SEVEN

"How come you didn't tell me about the fire?" Ava charged straight into the conversation with Rona, once the niceties were quickly dismissed.

Her sister was silent for a while and Ava imagined the thoughts going through her mind. For once, Rona appeared to be stuck for words.

"The fire?" Rona sounded cagey.

"You can quit acting ignorant about it, Rona. Nico told me."

"He said he didn't want you to find out while you were on your honeymoon." Rona replied.

"He should have told me."

"I side with Nico."

"You would."

"Why are you so upset?" Rona asked.

Ava exhaled an angry sound. "Why do you both think this is no big deal?"

"He was looking out for you. It's not like you could have done anything. Kim and I took care of it."

"How bad is it?"

"We've had a few complaints. A couple of people online have left a few bad reviews about your website. Our stock is starting to go down. Connor's garage still has quite a lot of our stock in it, but the good thing is he's no longer in a hurry for us to vacate it. He says he needs it done by next month though."

Ava relaxed a little. At least this was one less problem to think about. "Did you know that our latest shipment was destroyed?"

"Yes."

"Of course you know," said Ava, testily. "You know more than I do." She rested her face in her hands. When it rained, it poured, except right now Ava felt as though she was standing underneath a waterfall and drowning. That shipment might have helped keep them going while Andrea got herself together again. She had to go and see Andrea as a matter of urgency—or get Andrea to come and see her here, seeing that her friend no longer had a place to operate out of.

There were so many things to sort out. It was hard to believe that only yesterday she and Nico had been taking it so easy, enjoying the terrace and the Jacuzzi before taking a final walk along the sea.

It was all so different to the storm she'd walked into on her return. Still ... her eyes opened wide. There was still an order from d'Este. "Have the d'Este cribs arrived?"

"They did and you won't believe this, but we've nearly sold out."

"Really?" she asked breathlessly.

"Really."

She'd had a feeling they would be a good seller. "That's wonderful!"

"I moved them to the homepage on our site, and labeled them as bestsellers," Rona announced proudly. Ava had been amazed at how Rona had come on with tackling the updates to the website.

"You can't blatantly lie! They're not bestsellers yet, if we've only recently started to include them in our product range."

"They're bestsellers at the company you bought them from."

"That's because it's the only product they sell!"

"Well, technically, they are bestsellers now, because they've sold out faster than our other cribs did."

Technically, her sister had a point. And, if Ava remembered correctly, d'Este sent the products directly from their factory in Italy to Denver—which meant they didn't have to go via Andrea's warehouse.

Considering current circumstances, this had been a blessing. She knew that Andrea also preferred the manufacturer to handle shipping. Ava slid her hand over her stomach and felt the baby move. Perhaps things weren't as bad as they had seemed.

"Don't be mad at Nico," Rona told her. "He was only doing what he thought was right."

"I can't help it. This is my business, something I've worked hard at. What did he think would happen? That I'd fall to pieces with worry?"

Rona remained silent.

"I have to call Kim." Ava told her.

"Okay. But tell me, how was your honeymoon?"

"Great, until we got home."

"Don't be bitter, Ava. Don't take it out on poor Nico."

But even as she hung up, Ava couldn't help but think of what Nico's reaction would have been if she'd kept the news of the spa hotel burning down from him, assuming such a thing had happened.

She sat back in the bright and cheery office directly opposite their bedroom, across the large landing. Nico had a more traditional wood-paneled den that he liked to use downstairs and had given her carte blanche to design the workspace in this room. It would be her office from home.

It was white, and she had plans to bring in some ornamental desktop waterfall structures, and a couple of bamboo plants and she would decorate the walls with a few pictures. But mainly she wanted it uncluttered and clear.

She'd have to be careful about spending too much time in here, the temptation to continue working until the early hours, when working from home, was huge. It was bad enough with Nico and his crazy hours —she knew he would be back into the thick of things tomorrow. If she also became too obsessed about her work then what type of life did that bode for their child? She would have to make a conscious effort to find a balance.

When Kim didn't answer, she toyed with the idea of calling Andrea but decided to leave that until tomorrow. She felt another headache coming on, and when she looked down at her feet she noticed a slight swelling around her ankles.

With her deflated spirit only partially revived by news of the d'Este cribs selling out, Ava decided to have an early night.

The first thing she would do tomorrow was to arrange an appointment with the doctor. But then again, maybe she'd do that once she'd spent a few hours looking at the state of their inventory and analyzing her sales figures. It was time to put a price to the damage her business had suffered.

CHAPTER TWENTY-EIGHT

"You look well rested," Gina commented as she entered Nico's office.

Nico stared up at her with a distracted look. "And you look as though you've been overworked by a tyrant boss." He pushed his leatherbound diary away and beckoned Gina to come and sit down.

It had taken a couple of hours to sift through the hundreds of emails that he'd marked as non-urgent while they had been away and he estimated that it would take another few hours before he got through all of them and responded to the phone calls that had piled up in his absence.

He had all of this to take care of before he touched base with the managers of the other Cazale hotels. Only when he had taken care of all this, would he then give all of his attention to the spa hotel because he knew it would take up all of his time from now until it opened.

Don't forget the baby and the trip to Denver. And Ava too.

Last night the mood had been subdued after his admission of the fire. They hadn't christened the bed after all and Ava had been quiet for the rest of the evening and had had an early night. He knew it would take time for her to ease up with him.

Those little white lies on his honeymoon had cost him dearly. She'd come to bed and had slept with her back to him, right up against the edge of it. He'd felt alone in the huge bed with a distance as wide as the Mediterranean sea between them. But she must have felt it too, because she had gradually shifted position and moved towards the middle, finally ending up in his arms.

She would forgive him in time, he felt sure of it.

"I am well rested," he replied, addressing Gina. "The place is still standing, the staff look happy enough. But I'm worried about you." He examined her tired features and felt guilty that he'd left her alone, more or less, for so long.

"It was fine, in the end," said Gina, settling herself down. He knew that as long as he had Gina—and he'd have to make sure she never left—the hotel would be fine. She was too precious, too integral to his team, which at the moment only consisted of the two of them.

"What's been going on?" he asked, anxious to hear of any troubles. She hadn't called him much, and he knew from experience that running a hotel, even small ones like theirs, was not easy. "How have you coped?"

"It hasn't been easy. I won't lie to you. But there weren't too many problems, nothing that I couldn't deal with," Gina replied quickly. "Or I would have called you."

"I appreciate all of your hard work, and I know you did all of this alone. I knew you could handle it, there's no-one else I trust as much as I do you. I'm very grateful to you."

Gina shifted in her chair as he acknowledged her hard work. "Were you able to hold the weekly conference calls with the other hotels?"

She nodded. "Everything is running smoothly, Nico. I

want to know about your honeymoon. Tell me all about it. How was it?"

"It was one of the happiest times of my life," he replied, truthfully.

"Did Ava get to relax? Did you?"

He nodded his head, tried not to think of how much relaxing they'd done, and how much their lovemaking had been a part of it. "We did, and it was great while it lasted. Unfortunately, I had to come clean about the fire not long after we returned home."

"Ouch. How did Ava take the news?"

"Not too well. She's mad that I didn't tell her."

Gina nodded her head, not siding with either one of them. "I see her point of view, but I see yours too."

"She's keeping me at a distance."

"She seemed fine this morning," Gina admitted. "And she looked remarkably relaxed."

"It must have been big news around here."

"It was on the news and in the papers. But so was your wedding." Gina flashed a smile at him as he groaned. "Don't worry. Most of the pictures were taken from a distance at the church. They didn't get anything from the reception—which was out of this world. The wedding was beautiful, but your reception ... oh, Nico. It was the best."

Nico cheered up. "You had a good time?"

She nodded. "It was amazing."

Nico smiled. "We saw you talking to someone."

Gina blushed.

"Who was that?" he asked, probing.

"Just a friend."

"Just a friend?" Nico nodded, sensing that she didn't seem comfortable discussing the matter.

"Did you know there's talk about the fire at the warehouse

being a possible arson attack?" asked Gina, completely changing the subject.

"Andrea told me. Do they know who might have done it or why?"

Gina shook her head. "It only made the news for one day. It seems to have died down."

Nico understood. There was always something else to replace the churn of bad things happening.

"How's Andrea bearing up?" Gina wanted to know. "And what about Ava? Won't this affect her business?"

"It will. Ava found out last night the extent of the damage, and that her items were burned, including a large shipment that she'd been relying on."

"I can see why she's annoyed with you, even though you acted out of concern for her."

"She doesn't see it that way," said Nico slowly, recounting the stilted conversation in the car when he'd driven them both to the Casa Adriana this morning.

Gina watched him intently. "It's obviously going to be a huge shock for her to discover that her business suffered such a major setback. Give her some time, Nico."

He knew he had to give her some space and he was patiently waiting for her to discover the extent of how the fire had impacted her orders back in Denver. "As for Andrea, I haven't spoken to her since then. I need to talk to her." Nico wondered how Andrea would be. This was an enormous setback for her, but he felt some relief that she wouldn't have to deal with it alone, now that she had Leo working with her.

"In the meantime, what do I need to know? First of all, the course you postponed for me—when are you going?"

"Next month," replied Gina.

Next month was tough again. He had plans to go to Denver but he couldn't ask Gina to postpone her course again. "Book it," he told her. "Where did you get with the interviews?" If ever there was a reason for him to get the management team together quickly, this was it.

"I now only have two candidates lined up for you to interview. One of them dropped out but you'll be suitably impressed with the caliber of the two I found."

"You interviewed them yourself as well as dealing with everything else?"

"Here are their resumes." She slipped him neatly stapled documents in a plastic wallet. Nico drummed his fingers on the desk. "Good work, Gina. We'll talk later this afternoon, if that's alright? I need to speak to my project manager and check that we're on track to open in seven weeks."

"Seven weeks?" Gina echoed.

"It's not long is it? November is getting busy and I will be relieved when that hotel is up and running and bringing in money instead of draining me dry."

"You have the baby coming that month too," Gina reminded him.

"The baby, too." He was having palpitations just thinking about it.

CHAPTER TWENTY-NINE

'Terrible customer service. Still waiting for the crib and my baby is due any day.'

It might have helped if you'd ordered a few months in advance, thought Ava, drawing her lips together in a tight line.

'Will never shop here again. Ordered my products months ago and am still waiting!'

That was a blatant lie. She'd deliberately put a long time lag between delivery against all the product details, especially for the larger items such as the cribs and the high-chairs. She'd made it very clear on her website that she sold authentic products that were sourced in Italy. Her customers knew this wasn't a poor replica but the real deal. And her prices reflected the quality of her goods.

But the spate of bad reviews made her feel down and she couldn't stop herself from re-reading the vicious comments all over again. It didn't matter that she had an overwhelming number of good reviews from happy customers because her mind still chose to focus on the nasty ones. More of these had sprung up in the last few days and she knew losing that shipment was going to cause even more problems further down the line.

Her mood soured and she felt bitter and angry about what had happened. The fire was something she could not have foreseen but it was beginning to have a crippling effect on her business. Sales were much slower, reviews and comments were getting worse. She hadn't been prepared for the negativity. The problem with running an online store, especially one where she provided products for new babies, meant that timing was essential. Babies arrived by a certain date, and she always had that time pressure to think about.

She'd have to use air freight for the next shipment and that was going to cost a lot. She'd probably have to take a hit on making a profit this time around. Normally, she used ocean freight, it took weeks, usually about a month but it was cheaper. In the past this hadn't been a problem when she had regular shipments from Italy to Denver. With no shipments going out at the moment and with no idea when they would start up again, the stock she held was beginning to go down. Slowly, the business was beginning to stall, and she was shocked by how quickly this had happened. She had no idea how long it would take for Andrea to get up and running.

The only silver lining in all of this was d'Este. Whatever happened, she needed to place another large order with them, and fast.

She got thinking; did she really need Andrea to be the middle person? What if she went direct and dealt with d'Este herself? And why stop there? Why not go direct with the manufacturers of all the other products she sold? After all, it was she who had found d'Este and had suggested them to Andrea. Thinking about it more, she didn't really need Andrea to deal with sourcing products when she could do it all herself.

She sat back in her chair and wiped her hand over her brow. Andrea's fire had really caused her a serious amount of damage. The few who were being vocal about the delay in receiving their products had easily managed to spread the word about it. And online, reputation was everything. It was the same with offline businesses, but in the internet stratosphere, things spread more virulently and faster.

She'd become so complacent lately, basking in the goodwill of happy customers with a fast turnover of goods and a product line that was authentic and unique, she hadn't really stopped to think what might happen if she had a problem one day that would cause a bottleneck. Until now.

She felt her heart beating wildly and a dull ache starting up in her head. She didn't need this. Didn't need more problems heaped on top of her.

Last night there had been distance between her and Nico and she'd eventually gone to bed with her back to him. She couldn't bring herself to talk things over with him. It was wrong, she knew it was, but she couldn't help the way she felt. He'd lied to her. Her mind had been pre-occupied with damage limitation and how to turn things around in her business. But she couldn't sleep without his arms around her, and so she'd leaned closer to him. If he had any doubt that she was still mad, he found out for sure during the cold, stony silence in the car on the way to work.

She sat dazed and bewildered in her office wondering how quickly things had turned sour for her. It wasn't Nico's fault, but he was wrong to think that she wouldn't have been able to do anything. At the very least she could have sent out a newsletter sooner. She'd done so last night, but she was already weeks late. She sensed that she could have prevented some of the negativity she now faced if only she'd made an announcement sooner. Her customers would have understood. Kim and Rona had done their best, but Nico hadn't been able to give them any real direction except to tell them to keep the customers happy.

She felt like blaming someone and lately she'd felt out of sorts. Coming back home and hearing this news had given her another headache again. She was fearful of telling Nico exactly how she felt because his first response would be to tell her to slow down. Maybe he'd hoped that something like this would happen to her so that it would force her to take things easy.

This wasn't how it was supposed to be. She ran her hand over her belly, felt the baby move and smiled. She wasn't sure she needed to see the doctor yet and perhaps she'd leave it until next week.

The need to meet up with Andrea was more urgent.

CHAPTER THIRTY

"The infinity pool is in?" asked Nico, wiping his brow with relief as he listened to Bruno at the other end of the line.

"No need to worry about that, Nico." Bruno's reassurance was sweet relief to his ears. "But..." and there was always a 'but'. Nico didn't want to hear it but knew he had to. Why couldn't everything coast along? How had his father managed it? "But?" He pressed his fingers tightly along his brows.

"It's nothing too serious—and I didn't want to mention it while you were away—"

"The problem, Bruno. Just give it to me."

"It's the old hotel. We have a severe case of mold in a lot of the rooms along the east side of the old building."

"And nobody picked this up sooner?"

"We didn't realize how bad it was until we peeled back the old paper. It might delay us."

"We can't have a delay," Nico thundered. "The hotel must open by the end of November. There is no alternative. Tell me what it will take to get the job done." He knew he'd have to visit Ravenna tomorrow. It had taken him a couple of days to finish things up at the Casa Adriana and its sister hotels.

"We'll need a team to work on the mold."

"You know each day the project gets delayed, you incur a penalty?"

"I'm aware of that, Nico."

"I'll be over first thing tomorrow morning, Bruno. Be ready to go through everything with me then."

He liked Bruno and liked his straight forward manner—and the guy was polite. He had to be, Nico was paying out good money for his hotel for the new construction and the refurbishing of the old. If Edmondo had been here, Nico felt his father would have helped guide him through these dangerous waters for this was all new to him. He had no experience of the building process, or about the pitfalls in renovating old buildings. And old hotel buildings were much more complicated. Nico had only helped maintain his father's hotels—and he'd always had Edmondo to fall back on. What he'd done back then hadn't been as difficult. What he was doing now was akin to walking a tightrope above Niagara Falls without a safety net beneath him.

He felt very much alone and in shark-infested waters. Not only had he purchased an old hotel that was in bad shape, but he was also having a new spa center built on the grounds. He had ambitiously, hurriedly and maybe even stupidly taken on two huge projects neither of which he had much experience in. Though he'd hired the best people, he felt, once more, as though he was cheating; he was using his father's hard earned money and building everything up from that. He wasn't starting over—not like Edmondo had done. His father had created his own fortune from nothing.

Was he trying to prove to himself that he was as good as his father? He didn't know—and he had no time to dwell on such matters. He knew only that he had to get the job done and whatever happened, the hotel opening date could not change or be delayed.

This first week back seemed to be getting worse with each passing day. Things at home were not much better. Ava seemed as tense as he felt—he could see it on her face. At least they were talking again. She hadn't said as much, but she was warming up to him again and when she explained that she'd had a small spate of bad reviews, he understood her frustration. Neither of them needed this extra stress.

She'd left the office early today, complaining of a headache, and that in itself was something he found odd because she'd barely ever taken time off and gone home early. Maybe the state of things in her business was getting too much to handle. This was precisely why he'd suggested that she slow down. She was wearing herself out—she'd been taking too much on before the wedding but at least that huge event had passed and it was one less thing to worry about.

Yet he worried about her all the same. Whenever he told her to slow down, she'd take it the wrong way. He was proud of her, but she didn't need to kill herself to prove anything. They had plenty of money—he could easily provide for them all and give her a luxurious lifestyle. He knew that wasn't the type of woman he'd married. And he loved her for it. But could she not see that her health came before everything?

It was with these thoughts uppermost in his mind that he returned home later that evening and went straight to their bedroom where he found her lying on her side.

With her eyes closed like that, he left a gentle kiss on her cheek, then walked away to slip off his tie.

"You're back," she said, softly.

"I thought you were sleeping." He walked over to her and

sat down, stroking her face. He could never be near her and not touch her.

"I had a headache."

"Another one?"

"I'm just tired and ... some more bad reviews came in."

"Ratio?" It didn't matter how many were bad compared to the rest of them. She would focus on the negative things, he knew because he did the same. But for her he wanted to put things into perspective.

"I didn't check. I didn't care."

He frowned. This wasn't like her, she was usually so upbeat, so full of enthusiasm. "I get bad reviews too—without anything like a fire ruining my business. Your bad reviews have only started to creep in because of the fire and that was out of your control."

"I know. But sometimes, you just have a bad day. This is *my* bad day, Nico. Let me wallow in it." She crumpled before him again and he could see from the dark circles under her eyes how weary she was. But something about her alarmed him tonight. He'd never seen her looking so worn out. No matter what she thought of him for keeping the news from her, one look at her face told him he'd done the right thing. This was not how he'd have wanted her to spend their honeymoon.

"It will get better. It always does," he told her, thinking how easy it was to dish the advice out to others but how much harder it was to take. She kissed his fingers when he traced her lips gently. "Thanks." She mustered a smile, but her tired eyes looked even more lifeless.

"The baby's getting bigger and making more of a strain on your body," he said gently, palming her baby bump.

"The third trimester can be like this, apparently."

"I need to go to Ravenna tomorrow." But he wondered if he should leave her like this.

"I'm surprised you haven't been there yet."

"There was so much to sort out in the office. You know how it is. I've been in contact with Bruno since the first day."

"Will you be staying there?"

He used to stay over for a few days here and there before, but he couldn't bear to spend the night without her. And he would never contemplate leaving her, not when she was like this.

"I'll be back." It was a two hour drive to get there. Four hours of driving were doable—and worth it. He didn't plan to be away from her, which was why the looming Denver trip was something he kept pushing away to the back of his mind. Time was running out fast, and he didn't want to risk going when she was in the last month of her pregnancy. Which meant he would have to go within the next few weeks and leave the spa hotel again, as well as Ava. There was too much going on and piling on top of him.

"You don't have to rush back, Nico. I'm fine. Stay over if you have to, even for a night."

"You want to get rid of me?" He bent over to plant a kiss on her lips.

"I don't want you to kill yourself trying to do everything."

He almost opened his mouth to tell her the same but thought better of it. She would only assume that he was hinting to her to ease off her work and if he did that, he knew she'd defiantly stay at work to prove a point, even when she felt in need of a nap. "You rest. I'll make dinner."

"Maybe we ought to take on extra help with cooking—like you said." She'd come around to the idea? It took him by surprise. "I haven't been able to do a thing since I got—"

"Done," he told her, not giving her the chance to change

her mind. "I'm sure Helena could do three days a week of cooking for us and cleaning for the other two." He knew for a fact because he'd already asked her. "Does that sound good to you?"

Ava nodded, and he was happy. Having a cook and cleaner would be a huge help. He'd wanted to pore through the hotel plans again and go over all the project paperwork to check the clauses for the project going over time but he would do that later—maybe working until the early hours of the morning again. But maybe he could multi-task. He'd seen Ava do it plenty of times.

So he set about making the dinner while he looked through the hotel plans which he had propped up in a cookbook stand near the stove.

CHAPTER THIRTY-ONE

Any sense of apprehension Ava felt about meeting her good friend Andrea soon vanished. Andrea looked up from the sofas in the lobby area where she'd been looking through some magazines and smiled.

"Andrea," Ava beamed, waddling towards her. They embraced tightly.

"Look at you," Andrea exclaimed, her eyes shining as she looked Ava up and down. "You look ready to explode. But you look amazing," she said quickly.

"You think so?" Ava didn't agree with the last, seeing that she'd been unable to conceal the dark, puffy circles underneath her eyes.

"You're glowing, it's like you're lit from within, and the tan suits you," Andrea insisted. She always had a way of making Ava feel like a million dollars, whether Ava felt she looked it or not, though her skin did look great, she had to admit.

"Thanks," murmured Ava. Though Andrea didn't look so well, she noted. Her friend appeared gaunt and tiny lines crept around the undersides and corners of her eyes. "Let's go sit in my office. We've got a lot to catch up on."

"Is Nico around?" Andrea asked as they walked towards her office.

"He's driving to Ravenna this morning. He has so much to handle with the new hotel."

"I know. He said it was overwhelming at times. He called me a few days ago to find out about the fire," Andrea explained. "Would you say it's coming along, though? The new hotel?"

"It's coming." Ava drew in a deep breath. She found herself getting breathless quicker these days, and all she'd done was walk from the lobby to her office. "But he's in a race against time for it to open in November."

"A race with who?"

"With himself."

"Isn't your baby due in November?"

"He knows. He thinks he can take it all on."

"You two are so similar," Andrea commented, relaxing into a chair.

"I wish you'd been honest with me about the fire." There, she'd said it. Andrea stared at her blankly, then blinked rapidly a few times. "I'm sorry. We thought it would be best not to tell you the complete truth while you were on vacation."

"Nico owned up to it the night we got back."

"Please don't be mad at me. I didn't mean to make things worse for you. We all agreed that you needed to enjoy your break."

Ava softened. "I know you all meant well. I was more upset that my husband lied to me, and at a time when we'd both told one another we would have no secrets between us."

"I didn't think you knowing about the damage would have

done any good. You would only have worried and what would have been the point of that? Nico was concerned about how you might take it."

Ava leaned back in her chair, and tilted her face up to look at the ceiling, pondering over things. "I've heard his side of the argument many times but I still think this was something he could have told me. But let's not dwell on that." She lifted her head back off the headrest. "The only reason I mention it to you Andrea, is because we're friends. But I realize Nico put you in a tight place, I'm sorry he did that."

"Nico's not sorry, you do understand that, don't you? He cares about you, and he'd give his life for you."

What she didn't need was rhetoric from her friend about how great her husband was. She already knew that. "Tell me what happened," she said, needing to find out everything.

She listened as Andrea told her all about the fire and how it had happened while she had been away in Milan, how Leo had been knocked unconscious, how Riley had rescued him, and how the entire warehouse had nothing left in it except, miraculously, the office.

"I had no idea, Andrea. I'm so sorry." As worried as she was for her own business, she truly felt sorry for Andrea. Her own business was still intact, she still had customers, albeit a few unhappy ones, but she still had a base from which to work from, and an inventory, even if a significant proportion of it had burned away. She could resurrect herself and she still had something to come back from. Andrea had nothing. "How are you coping?"

"We're working out of temporary buildings in the same industrial unit," Andrea replied.

"That's a start. How's Leo? I heard he was hurt?"

"He's better now and it was almost as if he hadn't been injured."

That was reassuring to hear. "You're in temporary buildings?" Ava was more anxious to find out how soon they'd be fully operational again. Andrea nodded. "There were a few free units in Montova. These are small, but we managed to find two side by side. It's not ideal, but it is enough to house the new order of stock which is slowly coming through. I'm so sorry this has had such a knock-on effect on your own business, Ava."

"Don't be. It's not your fault. What was it? A fault? An electrical fire? Nico mentioned that it might have been arson."

"The insurance people aren't sure. They're still trying to reach a conclusion. Do you mind? I really don't want to talk about it anymore. It's consumed my life for the past few weeks and I'm sick of talking about it. It upsets me so much and I prefer to look forward towards the future and find a way to move on." She looked away, obviously not wanting to discuss it.

"Of course," said Ava. "But if there is anything I can do to help, you must let me know."

"I will."

"Oh, before I forget. That first shipment from d'Este—it's almost all sold out."

"Sold out?"

Ava nodded excitedly. "Kim told me the customers loved it and the reviews have been amazing."

"You'll want to place another order then?" Andrea asked, getting excited.

"I want to quadruple the order."

"Two hundred cribs?"

"Why not? Let me look through their catalog again and I'll email you an order in the next few days."

Andrea looked ecstatic. "Did you know they have another

company in Milan that makes nursery furniture? I'd gone there to meet with them when the fire broke out."

"Nursery furniture?" Ava's eyes lit up.

"When things are more settled at my end, I'll go back again and let you know if we can strike a deal."

"Yes, please." This was great news.

"And maybe they also handle the shipment, like the crib company does. Guess we were lucky they did."

Ava nodded. Otherwise these cribs would also have gone up in flames. "It makes it easy on you, doesn't it? Having someone else to do the shipment?"

"Definitely."

"I have a confession to make."

Andrea looked at her with concern.

"I have to admit that for a moment when I got back and saw how things had stalled in my business, I was tempted to go direct to d'Este. I mean, there's no reason why I can't send my orders to them directly, right?" Ava asked.

Andrea nodded, and the color started to wash away from her face.

"But then it occurred to me," continued Ava, "that I don't have the time to go around sourcing products. I saw these cribs and you were the one who went and set up the deal with the manufacturer for me. You get a cut, but that's because you're my middleman."

"What are you saying?"

"I like you being my middle man, or woman." She knew now why she couldn't travel around looking at products. She was in the business of selling—that's what she did best, and Andrea was in the business of finding good products. Together, they had a partnership that worked well and their friendship had come to mean so much more to her. She couldn't be angry at her friend for wanting to protect her by omitting to tell her the whole truth about the fire.

Andrea shook her head, "Why are you telling me this?"

"Because I realize now what you mean to me." They smiled at one another. "What happened at the wedding?" asked Ava, hoping to finally unravel the mystery behind Andrea missing the wedding.

Andrea rubbed her cheek. "I was hoping to explain it to you both by taking you and Nico out to dinner and catching up on your wedding and honeymoon—that is, after I'd finished groveling to you both for my forgiveness."

"Groveling for forgiveness? What are you talking about, Andrea?"

"For missing the wedding. You don't know how much I regret that. I should have come. I should have left him and come, I didn't even listen to Leo and he practically begged me to attend the reception."

Ava laid a hand on her friend's arm. "Left who?"

"Riley."

Riley? She waited for Andrea to say more but instead her friend rubbed her hands together.

"We missed you," said Ava, softly, "but it's not the end of the world. You must have had a very good reason for not being able to attend."

"That's just it." Andrea stared at her with shiny eyes the size of the moon. She was already thin, but as Ava cast her eyes over her appearance, Andrea seemed even thinner than she remembered. What had happened to the excited woman who, only weeks ago, had been so excited about the man she'd recently met?

"Maybe one evening the four of us could go out—"

"He left," said Andrea, in a voice as dull as dishwater. "We broke up soon after and now he's gone."

"Gone? For good?"

"He was a drifter anyway. I should have known better."

"What happened?"

"He left."

"On the day of our wedding?"

"No, he was ill on that day. That's why I chose to stay by his side. Looking back I don't think he was really that ill. Sick in the head, maybe. He used me. He played me for the fool I am. I didn't need to spend all day by his side when he was sick but I did, because that's who I am. Loyal and caring and I thought he cared about me."

"You're not a fool."

"You don't know that."

"I know. You're not a fool, Andrea. You're an angel and you have a heart of gold."

"He saw me coming."

"You were infatuated by him," Ava reminded her, still no clearer as to what had happened.

"I knew I didn't love him. Isn't that strange?" Andrea's face twisted. "I might have *thought* I loved him, but when it came down to it, I couldn't bring myself to say the words. But infatuation, lust, carnal desire ... I mistook that as being a good enough reason for wanting to be with him."

"Infatuation can be misleading."

"Infatuation can be fatal," said Andrea and Ava waited for an explanation. Her friend seemed on the verge of tears and she guessed that this man must have broken her heart.

Andrea plucked at the leather corners of her folder and said nothing.

"He's gone, and with time you will get over him," Ava said gently, sensing there was more to it but she wasn't going to pull it out of Andrea. She'd wait for her friend to tell her in her own good time. "You don't seem ready to talk about it," said Ava, carefully. "But when you are, I'm here, at the end of a phone, or here, in person. All you have to do is call me, and I'll come."

"You're going to have your hands full, soon."

"I'll always have time for you. You're my first real friend in Italy, Andrea. I like to think we can count on one another at any time. Who knows, if things get really bad for me, I'll need a listening ear too."

"You have Nico."

"He's so busy. I hate to concern him with my problems. The spa hotel takes up so much of his time, and he's trying to hire a few managers as well. I can't and I don't want to burden him unnecessarily."

"He wouldn't see it like that."

"But *I* would," said Ava firmly. Her husband was strong. She knew how strong he was and what he had gone through, what he'd lost and how he grieved for his father. She also knew that he hid his sadness well, and put on a brave front, that he worked harder than ever in order to hide the pain and sorrow, and that he was on a quest to prove himself.

But he wasn't unbreakable.

CHAPTER THIRTY-TWO

"I 'd like to hold the interviews next week. Do you think you could get them all to come in on one day? I'd like to get this dealt with in one hit."

"I'll see what I can do," replied Gina. Nico hated that he was treating her as his secretary. Was that another position he needed to hire for?

But between the two of them they were able to carry out admin tasks and seemed to be getting by.

"What are you thinking about?" asked Gina, hugging her folder to her chest.

"That maybe I need a secretary and that I shouldn't treat you like one."

"You don't, Nico. We see a job that needs doing and we do it."

"All the same, hiring an admin person would be a great help."

"And filling out the bigger positions before that would be an even bigger help."

"And that's why I'm asking you to set up interviews next week." Perhaps once November was over—for that was the busiest month and a lot depended on it—he might consider getting an admin person in. With more managers, there would be more paperwork and more to manage.

"Let me call them and see if I can arrange it." Gina walked towards the door, just as Nico considered taking Ava out for lunch. He got up. "I'll ask my wife whether she'd like to go out for lunch today."

"She's not here," Gina told him, pausing. "She was in a rush to get to her appointment, just as I came in."

"Appointment?"

"To see the doctor," replied Gina, looking puzzled.

"She's gone to visit the doctor?" he asked, wide-eyed. "Are you sure? She hadn't said a word to him about it.

"I thought you knew."

"No," Nico muttered to himself, rubbing his face.

"I'll get going," offered Gina and left abruptly.

"Thanks." He let out a heavy breath before picking up his cell phone. But when he called Ava she didn't answer.

Why in the hell had she gone to see the doctor without telling him? He returned to his desk and finished sending a few more emails, then went into Ava's office and waited for her, trying to keep a lid on the anger that was welling up inside him. After a little while he got up, unable to sit still waiting for her and he walked out into the hotel lobby. He wandered over to the sofas and picked up one of the magazines that had been lying there.

On the cover, interspersed with photos of other couples in the news recently, was a photo of the two of them walking hand in hand on their honeymoon. He scanned over it, then flicked through the glossy pages and found a half page article on both of them. He stared at the image of them, near the sea and quickly read the article. There was nothing derogatory, so he breathed easy, and hastily put the magazine back into the rack as soon as he heard Ava's voice. She was on her cell phone as she walked through the doors.

She stopped as soon as she saw him. "I haven't forgotten. Let me put the order together and I'll be in touch. Thanks, Andrea." She slipped her cell into her bag walked over to him looking puzzled. "Nico," she said, a little too breathlessly. "What are you doing here?"

He took her hand and the hardness that had tightened his facial muscles, seemed to melt when he saw her. "I've been waiting for you to get back."

"Is anything wrong?" She looked around the empty lobby.

"I could ask you the same thing. What did the doctor say?" His tone was hushed because he was aware that they were in an open place. "And why didn't you tell me you were going there? I always take you to your appointments."

"This wasn't a routine appointment, Nico." She, too, kept her voice low.

"Then?"

"I needed to see the doctor. To get some peace of mind. I promise you, nothing is wrong. Must we have this conversation here?"

He needed to know, and he was done waiting any longer in order to find out. "If nothing's wrong, why did you go to the doctor?" The worry in his voice kept the anger at bay. He saw the tightness of her mouth and knew she was considering what to tell him. "I need to know, Ava."

"I've been getting headaches and feeling overtired. My heart's been going wild, it's ..." She looked flustered. He suspected that the combination of her working too hard all the way up until the wedding, and then the stress and worry of recent events had all combined to make things worse.

He had plenty to say to her but held it in check for fear of upsetting her. Everything she had gone through was beginning to take its toll and at seven months pregnant, it was dangerous. This was what he'd been worried about.

"Everything is fine. My blood pressure is a little high, and I need to keep an eye on it."

"High blood pressure?"

"I promise you it sounds worse than it is."

"High blood pressure is never good, especially with a baby."

"Mine isn't crazily high," she countered. But he'd already made his mind up that he wouldn't risk it.

"How long has this been going on for?"

"Since we went on our honeymoon. Maybe a few days before."

"Before the wedding?" He raised his voice. *She'd kept this from him that long?*

"It was only a few headaches, Nico, and ..."

There was more?

"What else, Ava?" He spoke softly, touching her arm.

"I was getting double vision—only a few times."

Double vision? Fear coursed through his veins and his insides seemed to empty. If anything happened to Ava ... or the baby ... His gaze fell to her stomach. "Why didn't you see the doctor before we went?" He tried to hold back his anger at being kept in the dark about something as important as her health.

"I should have, you're right. But I had so much going on."

"You're carrying our baby. Don't you know how much you both mean to me?"

She froze, not saying a thing.

In a softer voice he moved closer and rubbed her hand. "You're all I have, can't you see that? I don't want to risk anything happening to you."

"It's nothing serious, Nico."

"What did the doctor say?"

She seemed to hesitate before answering. "That he was concerned and to keep an eye on it."

He scrubbed his jaw. "But you could have told me. Don't I need to know?"

"You have a lot on your plate, Nico. The baby's been kicking each day, and apart from a few headaches, and the tiredness, I feel mostly fine."

"You're my priority. Your health, the baby's health. I don't care for much else."

"But you do. You're driven to get this hotel up and running. You're convinced it must open and I'm thinking maybe you should forget about the trip to Denver."

"Don't worry about me or the trip to Denver or what I can or can't handle."

"Is that fair? What if I told you not to worry about me?"

"You might not have said it in as many words, Ava, but you implied it. You cut me out and hid the news from me. I only found out you'd gone to the doctor because Gina mentioned it casually."

"I'm sorry. I didn't want to worry you."

"This concerns our baby, Ava! It concerns you."

"See," she countered. "You're getting irate."

"You are my life, and what concerns you *is* my business."

"It didn't seem like such a big deal. I wasn't getting these symptoms every day."

He slipped a finger under her chin and tilted her face upwards, forcing her to look at him. "Our baby and you are the two most important things I have in my life. Nothing else matters."

"I get it," she said, suddenly, her voice soft again. "I understand. But how do you feel now? This isn't too different from you hiding the warehouse fire from me because you didn't want me to worry."

"Is that what this is about?" Nico asked, raising his voice slightly. "You surprise me, Ava."

Two finely dressed women in pearls and twin sweater sets glided past them, watching them discreetly, while trying not to make it so apparent that they were staring in their direction. Nico forced a smile and, when they had passed, he took Ava by her arm and guided her over to a sofa by the corner. It clearly wasn't safe to walk towards their offices, which meant going past the reception area where the two women hovered.

He leaned in and whispered. "Did you keep this from me to get back at me about the fire?"

"No," she returned, indignantly. "I really didn't think it was that much of a deal, and I can see you're under so much pressure. I wanted to make sure first."

"You and the baby *are* a big deal to me. Never forget that."

"I'm sorry."

"I know we've both been under pressure since we got back. It's a tough time, that's all. It will pass." He remembered his father often saying that, and his father's words now reminded him that all would be well again. "How's my daughter doing?" He placed his hand gently on her stomach.

"Your son is doing great," she replied, with determination.

"You didn't secretly find out what we're having, did you?"

"No! I wouldn't do that. And we agreed not to find out."

He got up and walked quietly to the center of the lobby, scoping out the reception area once more and was relieved to see that it was now clear. He walked back to Ava. "Let's go to my office. Apparently, we're well known faces here now. For a while, at least."

"Well-known?" she asked. It would be better for her to know. "This," he said, picking up the glossy magazine again.

He flipped it open to the relevant pages. She took one look and was immediately horrified. "Don't get stressed about it." He attempted to take the magazine off her but she held onto it tightly, and was flicking through the pages.

"They were there, on our honeymoon?" she gasped. He knew what that felt like, the shock of finding out that they had been followed, had been watched without them knowing. He prayed that the photographers hadn't used any long-range lenses. He'd tried to be careful and wary in their honeymoon suite but he was sure there had been a few occasions when he hadn't closed the terrace doors and he and Ava had ...

She clasped her hand to her chest.

"We're B-list, darling, and hopefully quickly slipping down to Z-list celebrities."

"We're on the front page!"

"With others. It's a shared cover." He tried to downplay it as she examined the pages inside.

"What does it say?" Ava asked, her face draining of color.

Written in Italian, he translated the general tone of it. "Nothing bad, just that you and I were on our honeymoon in Amalfi and we stayed at the expensive ..." He yelped in surprise. "It wasn't fifteen thousand Euros per night." But he was well aware of the media's blatant manipulation of events and the way they liked to twist the lies in with the truth.

Ava looked angry. "I wonder what other lies they'll print."

"It will die down, Ava. This magazine is a week old."

She didn't look convinced. "At least they don't have any pictures of the wedding."

Nico's face fell.

"They do?" She was quick to notice. "Where?" She chewed her lip then, looked at him with wide, frightened eyes.

He traced the side of her face with his finger. "It was last week. Gina mentioned they had some shots in the papers, taken from a distance at the church."

"Why didn't you tell me?"

Because he knew it would wind her up, as if the fire and the burnt shipment hadn't already given her plenty to be mad about. "I don't want to worry you and have you get all angry, especially now." He gestured at her belly. He needed everything to be peaceful and calm around Ava now, especially with this recent news about her health.

"It will die down, and I can't let this upset me," she said all of a sudden, putting the magazine down and taking his hand. "The receptionists at the doctors were full of questions. They kept waiting for you to come through the door."

Nico almost smiled. "Next time, I will go with you. No more sneaking off without me."

"No more sneaking off, I promise."

"And more of taking things easy," he told her.

"Did you not see the way I let go of the magazine photos?"

"Let's see if you can keep that up." He squeezed her hand and kissed her on the lips. "I love you."

"I know."

He led her past the now empty reception desk and to his office. As soon as they walked in, he enclosed her in his arms and held her tight. Of all the debris that seemed to surround him, and the troubles looming in the near horizon, she was the only thing that mattered—her and the baby.

"I'm sorry." Her voice was muffled as she buried her face in his chest.

"Promise me you'll let me know what's going on? That you'll take it easy?"

"I'll try."

"You have to do more than try, darling."

"What do you mean?" She lifted her head.

"Just that ..." He had to say it, even if she bit his head off for it. "You had Lizzi helping you out before, why don't you get her back to help you for a few hours a day?"

"Because she's returning to college soon. And I can manage."

"Clearly." He cleared his throat. "I'm only asking you to take things easy, Ava."

She pulled away from him. "But you know I can't. How can you ask me to do that, Nico?"

"It's not impossible. Think about it."

"I *am* thinking about it. I am putting the baby first. I can't sit around doing nothing. That's not me." She started to walk away. "This is always your answer. Always."

"No, it isn't," he countered, firmly.

"You'll do anything to have me stop working. You want a wife who's reliant on you. You want a trophy wife, Nico. I was never one of those. I worked hard to build up my business, as your father did, as you are."

What? Where was this coming from? All he wanted was for her to be safe, for the baby to be safe—why couldn't she see that?

CHAPTER THIRTY-THREE

I t was rest she needed, not drama.

"Calm down, Ava. I don't want you to sit around doing nothing. I'm proud of you, I always have been—"

"Then why is your first answer to everything for me to slow things down in my business? You said the same thing before, when things around the time of the wedding were becoming too hectic." Rage simmered silently below her belly.

"Calm down." Nico looked anxious.

"You must have been pleased when the fire happened." But she regretted her words, spoken in anger in the heat of the moment. She could tell that he was holding back, that he wanted to respond but that he was being careful. Her accusation had been unfair. She closed her eyes and released a small sigh.

"Why are we fighting so much?" he asked, looking pained.

She looked away, not knowing the answer, and also hating the constant friction between them.

"Sometimes it just seems as though you don't take my business seriously. As though you seem to think that it's still a hobby of mine."

"You are so wrong, my darling. I've always been proud of you and your achievements, and I've always tried to encourage you. Not that you need much encouraging. The only thing I'm guilty of is wanting to keep you and the baby safe. Worrying about events you had no control over wasn't going to help. I'm sorry you see things differently."

"Is it us, or is it the pressure?" she wondered out aloud, turning to meet his gaze again.

"It's the pressure, and circumstances, Ava. Don't doubt us." He took her hands in his once more, but his phone rang. He ignored it.

"You'll need to get that," she told him, and moved towards the door. "I have work to do as well."

He gave her a helpless glance as she turned her back on him and slipped out of his office.

The doctor had told her to take it easy—that the last thing she needed was to raise her blood pressure. But she wasn't going to tell Nico that; he'd have her confined to her bed until she went into labor.

He could try, she thought bitterly.

His typical response—as she knew it would be—was to attack her business and to get her to slow down, probably with the hope that she'd ease right down on it. She was stubborn, and she wasn't about to back down. Women had babies every day. She was a healthy woman and not too old either. She'd be fine. Lately though her hormones, her temper and her feelings were all over the place.

Instead of returning to her office she wandered out into the garden and sought out the pergola which her mother loved so much. There was a peace and tranquility out here that was unparalleled anywhere else and she sank gratefully into the wicker chair, resting her hands over her ever growing bump. The doctor's words had given her a warning and she was mindful of not overdoing it. She'd been right to listen to her body recently when she'd gone home early a few times to take a nap. She'd never done that before, and it seemed right that she'd been more in tune with her body than ever.

They'd been married less than a month yet already she was starting to feel more trapped than ever. Things weren't meant to turn out like this. They weren't. She and Nico were a solid couple, or they had been until recently. The constant unease between them wore her out.

If Nico's only recourse for her was to get her to give up her work, she couldn't battle with that all the time, not when she was also trying to regain the momentum in her business. She hadn't meant the things she'd said to him. She knew he hadn't done anything to hinder her progress. The negative effect on her store was due to events and timing, and Nico was right, what would she have been able to do if she'd found out about the fire on their honeymoon? Nothing, except a whole lot of worrying.

She closed her eyes and sat in the stillness of the gardens with only the singing birds to remind her that she was not alone.

"Mi scusi." Salvatore's craggy face and thick set eyebrows were the first thing she saw when she opened her eyes again. He tipped his head to her and was about to move on, she thought, but he stopped and paused by the entrance instead. "Good honeymoon?"

She nodded. "It was wonderful, thank you."

"My family enjoyed your wedding very much." She smiled again, thinking how far away it all seemed, the wedding day, and having her family around her, and her saga with the dress. "That's what we wanted," she replied, staring up at his heavily lined face. "We wanted our family and friends to have as great a time as we did."

"Your mother? She does not like Italy? Or your sister?"

Ava smiled, wondering at his choice of words. "My sister had to return with her husband and child. Her daughter turned one a few weeks ago." She found herself gesticulating more with her hands when she spoke to Salvatore. It wasn't that he didn't understand her, he did. But with his heavy Italian accent, she mistakenly assumed that he didn't and the fault was more hers than anything else.

She forced her hands to remain still as the feeling crept upon her that he was fishing for more information about Elsa. He didn't have any real concerns about whether Rona loved Italy or not. "My mother decided to go back." Ava shrugged. "I wanted her to stay for longer, until the baby came. But she wanted to go back."

"She will be back for the baby?" Curiosity piqued in the man's tired old eyes.

"I hope so," said Ava, slowly, not wanting to raise his hopes too much, for she got the feeling that he was interested in knowing more about Elsa's schedule.

"November? Si?"

"Si."

Salvatore smiled at her again. "Ciao," he said gruffly, nodding his head as he trailed off in his thick brown wellington boots with a bucket in one hand.

CHAPTER THIRTY-FOUR

"What's wrong with the existing elevator?"

"The preliminary safety inspection showed that we need to replace it. It's old."

"I thought there wasn't a problem?" Nico growled. As the weeks passed quickly, and their honeymoon days soon became a distant memory, the troubles seemed to escalate.

Bruno ducked a pencil behind his ear, then removed it again. "I thought so too, but I'm hearing back from my contact at the department that the elevator isn't going to pass. I had concerns about it myself."

"Why didn't you bring it to my attention before?" Nico barked. They stood in the mobile office which occupied a corner next to the spa center. The pristine new and white building with its shiny atrium and gleaming white windows, gave him hope. It was only when he turned and looked at the old building, where the old hotel had been, that his heart sank.

Edmondo had known that it needed a lot of work. Nico had known, too. Maybe he'd have been better off if he'd knocked the whole place down and built it back up again from scratch. Trying to upgrade the interior and fixing any problems they came up against looked to be the worst option. But he had to stick to this now. They didn't have much contingency in their project timeline.

"I thought we could get away with it. You could in the past. It's not dangerous, but the laws are becoming more strict these days. The officials at all of these government places are into customer safety and all that."

Nico scratched his neck. "I get that it's not your fault, Bruno, but it's going to cause me a problem if we get delayed. It mustn't happen." He was getting customer inquiries about the new hotel, particularly from guests who stayed at the sister hotels.

"The rest of the project is on time," Bruno continued. "It's coming along nicely."

"Just as long as you don't hit me with any more nasty shocks."

"I'm not planning on it."

"How's the treatment for the mold coming along?"

"It's under control."

"I take your word for it," said Nico, not wanting to get into the nitty gritty of it. He trusted what Bruno told him, and knew that this project manager, with over a decade of experience behind him, knew his stuff. "I'm away around mid-October for a week. By then, do you think the elevator will be in?"

"No. We can't start that until the mold is treated—it's along the same side of the building. You don't want too much congestion in one area."

"When, then?" Nico asked, gritting his teeth.

Bruno nodded, as if thinking it over. "The first, maybe the second week of November, at the latest."

"That's too late. It needs to happen by the first of

November but don't we have a final inspection around that time?"

"It's a tight squeeze. I'm conscious of your timeline." Bruno scratched the back of his ear with the pencil. "I'll try to do it as fast as I can but it's out of my hands. It depends on the firm providing the new elevator."

Nico narrowed his eyes at him until the man was forced to reconsider. "I'll see what I can do." Bruno replied, in a tight voice.

"Our baby is due mid-November. So you understand why I need to have everything running according to plan? No delays."

"I'll do my best," answered Bruno, "but you've taken a lot on, Nico."

"I don't need you to remind me," Nico replied, uneasily.

"We're not in a bad position."

"Don't speak too soon," warned Nico. "I'm going to head back."

"You're not staying the whole day?" Though Bruno looked somewhat relieved. Nico wondered whether he came across as a tyrant to his workmen.

"I can see you're in charge and handling it well. I'll leave you to it. I might try to fit in another visit before I go to Denver. Keep an eye on the safety report. Use your contact." If there were any early hints to be gleaned he'd need to act on them fast.

He got into his car and drove off. There was no need to spend too long here, unlike in the early days when he'd spent a lot of time working with the designers and architects. Over the months he'd seen the spa center slowly coming together. There were some days he seemed to be going backwards, but over time, they were making strides.

These days his time and attention was needed more at the

Casa Adriana. They'd taken on two new people but they wouldn't be joining until the beginning of December. It was much later than he'd liked, but they'd had to give their notices to their current employer. He'd need to give them guidance in the initial stages. And as always, there was Ava who was his main priority. She was getting bigger and slowing down a lot more. She hadn't complained of any more headaches or double vision lately though he hated the idea of leaving her all alone in their mansion while he was away. Attempts at getting Helena to stay over had been met with severe resistance and she'd suggested having Andrea over instead. It made sense and he felt relieved that Andrea would be with Ava.

When his cell phone rang he dropped his keys in a rush to answer as soon as he saw Ava's name flash on the screen. "Hey."

"I can't believe it." Her words were strangled, her voice strange.

"Can't believe what?" His insides froze.

"There are pictures of us on the internet. Intimate photos, Nico." She sounded as though she was going to cry.

"What?" he bellowed. His heart thundered beneath his ribcage. "What photos?"

"From our honeymoon," she whispered.

What the hell? "I'm coming. Wait for me." He thrust the ignition on and floored the accelerator, speeding away as though he was racing in the Grand Prix.

CHAPTER THIRTY-FIVE

Her fingers hovered over her mouse as she stared at the grainy images. It was obvious that this was an intimate scene between her and Nico—on their bed, in their honeymoon suite. She tried to remember when it was—there had been so many times. Luckily, he was on top of her, and her modesty was covered.

Until she flicked over and saw the next image.

Her topless, with her stomach showing, wearing bikini bottoms. Remembering that time, she buried her face in her hands as her insides flipped. "Oh god," she wailed, shrinking back in fear as though the perpetrators of this hideous crime were going to climb out of her computer screen.

Her hands hung limply by her sides and moments passed as she stared at the screen blankly. She felt lifeless, even though the blood rushed through her ears, reminding her of the sound of the waves at the sea shore.

Her office phone rang and she ignored it, feeling powerless to move. She couldn't deal with this—the idea that these private images of a moment tender and sacred between her and Nico, were on the internet for the whole world to see.

What would her mom think?

And her friends? And all the people at the wedding; the hundreds of friendly faces they'd spent their precious day with. It didn't matter that she hadn't committed a crime, or done anything remotely wrong. She hated the thought that others would see *this*. A moment that was never meant to be shared with anyone else.

Her fingers crept back up to the mouse and she inhaled deeply before taking another look. There was also a third image of her looking out onto the sea from the terrace. How long had these parasites been watching them for? She suddenly felt as if the whole of their honeymoon had become tainted by the intrusion.

A sound at the door failed to extract a reaction from her and in the next second Gina rushed in, looking worried. "You *are* here," she cried, as if she'd expected to find an empty room. "I called from reception but you didn't answer. What's wrong?"

Ava closed down the offending images on her monitor. "Nothing."

"It's not *nothing*," replied Gina slowly and angling her head as if she was studying Ava. "Are you feeling alright? You look pale."

Ava took a few short breaths and tried to disguise the situation but she had never been a good liar. "I've read some more bad reviews," she said, trying for a lie. "Did you want something?"

"I'm sorry to add to your troubles but," Gina winced, as if it was difficult to finish the sentence. "You have a visitor and she demanded to see you. I tried to explain that you were very busy but she wouldn't take 'no' for an answer ..."

"Who is it?"

"Silvia." Gina's face pinched. "I'm sorry. I should have told her you were in a meeting."

"No," said Ava, rising up slowly. She needed to take her frustration out on someone. Silvia would do nicely for now. She followed Gina out of the office to find the platinum blond hulking at the other side of the reception desk. As always, she dripped with designer labels and shot Ava a sickly smile.

"Silvia!" chirped Ava, in the most put-on voice she could find. She couldn't be bothered to make an effort to be polite to this woman but she could do put-on. "How ... *interesting* to see you again." Ava walked over to the other side to greet her enemy face to face. She wanted to show off her huge swollen stomach and gently stroked it in case Silvia had failed to see it. A bright red arrow pointing to it could not have done a better job.

"You've put on weight," commented Silvia, not once staring at her stomach. "It suits you—you were too bony before."

"What brings you here?" Ava asked, stroking her belly slowly. "Has the fashion show season ended?"

"I hadn't seen you both lately. I don't spend much time here anymore, and as I was passing by I thought it would be only polite to pass on my congratulations."

"Thank you," Ava replied graciously. "Was there anything else?" Meeting this platinum witch had taken her mind off the internet photos for now, and she was taking great pleasure in behaving like a bitch.

"A couple of my friends passed by here a few weeks ago and they said they'd heard you and Nico arguing. I hope everything is alright between you both?"

Ava frowned. "No trouble in paradise, Silvia. Sorry to disappoint you."

"Really?" sniped Silvia. "Because that's not what they

said. I recommended the afternoon tea here, and they were thrilled to see the happily married couple in the lobby, but they were as equally as amazed to find you two bickering."

"It might have been an insignificant little *disagreement*," replied Ava, not caring what her friends had or hadn't seen. "But don't you worry that tiny brain of yours. We made up afterwards, I can assure you."

"I remember those days. Nico was an absolute god when it came to make-up sex."

Ava resisted the desire to plant her palm across the woman's puffed up face. Even now that they were married, and this supposed gold-digger had found her own sugar-daddy, Silvia couldn't seem to keep her claws or her carcass away from Nico. It was as if she had a fixation with him.

"He's my husband now, Silvia. He married *me*, and we're having a baby soon. You'd do well to remember that."

"Believe me, I can't forget it, try as I may."

"Can't you find it somewhere in that heart of yours to leave us in peace? If you can't say anything nice to us, then don't say anything at all."

Silvia ran her aubergine colored nails over her lips, contemplating. "I *do* wish you well," she trilled, smiling at Ava. It was then that Ava realized her puffed up face looked plastic; there were no wrinkles, or creases when she released a faux-smile.

"I can't tell whether you do or not," replied Ava, suddenly tired and feeling as though the woman had sucked the energy out of her. "I can't read your expression. Too much Botox can have that effect."

"Where's Nico?" asked Silvia, ignoring her completely and looking around.

"He's away, on business."

"On business? Are you sure?"

Ava chose not to rise to the bait. Once, this woman would have riled her up and gotten her worried, but Ava was now secure and confident in what she and Nico had between them and this thin bone collection of a mannequin wasn't going to take that from her. "Yes." Her reply was immoveable, secure. Enough.

"He's got another hair brained idea, I hear? Some new hotel in Ravenna that he's working hard on. He has his hopes pinned on that place, doesn't he?"

Ava forced her smile wider and refused to give in to the woman's bitterness. "How's the politician working out for you?" she asked, finding it easier to turn the attention on Silvia's own state of affairs.

"He's extraordinary."

"Viagra can have that effect, so I've heard." That one slipped right out of Ava's mouth unbidden. "You have a happy time together," said Ava. "Thank you for feeling the urgent desire to pass by and give us your best wishes. I'll be sure to let Nico know." She turned and headed back to her office, rolling her eyes at Gina as she walked past.

CHAPTER THIRTY-SIX

He raced up the steps of the Casa Adriana, burst through the double doors and collided straight into Gina.

"Sorry!" He rushed past her.

"Something's up with Ava, but she won't tell me what," Gina cried out after him.

"I know," Nico shouted back. "I'm on it."

"There's something else you should know too," he heard her say but he didn't stop. One push of the door and he was into Ava's office. She looked forlorn, as she sat at her desk typing away. She looked up at him in surprise, then glanced at her watch. "You got here fast." Disapproval spread across her face quickly. "I hate it when you drive like a maniac."

He rushed to her side. "Come here." He gently raised her to standing before enfolding his arms around her. Every fiber in his body wanted to protect this woman.

"How could they do this?" she murmured into his chest. He drew back his head, and tilted her face up to him, his heart breaking to see her eyes so full of anguish. The bastards would have to pay—he'd take out every injunction under the sun.

"I know," he whispered. "I know," then he placed a hand over her belly. "How're we doing?" He was always anxious about her health and that of their baby. If anything happened to either of them, especially because of this, he would ruin the bastards. He'd already spoken to Pelosa. "Show me," he urged and pulled up a spare chair next to her.

"Nico, they're private, intimate moments ... of you and me in the hotel room ..." His eyebrows snapped together. Even he hadn't been prepared for this new level of lowness. In his misguided past they'd had plenty of opportunity to take such incriminating shots of him but none of these had ever surfaced. This, using Ava and their private moments, was a new level of dirty.

He stared at her computer screen and felt the muscles along his neck and shoulder freeze. There were pictures of them walking along hand in hand outside, one of Ava standing on the terrace, looking out. She looked happy—content, and beautiful, and, for one peaceful moment, he was instantly taken back in time to their honeymoon days.

Until she showed him the grainy images of them naked on the bed.

Were these even legal?

He was sure they were a clear breach of privacy. The photos were taken from a distance, probably with a long range lens. In one he was naked, and it showed his whole body from behind, and in the other, she was topless for all to see.

He smashed his fist on the table. ""Bastards. They can't get away with this."

"Will this be in the papers and or magazines?" Ava whispered. He shook his head. They wouldn't dare print these because these photos were such a blatant intrusion of privacy. However he couldn't vouch for some slimy, desperate magazine taking the risk.

"How did they even see us? We were inside the bedroom."

But they'd been near the open terrace. He was aware of the strength and range of their lenses. Anger started to seep out of every pore. He would see to it that they didn't get away with this. "Bastards," he snarled, forgetting his resolve to handle this calmly, knowing how upset Ava was. He sat back down again and covered her hand with his. "Are there other photos?"

"Just these."

A few photos—for now. He wondered how many more were in circulation. He and Ava weren't celebrities but, obviously with him marrying a beautiful American woman, one who ran her own business and had her own interesting backstory ... it had made them a target of interest.

He had to face facts.

The media interest wasn't only in him anymore, Ava was a target too, and for the wrong reasons. Now he worried that their baby would also be at risk.

"I can't have people seeing this, Nico. I'm so embarrassed."

"I know, darling. I know."

"I wish I was invisible again. I wish nobody knew who I was."

He saw the worry on her face and wanted to put a fist through the photographers faces as well as their cameras. He couldn't begin to imagine the embarrassment she must have felt.

Briefly he considered hiring a PR firm to help but the truth was he didn't care what it did to the Cazale name. He only wanted to protect Ava. And he'd already let her down. An invasion of her privacy had always been one of her biggest fears.

"I've got Pelosa on the case and I'm going to let him deal with it. We're going to sue."

She held her head in her hands. "Will that stop them?"

"It might make them think twice." But it wouldn't stop them. He held her again, knowing that any words he offered wouldn't help. Only time would help make these wounds better, and as long as the photos didn't get into mainstream circulation. He hoped that Pelosa could handle this quickly. The man had a good team behind him and Nico was confident of it, but the damage already done to Ava would be harder to fix.

"How did you come across them?" he asked, curious.

"Zanobi told me that my wedding dress had been featured in a magazine, so I Googled our names."

"Does Zanobi know what happened to the dress?" He tried to take her mind off the photos.

"I haven't said anything yet. I'd like him to fix it, though, so I can put it away safely for our daughter."

"Aaaah. So you agree with me? That we're having a daughter?" He felt relieved to see her smiling again.

"This one's a boy, the way he's kicking," Ava insisted.

"Our daughter would find that remark sexist."

"Our daughter will be baby number two, or three or—"

He kissed her deeply then, massaging her tongue with his, feeling her soft lips over his. "Or five, or six," she said, breathlessly, when they pulled apart. "I love making babies with you," she murmured.

"Let's go home," he whispered, already thinking of a way to take her mind off the stress of the situation. "I know a good way to make you relax."

"Ummmm." She pressed her lips against his before sucking his bottom lip hard and surprising him. The Ava of old would have been more difficult to derail and she would never have contemplated going home early, much less going home to make love in the middle of the afternoon when there was so much work to be done. It pleased him to see her beginning to take things easy, especially in light of this current shitfest.

He lowered his head and blew soft kisses all over her bump. "Shall we go?" He looked up at her, his hands moving over her bump as he tried to detect the baby's movements.

"Yes," she whispered, her voice low. "I can tell you all about Silvia's visit on the way."

"Silvia?" He groaned loudly. "I thought *I'd* had a bad morning."

"Wait until I tell you what she said."

"Wait until I make it up to you," he promised.

stroked her hair. It
of her.

"I know," she s
have a safe trip and
me." She sensed he
of being left alone
him to stress about
with.

"I'm looking fo
the family again,"
wistful.

"And meanwhi
you're away." It w
week bearable.

"Look after her
"*He'll* be fine."
until they had to pa

Tears welled i
Adriana. She felt a
sat in her office, mo

Was this really
She missed her
loved the romance
spring and the sun
tip-toed in, bringi
found herself con
Especially after all
unknown stranger
wasn't sure she cou

She longed for
If only she could t
Denver.

Yet she'd escap

CHAPTER THIRTY-SEVEN

The next few weeks passed by in a sea of calm. It had taken her a while to come to terms with the photos on the internet and even when those private photos had been removed and the photographers in question had been handed permanent injunctions preventing them from stalking the couple, Ava still remained wary.

Other images of them walking around Amalfi remained and soon found their way into magazines anyway, and so it seemed like a hollow victory.

That these photos, even now, months after their wedding, would be of interest to nameless, faceless people she did not know, left Ava feeling uneasy. The shock of having her private life intruded upon never left her and her heart raced with fear each time she stepped outside. She always wondered who would be watching.

But she would have to get used to this. There was no alternative, not now that she was married to a man like Nico and was soon to have his baby.

Had she moved too fast?

It was a question that sometimes haunted her, even now.

She couldn't shake i
like this she wished t
inconspicuously inqu
in her life. Nico was
worry him too much
at this moment.

Not only was he
was slowing down,
used to. Taking into
took things easier, tri
problems and made a

It helped.

Her headaches h
blood pressure sho
worrying levels. Sh
rested whenever tire
for Nico because, as
pressure continued t
his impending trip to
be strong.

When he couldn
during his absence,
about leaving her h
come up with a good
over instead. This so
day of his departu
spending time with h
away more bearable.
deeply about things,
welcome prospect fo

As he got ready
heart that she was un

"I'll be back soo

love not only with her soulmate, but with his country too. She'd looked forward to starting a completely new life, but media intrusion had shaken the very foundations of her world. She worried about her baby, and doubted that she would ever be ready for this role.

She couldn't leave either, for she loved Nico with her heart and soul, and she looked forward to the arrival of their baby but all the same, this—a new life in Verona—was suddenly not looking as rosy as it had before. Walking around his mansion, sitting in his office at the Casa Adriana without Nico around felt strange to her, as though she was renting out space.

With Nico she felt complete. Perhaps that was why, with his departure, she felt at a loss. Five days, and he would be back. At least she would have an opportunity to find out what was going on in Andrea's life. Ava's uncanny sixth sense told her that her friend was holding something back and she wondered whether Andrea would now start opening up to her.

A fluttering in her belly pulled her from her gloomy thoughts. *It's going to be alright,* she told herself. In time, things would look up again and when the baby arrived she would be too busy to wallow in self-doubt, or worry about photos and vultures like Silvia.

How odd that Nico would soon be in her hometown, meeting her mom and family while she was here, alone in *his* hometown.

———

"Your home is like a palace," gushed Andrea.

Ava had to stop herself from saying, *'Nico's home,'* because she was still getting used to this being her home. "I still have to pinch myself," she said as she guided her towards the guest bedroom, having shown off her newly redecorated room and the new nursery. It occurred to her that Andrea would have seen Nico's room once, a long time ago, when they'd been together. But the women never talked about that anymore. "Helena made us meatballs and spaghetti," said Ava. "I don't know about you but I'm starving."

"Who's Helena?"

"Uh ... she's a lady who cooks for us."

"You have a cook?" cried Andrea, enviously. "I bet you have a cleaner too?"

"Helena cleans a few days too," replied Ava reluctantly. Getting used to this was going to take time.

"You're so lucky, Ava."

"I know," she replied, because there was no other answer she could give. She *was* lucky. She had everything; if only she could settle into her new life and feel at peace, too.

They sat and ate Helena's meatballs, enjoying the taste of authentic, home cooked Italian food as they talked about their day. Andrea had re-ordered the stock that had burnt down in the fire, and Ava's new shipment had been sent to the US a few weeks ago.

"Your stock will be replenished once the shipment reaches Denver." Andrea told her. "I can send another shipment sooner, if you want."

Ava sensed the guilt Andrea felt, and not wanting her friend to feel bad about it, reassured her. "Sales are slowly starting to pick up," she said. "There were a small handful of customers who were nasty, literally, like maybe a handful, but all the others were so understanding."

Andrea curled spaghetti around her fork. "People like it when you're honest. Most of the time customers want to know that they're dealing with a human on the other side, and not a machine."

"How're things at the warehouse. Did you find out any more about the arson?"

"They're still carrying out investigations," replied Andrea, looking down at her food.

"*Still?* It's taking a long time," commented Ava, in surprise.

Andrea nodded her head dismissively. "I suppose they have to be certain."

"Do you have any idea why someone would set fire to your warehouse?"

Andrea shook her head and Ava could tell she didn't want to talk about it anymore. She changed the subject.

"And you never heard from your friend again?"

Andrea laughed. "I don't expect to hear from Riley James ever again."

Ava still wondered what had happened between them. This was the man Andrea had swooned over; the sex-god she'd been drooling over. How had it all turned so sour so quickly? While she didn't want to push Andrea to giving her an answer, she was itching to know, woman to woman, exactly what had gone on.

Andrea wiped her mouth with her napkin. "He wasn't the man I thought he was."

Ava swallowed, intrigued, not daring to take a bite of the meatball that balanced on the edge of her fork. "So, he's gone and that's that? You were crazy about him."

"I was more than crazy about him at first. If you could bottle sex, Riley was the Paco Rabanne of orgasms."

Ava almost gagged on her meatball. Andrea laughed bitterly and picked up her glass of wine. "He sure gave me plenty," she murmured, the look in her eyes was almost wistful. Ava stared, open-mouthed.

"I can't describe to you the effect that man had on me. It was something I'd never experienced before. Not only was he gorgeous to look at but in the early days he was wonderful. I soon discovered that he was all sex and no substance. I don't think he had a caring bone in his body."

Ava chewed thoughtfully and wished that she had at least clapped eyes on this sex-god so that she had a real image of the man in her mind. Instead, she was feverishly trying to put a face to him. She swallowed, and felt thankful once more for *her* sex-god and gentleman all wrapped into one delicious package. She was going to hold onto Nico for life. "I'm sorry it turned out that way for you," she said softly. As interested as she was in finding out what happened at the end, she wasn't going to push Andrea. "You'll meet the right man, when the time is right."

Andrea gave her a bitter laugh. "That's the kind of thing people say when they've already found their soulmate. I don't mean to sound ungrateful, Ava. But that's not always true."

Ava managed a smile. "I'm sorry. I didn't mean to sound patronizing. I know what it's like to have the wind knocked out of you. Remember, Connor walked out on me weeks before our wedding. It took me a while to understand that he'd done me a favor, that things weren't as wonderful as I'd made them out to be. Looking back, I was in love with the idea of love, of having someone and of finally settling down. After all, my sister had Carlos, and a baby and she got married years ago. I was getting older, I had my business, but it was more of a hobby back then. I was working as a freelance copywriter. Connor was a high-flying corporate lawyer and I thought we were going to have a beautiful wedding and make beautiful babies, and he'd live the corporate lifestyle and I'd become a mom who worked from home. It never happened like that."

Thank god it had never worked out that way.

Andrea put down her wine glass and listened. "You hit the jackpot, Ava. You have one of those fairytale romances we read about in those glossy magazines you hate so much."

Ava sighed. "Those glossy magazines don't always capture the real moments. They fabricate lies and feed them to people hungry for the glimpse of a life they wished they had, but most of the time, it's not really like that anyway."

She knew her life seemed idyllic to others—and it was, for the most part; there were many times she had to pinch herself to believe that this was now her life. But it wasn't without its downsides. "It's worked out far better than I could ever have imagined. Connor leaving me was the best thing to happen to me. There were so many things wrong with us that I didn't see back then. I accepted a lot of things, when I clearly shouldn't have. Even when Connor admitted—the day after he dumped me—that he'd cheated on me, I wondered if it was something that *I'd* done wrong. If he hadn't left me, if he'd confessed to me—I might have forgiven him."

"You'd have gone back to Connor?" Andrea asked slowly. Ava shuddered at the thought.

"Do you know why I'd have forgiven him?" Ava asked, "because the church was booked, and I had my dress, and the invites had been sent out, the wedding reception had been booked, we'd chosen the cake. All I had to do was show up and walk down the aisle. It was easier to sweep my self-esteem under the rug than to let down all those people and tell them that my marriage was a sham. Connor saved me from that by walking out first."

Andrea looked as if she didn't agree. "I know Connor leaving you was a huge shock, initially. But your fairytale began when you met Nico and now you have all of this." She waved her arm around the dining room, before placing it on her chest. "I'm not jealous, Ava. I love you as a friend, I'm happy for you and maybe I'm in a dark place in my life, but it seems to me that you have it all—and that you're trying to convince me that I too will have my fairytale ending. Sorry, but I don't buy it."

Ava felt the color rise to her cheeks. "I'm sorry. It's not what I mean at all. I was lucky, I *am* lucky. I met Nico, but we almost never got together. And even when we did it wasn't all smooth sailing. Did you know I was dead set on living in Denver without ever telling him that I was pregnant by him?" She wanted to tell Andrea it was because of her, because Ava had wrongly assumed that Andrea had feelings for Nico, but raking that up now, when it wasn't true, seemed pointless. "I took a chance, Andrea. And he took a chance on me, and that's how we've made it this far."

Andrea rubbed her brow. "I hear you, and I'm so happy it worked out so well for you. You've married one of the few wonderful men left on this planet. Call me jaded, but I don't see myself having the same luck."

"Don't push the idea away. I'm not saying be all wide-eyed about it. I sense that you've been hurt badly and that you need time to get over it. But you also have every right to find happiness. You're a wonderful friend and a big-hearted woman, Andrea. All I'm saying is—don't be so sure that there isn't someone like that out there for you."

"What would you have done if you hadn't met Nico?"

"I'd have returned to Denver and thrown myself into my business. I'd still have met you, right? My business taking off is down to me selling your products. As for men, who knows?" Ava shrugged lightly. "Either I'd have met someone in the US, or here in Italy, and he might not have been an American or an Italian, the world is so small, you never know who you might meet." But all the same, she was more grateful than ever that she had her fairytale ending with Nico.

Andrea shrugged. "I don't even want to consider romance at the moment."

"You're hurting because you felt something for this guy."

"I don't think I loved him."

"I know. But maybe you *wanted* to, I mean, in the beginning, from what you've told me, he was everything you could have dreamed of."

"I *could* have loved him, if he'd been the man I thought he was. But he was far too damaged."

Ava raised an eyebrow, wanting to get to the bottom of this but Andrea remained silent. "Instead, I have Leo helping me to get our business off the ground again."

"How's that going?"

"We're looking for a bigger, permanent base and I've re-ordered most of my inventory. We're getting on with things. Nico's gone to find a warehouse in Denver, did you say?"

"Yes. And hopefully this week we'll have a huge place we can fill from top to bottom. Kim has a few places for him to look at. He'll check them out, sign the necessary paperwork, get the finances in order, help get the security and business insurance in place and help the girls to move the stock out from the residential places into that unit."

"He's hoping to do all that in five days?"

Ava nodded. "He's also got to empty out Connor's garage. There won't be much in it, and I expect he'll be mad because he wanted it empty weeks ago." Not that Connor had any reason to be mad, seeing that he was still holding on to a chunk of her money. Something she still hadn't told Nico about.

"Are you and Connor still in touch?" Andrea made a disapproving face.

"Out of necessity. It helped when he offered to let me stock my products in his garage."

"The sooner you get your things out the better." Andrea looked displeased.

"Nico said the same thing."

"You'll need a big place if you want to store those two hundred cribs you ordered."

"They're almost sold out, did you know that?"

"They are?"

"Rona updated the website, increased the prices, and still we managed to sell about half of them, and they're not even in Denver yet."

Andrea's eyes almost bugged out of her head. "Sweet! That's fast. Don't worry, they're due to reach there by next week."

Ava nodded excitedly. Her store was slowly starting to recover from the recent setback. "I'll place an order for five hundred cribs soon."

Andrea stared at her wide-eyed.

"If I have the storage space, why not?" Ava retorted.

"Why not, indeed?" asked Andrea, re-filling her wine glass.

"I'll place the order tomorrow." Andrea's face lit up at this. "How's Leo?" Ava asked. "Did you know that his ex-wife's father is—"

"I know," said Andrea, "Nico's lawyer. Leo told me."

"How's it going with him? He seemed kind of nice." Ava felt hopeful.

"He *is* nice."

"Is he ... single?"

"How should I know?" asked Andrea, a little too defensively, thought Ava.

"You work with him."

"Are you trying to pair the two of us off, by any chance?"

"Who, me?" asked Ava, wide-eyed and innocent.

"We work well together," said Andrea, "but that's about it. How about after dinner we sit down and watch a nice girly chick flick?"

And that, Ava decided, was the end of that conversation.

CHAPTER THIRTY-EIGHT

"You're still up?" Ava asked, sounding shocked.

"It's after midnight here." Nico felt out of sorts. Overtiredness had come and gone but getting used to the time zones and adjusting his sleep would take days and before he knew it would be time to return to Verona.

He hoped to find the ideal warehouse in the first few days, tomorrow even, so that he could rest easy knowing that his main job was done.

"Oh, baaaby," she cooed. "It's Tuesday morning here and I just got to work. Andrea dropped me off."

"That's good of her. What's it like having her stay over?"

"She's a good replacement for you. But I still miss you."

"I miss you. I'll be back before the two of you have had a chance to discuss all your old boyfriends."

"Is that what you think women do?" she cried haughtily, and before he could reply, she answered. "I don't have a long list of boyfriends to go through. Neither does she, I don't think."

Time to change the topic, thought Nico, since they both knew that he and Andrea had been an item once. "How was your night? Lonesome without me?" There was a certain presumption in his voice.

"I'd like to say yes, but Andrea and I spoke for hours and the time flew. We started to watch a film but we ended up talking."

"That's women for you."

"She's still hung up on that Riley guy."

"She is?" Nico got into his bed. He'd long since been back from dinner at Elsa's. Carlos, Rona and Tori had come over too and it had given him the perfect opportunity to catch up with them all. Naturally, they had wanted to know about the honeymoon and married life, and they'd asked about Ava and the baby.

"I might be wrong. She's not saying much."

He positioned the pillow against the headrest and leaned back. "I'm sure you'll wheedle it out of her."

"I can try."

"I had dinner at your mom's. Carlos and Rona came over too. We missed you."

"Aaaaaw," she murmured, sounding sad.

"Your mom said she'll try to come around the beginning of December."

"That late?" cried Ava. "I was hoping she'd be here in time for the birth."

"Junior told you she's making an entrance on the twelfth?" he asked. He'd noted the due date down in his diary and on his phone. It was right up there along with his project milestones for the new hotel.

"I could do with having my mom around," said Ava. "And I'm hoping Junior arrives sooner than his due date. Lying down is getting uncomfortable for me."

"Keep your legs closed," Nico told her. "Don't you go having that baby while I'm away." She was eight months pregnant and he was hoping the baby stayed firmly inside until he returned. He'd been reluctant to come here, but he had no choice and it was better to have this visit over and done with now, than closer to her due date. He yawned loudly. "Sorry, darling. I'm feeling sleepy. I've been up for over twenty-four hours and I can't keep my eyes open anymore."

"It sounds as though you're getting lonesome without me."

"I'm a lost cause without you." He meant it, even though he said it laughingly.

"Go to sleep," she told him. "I'll speak to you later. I love you."

"I know," he told her. "I love you more." He hung up, and sleep swept over him within seconds.

He awoke the next morning and found himself lost for a few short seconds.

For a moment he wasn't sure where he was, and wondered if he was still dreaming about the spa hotel. And then he remembered it had only been a dream and that he was here at the Westin Hotel in downtown Denver. He breathed easier knowing that the spa hotel was still standing and hadn't been knocked down.

Forty five minutes later he took a taxi to Ava's apartment, where Kim and Rona were expecting him. It was his first time there, and he tried to imagine her returning home to this place in that other universe she'd once lived in, where the two of them had not even met yet. He rang the bell, and a woman he'd never seen before, opened the door.

"Nico?"

"Kim?" he guessed, by elimination. He heard Rona's voice in the background.

"Nice to meet you!" Kim fixed him a warm smile and shook his hand firmly. "We've been looking forward to you coming over."

He walked inside and picked his way through the piles of boxes that were everywhere. Surprise ran across his face as he glanced around. Ava had told him it was small but it seemed even tinier now that it was filled with boxes of products stacked everywhere.

"Hey." Rona put down the phone and nodded at him. "You should have called me, I'd have picked you up from the hotel."

"It's not a problem," he replied, still casting his eyes around the room in wonder. "This is where you ladies work?" he asked, walking into the small kitchen area. He saw the small table and laptop in this relatively uncluttered space.

"I'm working out of my place, mostly," Rona explained, "Ava has me doing more of the backend stuff."

Nico was well aware that Ava's whole reasoning had been to keep the two women working apart.

"It's not too bad," said Kim. "It makes sense for Rona to be at home and for me to work here."

"It's not ideal," he murmured. "I can see why Ava was anxious for me to resolve the space problems."

"How's she doing?" asked Kim with interest. "And by the way, your wedding and the honeymoon looked awesome. We saw the pics."

"You did?" he asked, weakly.

"Rona had a million shots."

"I had to show my friends. They were dying to hear all about it," chirped Rona. Nico smiled, more with relief than anything else. The offending images had been removed and the injunctions had been served. He couldn't stop journalists posting pics of him and Ava out and about, but he was suing for the release of the intimate photos.

"We're going to find a place today," he decided. Even if they didn't find anything ideal, something bigger and *not this*, would be better.

"I have some brochures for you to look at and I've set up appointments for the places Rona and I liked," said Kim, showing him a sheet where she had listed all potential warehouses. He looked through them quickly.

"I like that one." Rona angled closer to him and pointed.

"Only because it's close to your house," countered Kim. "I prefer this one." She pointed to one that was slightly more expensive, but bigger. "Or this one, but it's a twenty minute drive from where I live."

"And half an hour from where I live," whined Rona.

"But if you return to work, then it won't matter where the warehouse is," Kim stated calmly.

"I haven't decided yet."

"Okay," said Nico, knowing he had his work cut out. Something was clearly going on with these two. Whatever happened, he had to find a place this week, and get back to his pregnant wife by the weekend. "We're going to find a place today. Shall we go?" he asked, looking at Kim.

"Here's your copy of the listings." She handed them both their own copies. "Let's go." She stood ready with her folder and pen close to her chest.

"Lemme pop to the ladies room," said Rona.

Kim gave Nico one of those here-we-go-again looks. He returned it with a smile. "I hear you have a young child?"

"Danny," replied Kim, breaking out into a smile herself. "He's eight."

"How're you finding this?" He looked around. "The work and everything?"

"I love it. Ava saved me."

"She did?"

"I was working as a virtual assistant doing odd jobs for different clients. It was all very bitty. Ava gave me a chance to work for her full-time. Turns out, I prefer working for one person and having a big meaty job to do—something that I can work on every day and see it grow. And Ava's a wonderful boss to work for. I've worked for a fair amount of women, with the kind of admin duties I do, and I hate to say that some of them are as nasty as the men. Maybe they think an admin person is the bottom of the food chain. Ava treats me like I'm on par with her. She asks me for my opinion, as if it really matters to her and she makes me feel like a part of this." Kim's voice dripped with sweet admiration and he could plainly see the enthusiasm as she spoke of her work. Listening to her now, Nico understood exactly why Ava had taken Kim on full-time. His wife was lucky to have *her*.

"Ava's completely grateful to you," he told her. "You saved her. She's had a lot on recently." He lowered his voice, "but she knows that you hold all of this together. Rona works well on the backend side, but you, this, the orders, and the distribution side are the crux of her business."

Kim smiled. "I'm glad to help."

"Ready?" trilled Rona, flouncing back into the room with her hair fanned out across her shoulders. "Oh, wait. Let me grab a can of Pepsi."

CHAPTER THIRTY-NINE

Nico had been putting off the trip to Connor's garage but come mid-week, he knew it had to be done.

He would have been happy enough to go alone but Carlos had reminded him that he had no transport and that he had a hulking big pick-up truck they could use. He hadn't needed much convincing and had waited for Carlos to finish his shift at the restaurant early. They'd gone straight to the garage, armed with keys from Kim, and hopeful of avoiding Connor. But the man had obviously seen them and now hovered around them like a mosquito.

"How did it go, the wedding with my ex?" Connor's question speared him like a harpoon, and Nico straightened himself to his full height, feeling the need to throw him a sucker punch. Carlos' steady gaze just behind Connor, stopped him from making a rash move.

"Dude, *manners,*" Carlos growled, hefting a box out of the garage. "We got this, buddy," he told Connor, stopping directly in front of him. "You can go back to your apartment and we'll let you know when we're done."

"It's not a problem," insisted Connor, completely missing

the point that *he* was their problem. He stayed put, leaning against the outside wall, surveying the two men without any offer of help. His presence only made Nico work faster as he and Carlos shifted the boxes to the truck. He couldn't wait to sever what he perceived to be the final link between his wife and her ex. Once they had removed her stock, she would no longer need to use this asshole's garage.

He'd been wary of meeting Ava's ex-fiancé but the thought of putting an end to Ava's reliance on him had sweetened the deal. It was still awkward seeing the guy, despite Ava's protestations that Connor 'wasn't really so bad'.

Nico didn't share her opinion. He didn't *dislike* the guy, he just didn't *like* him, nor could he forget the way he'd treated Ava, even if it was Connor's behavior that had helped direct Ava into Nico's life and eventually into his arms.

Still, Nico didn't forget, and he didn't forgive easily either. It wasn't a case of him being jealous, and he was in no way insecure, but he simply wanted to ensure that there was no further need for Ava's ex to remain within sniffing distance of his wife.

"The wedding?" asked Connor again. "How was it?"

Nico eyeballed him. "Great," he replied stiffly, and walked into the garage to lift two more boxes into his arms.

"I've been waiting to get this cleared for weeks now. You guys came much later than I expected," Connor complained.

Nico grunted and moved away to the truck.

"Tell Ava I'm sorry I had to ask her to vacate this place but I'm moving to a smaller apartment and I don't have a garage there," said Connor.

Nico's interest piqued. "Moving?" *To Alaska,* he hoped.

"I'll still be in Denver. You guys be sure to visit next time you're over."

Nico wandered back in and picked up a few more boxes.

"Smaller, did you say?" He narrowed his eyes and ignored Connor's invitation as well as the weight of the boxes.

Connor winced. "I got laid off."

Nico's eyes widened. "I thought you were a hotshot lawyer?"

"Even top lawyers get laid off, especially if we can't bring in the dollars and the clients. I'm not such a hotshot anyway," Connor claimed, forcing a smile. "But Ava used to think so." His voice was flat, as though the life had gone out of it. "But things could be worse."

They could be; she could have married you.

"I'm starting with a smaller firm. Maybe not working such crazy hours anymore. Maybe I can have a life again."

Nico exhaled slowly, not quite warming towards the guy but feeling less of an urge to punch him. "I hope it works out for you."

Connor nodded, and stared straight into Nico's eyes. "Thanks," he mumbled as Carlos approached them. "I'll take these." He took the boxes from Nico.

Connor waited for Carlos to leave again, before lowering his voice. "I'm sorry I asked for the money. I didn't know who else to turn to. But thanks."

Nico jerked his head back. "Yeah?" was the only word he managed to get out.

What money?

"Tell Ava I'll pay her back real soon, as soon as I start at the new place."

The muscles along Nico's jaw tightened and rage whipped through him.

Ava had lent this asshole money? And she'd not said a word to him about it?

Exactly how much were they talking here?

"I know it can't be an easy time for her," Connor

continued. "Rona told me last time she was here that the online store suffered recently, slow sales and all that because of a fire at the factory or something?"

Nico didn't bother to correct him, but his insides steeled. He couldn't find the words to answer.

Why had Ava hidden this from him?

"We're almost done, buddy," Carlos squeezed his shoulder and walked past. "I got these last few." He heard the words but the pounding in his ears was louder.

"She's had a bad time of it lately," replied Nico finally, his voice cold. At least she didn't need to worry about living expenses or anything like that. Even if he wanted to help her, he had to be careful—Ava was so guarded about her business, and lately any time he'd tried to start a conversation about it, she became defensive and took things the wrong way.

He'd left her to concentrate on it—not knowing how much her business might have suffered. Or what sort of financial condition she was in. But one thing he was sure of, if she'd lent this douchebag money, she would be that much worse off.

"I hope things turn around for her. She's worked hard," Connor replied, thoughtfully. "At least she's got you to fall back on."

Connor's words made him see red. This was what most people thought, this same assumption now shared by this dufus; that Ava was rich. She was, thought Nico, happily. She had everything and anything that she could want, but he also knew his wife didn't see things that way. And he hated that parasites like Connor assumed she was suddenly a money tree for them to take advantage of.

"What do you mean by that?" he asked, his nostrils flaring. His tone startled Connor, who straightened up, not leaning on the wall anymore.

"Nothing, I ... I mean it's not so hard for her anymore. I didn't know who to turn to."

The muscles in Nico's neck corded. He was having difficult in understanding why Ava had neglected to mention a word of this transaction to him. He wasn't sure what he was angrier about—that Ava had lent money to this scrotum-less shmuck or that she'd neglected to tell him about it.

Did she think he would be jealous? Or that he would try to stop her? "You understand that she's trying to set up her own business? That she doesn't have the comfort of a regular paycheck? That Ava is the type of woman who is too proud to ask me for help? You understood that about her, didn't you? That she's independent and stubborn, and big-hearted enough to help others when the person who probably needs the most help is her?" He couldn't keep the rage out of his words.

"Is there a problem?" asked Carlos, hovering in the shadows. Nico shook his head and Carlos made himself invisible once more.

"I'm sorry, I thought you should know why I hadn't paid up yet." Fear colored Connor's voice. "I knew it was wrong to ask just before the wedding—"

Just before the wedding? Nico flexed his fists. He knew she'd had maximum stress at that time. He rubbed his hands together, his fingers tingling from the rush of adrenaline to his brain.

"—and I know ten thousand dollars is a lot of money, but I was maxed out on my credit cards."

Ten thousand dollars?

His gut caved in as if he'd been jabbed straight in it. Gritted teeth and tight muscles made him want to take a swing at the man and he'd have done just that were it not for

Carlos' strong and restraining hand on his shoulder. "We want to get this done, Nico. And leave. Right?"

He didn't know how much Carlos had heard—probably most of it—but Carlos was right. Nico held back.

A corporate lawyer with no money?

"You maxed out your credit cards?" Nico asked, moving towards him. "What were you buying? Heroin?"

Connor mistook this for a joke. "If only," he replied, smiling. "You know how it is, things got out of control."

But Nico didn't know how it was. Even when things had gotten out of control for him, he would never have sunk so low as to ask a pregnant woman for a large loan just before her wedding. "When do you think you can pay her back?" Because he was going to make sure that this pile of horse shit *did* pay her back, and soon. But telling Ava that he knew of this transaction was another matter.

"Soon. I swear. Give me a while to settle into the new job."

"A while? What's a while?" Nico barked.

"A month," stammered Connor.

"A month." Nico committed the date to his memory. "Don't go over," Nico warned, in the same voice he used when speaking to his project manager. *Because it won't be in your interest to delay.*

As a wealthy man Nico was accustomed to people asking him for money. Family members and friends—usually not such great friends either—occasionally came up from beneath the woodwork.

The Bank of Cazale—Edmondo had called it and had been well aware of this phenomenon but Nico had never understood it until he had recently become the target himself. It had never occurred to him that Ava might also be at the receiving end. While he was given to thinking that it might have been because of the upcoming success of her store, he knew she kept that news to herself and the people close to her, which was why it led him to believe that she'd been targeted in this instance because she was married to him.

It was because of his wealth that people would ask her for financial help.

"Shall we go?" Carlos asked, raising his voice as he waited patiently by the pick-up truck.

"There was a table and chair in there," cried Connor, inspecting the empty garage.

"That's yours?" asked Carlos, moving over to the back of the truck and finding the items.

Nico shook his head. What a loser. The guy had borrowed ten thousand dollars from his wife and yet the idea of her accidentally ending up with his table and chair had riled him.

"Tell Ava I said 'hi'." Connor held out his hand.

Nico stared at it and fought the urge to take it and smash it against Connor's face. "Yeah," he grunted in response, then took a breath in and reluctantly shook his hand. He walked away, leaving Connor's face intact.

"Look me up next time you guys are here." Connor shouted as Nico piled into the truck. He'd rather take a walk in the sewers.

They were silent as Carlos drove to the new warehouse they had secured only yesterday. The search had been remarkably smooth, made more so by Kim. She'd done a lot of the groundwork and her list of warehouses to view, by price per square foot and leasing details, made Nico's attempt at finding and securing the right place was a breeze.

Even with Rona in tow for entertainment.

It took a few days but by midweek they'd found the perfect place. Between the four of them they had slowly managed to move items from various storage places to the new warehouse. He had purposely saved Connor's place until last, and was glad that he had, for his mood had soured.

He sensed that Carlos could tell as much, for the jovial man who was always prone to talking and making jokes, was quiet the entire journey back.

After they offloaded quickly, Carlos persuaded him to come for something to eat at one of his family's restaurants. Nico was thankful for the offer and knew he wouldn't be able to relax alone in his hotel room. At Elsa's insistence, they'd all been having dinner at her place for the past few days and he was wary of putting her out again, not that she would have seen it that way.

"Come on in," said Carlos, proudly opening the door and leading Nico in to one of the family restaurants.

"Are you sure I'm not getting in the way?" asked Nico, sitting down at a table as Carlos slipped in opposite him.

"No way, man. Sit down. I'm off for the rest of the evening and we can chill out together. We've earned it."

"Thanks for your help. Couldn't have done it without you."

"Don't mention it."

Every now and then Carlos introduced his new 'brother-in-law' whenever someone walked past and within ten minutes of getting there, Nico was sure that he'd met most of Carlos' family.

They ordered beers and the freshest pizza Nico had tasted this side of the Atlantic.

"Good? Huh?" Carlos asked, looking on eagerly.

The tension that had spread through Nico's body slowly melted away as he settled into the thick, cushiony booths. With Formica tables and bright colored lights, the place had a retro feel about it and he immediately felt relaxed and at ease.

He took a bite of the pizza slice and his face lit up. "It tastes like the ones in Italy."

"It should do," said Carlos smugly. "I got the recipe from one of the restaurants in Verona. The secret is in the base, right?"

Nico couldn't vouch for that, not being a cook himself, but he quickly took another bite, eating hungrily because the pizza tasted so damn good. "This," he said, talking with his mouth full because he couldn't help it, "is great, Carlos. Anytime you want to come and work for me, you let me know."

Carlos laughed and started to eat. For a few minutes there was silence in appreciation of good food.

"What's happening with Rona?" Nico asked, finally. "Is she returning to work or what?" Nico wasn't sure, and he'd never managed to get a reasonable answer from Rona.

"I wish I could tell you. She's so laid back about making up her mind. The college is pushing her for a date though, and she'll have to decide soon enough."

"What does she do?"

"She works as a secretary at a local college but she doesn't like it so much. She took a year off before she had Tori and now the shock has hit her because the year has gone by so fast. She's been putting off her return to work, what with the wedding and all that, but they're expecting her back and she has to let them know soon. She's not sure she wants to go back."

"She wants to carry on working for Ava?"

"She wants to do a few days here and there, and she likes the idea of working from home. I don't know if we can manage it. It's been hard living on one income. But with her working for Ava, and enjoying it, that took the pressure off the money situation."

Nico considered what Carlos had told him. It wasn't easy, he imagined. He'd never been in that position, living from paycheck to paycheck. Or even in Connor's situation, a man with a seemingly high flying career and still struggling for money. But Nico didn't put it past the man to have asked Ava for money when he might have had savings he could have dipped into.

"I keep telling her to speak to Ava about it." Carlos continued.

"Could she go part-time with the college and still work part-time for Ava too?"

"They want her back full-time. It's not really that big a problem. I'll manage and we'll make do somehow. I can always work extra shifts. Rona says she'd rather work full-time for Ava, but I don't know if Ava can afford that, and between you and me," Carlos dipped his head closer. "I'm not sure Ava would want my wife working five days a week." Carlos gave him a knowing smile which Nico returned. He knew about the past friction, even though Rona had been a great help when she'd been in Verona, he'd seen with his own eyes how easy-going, to the point of lazy, she could be without supervision.

"She means well," said Carlos defensively, his face turning into one big smile. "But she doesn't see things the way others do. I still love her to bits. Can't change that, crazy fool that I am. I'm hoping we'll have another baby at some point. There's that to think about."

He sensed that Carlos was trying to find the answers from him. Nico wasn't sure how Ava's financials looked. Now, knowing she had ten thousand dollars less to her name, he wanted to ask her, but it was a touchy subject and he didn't see himself raising it with her unless she brought it up herself first.

"You can't work more shifts, Carlos. You already work more hours than anyone I know."

"So do you, according to Ava." Carlos replied. "I love this job, Nico. I know it's not as fancy as what you do—"

"Hey," Nico said, not wanting the man to think he was any less because he worked in a restaurant. He knew restaurants were hard work too. "A job is a job, but this is yours. This belongs to your family just like the hotel business was something my father passed down to me. It's a family business, irrespective of the work we have to do for it and that's probably why it doesn't feel like a job. It's not that either of them are better. If it's what you love to do that it then it doesn't feel like work."

"I'll drink to that," replied Carlos, lifting his bottle for Nico to touch with his.

CHAPTER FORTY

"What article?" Ava's breath hitched in her throat and the warm tomato, basil and mozzarella panino hovered inches from her mouth.

Whenever Geraldino called her lately it seemed to be bad news. "You haven't seen it?" he squealed.

Hadn't seen what?

The obvious delight in his voice worried her. No doubt he believed he was the first to pass this on—whatever gossipworthy tidbit he'd sniffed out.

"I see why you and Nico took such a long honeymoon. Niiiice shot," he drawled.

What shot?

Shock glued Ava's throat together, making her heart sink to the base of her stomach.

"Type in this URL. Ready?"

She put down her panino as the breath stole out of her lungs, and typed in what he told her. A webpage flared into life and she scrolled through it, her body knotting with tension. But she saw no naked skin or risqué photos.

She breathed again.

Until her eyes scanned the headline. *"Magnate's wife living the high life,"* and subheading: *"Forgets the people who helped her up."*

Beneath it was an image of her looking out from the balcony, smugly, it seemed now, in light of the caption. Another photo showed Nico alone. It was a typical playboy shot and he looked charming; rich and moneyed in a Tuxedo with his hands in his pockets and a cheesy grin on his face. There were other photos, the familiar pictures of them in Amalfi. One taken on the lemon tour they had gone on and the other in Sorrento. Her heart tanked.

Had they never truly been alone?

"Can you believe some people?" Geraldino chortled. "I mean, the nerve. This shit isn't even true. Is it?" His words were like white noise as she scanned through the rest of the article which chronicled her failed engagement and her escape to Italy, into the 'arms of a wealthy playboy'. It went on to detail how she'd once been a 'dirt poor waitress struggling to build up a side business.' Ava scowled.

A waitress?

"It's *diss-gusting,*" said Geraldino, voicing his faux-outrage. "I thought I should bring it to your attention. I must go," he told her and hung up.

"Thanks," she said, vacantly, and continued to read in silent shock. The article also made out that she didn't care any more about her online store or her customers now that she'd 'married up' with her 'filthy rich husband' and implied that she'd let her business fail while she cavorted around the Amalfi coast after her 'million dollar wedding.'

She sat back and heard the pounding of her heart as it thrashed inside her ribcage. This would never end. Just when she thought they had overcome the last nasty episode, here was something new, something she'd never seen coming and the last thing she expected. She placed a comforting hand over her belly and ran it smoothly over the tight skin of her stomach, willing herself to calm down.

Hurry back. She thought of Nico and couldn't wait for him to return tomorrow. It had been a long week without him, and her recent happiness at his having secured a large warehouse for them soon evaporated.

She re-read the article twice more, then deleted the order for five hundred cribs that she'd been in the middle of placing. It was time to go home early, she decided.

———

"You have to see this," Kim beckoned Nico over, her face clouding over quickly.

"What is it?" he asked. He'd stopped by the warehouse to examine it for the last time before returning to his hotel room. He had some last minute business he needed to tend to and Bruno had some questions about the new elevator.

"I got an email from an irate customer and … she alerted me to this." Kim clicked on a link and showed him an article online.

'Magnate's wife living the high life'

"What's this?" he muttered, as his face fell. He read the text quickly.

Again?

He scrolled down it quickly looking for images he prayed he would not see and was relieved to discover that the images were safe. But, when had they taken these photos? Some were different from the last ones. How long had these vultures been following them for?

"A struggling waitress?"

"I can't believe people can be so vicious," voiced Kim in

outrage. "I wanted to show you first. I don't know if Ava has seen it."

"This is all bullshit," Nico raged. "Those goddamn cockroaches." He hung his head, knowing how hurt Ava would be if she had. It pained him to know he was so far away from her and could not make it better even if she had. Scrubbing his forehead, he pondered the chances of getting a late flight out tonight.

"Why do they print such lies?" Kim asked.

"Because they can." He felt nothing but hatred for the faceless so-called journalists who made up lies for money without a care in the world for the people they hurt.

"Is this what it's like—being famous?" Kim asked.

"I'm not famous," replied Nico quickly. "At least, I don't consider myself to be. I was in the public eye because of my father and his wealth, and because I seemed to fit into the lifestyles of the rich and famous. I partied and had fun. I'm used to this shit and I can handle it, even though I hate it. But I know it's hard on Ava. She values her privacy and she's not used to any of this. I'd rather you didn't mention anything to her until I return to Italy."

Kim nodded, agreeing. "Don't worry. I'm not going to say a word. I handle all the customer emails and queries, so Ava won't even get to see them if any customers refer to this article."

"Will you tell Rona, too?" That would cover all the bases.

Kim nodded. "I guess this sours the evening? It's okay if you want to cancel."

He had arranged to take them all out to dinner on his last evening but he was now worried about Ava and he started to rethink. "I'm going to try to get a flight out tonight —and I'll take it if I do. Can I borrow your laptop a moment please?"

Kim moved out of the way. "I'll go tidy up our super huge warehouse."

"Wasn't Rona supposed to help you?" It was already midday.

"She's working from home in the morning and says she'll be here in the afternoon."

Nico rolled his eyes marveling at Kim's enthusiasm, then began to search online for flights. Missing Ava, he decided to give her a call; she'd be settling down to dinner about now, he imagined and he was most anxious to hear her voice again. He knew he'd be able to tell immediately if anything was wrong. When she answered, the dull tone of her voice made him worry. "What's wrong?" he asked, anxious.

"Nothing. We were getting ready to have our last dinner together."

"Your *last* dinner? It almost sounds like the last supper. I didn't realize you and Andrea getting together was such a holy event."

Ava laughed and in the background he heard Andrea say something in a loud and happy voice.

"What's so funny?" he asked.

"She wants me to tell you that she's working her way through your wine cellar."

"She's more than welcome to it."

"Not me, just Andrea."

"I know," replied Nico. He knew Ava was careful with what she ate. And hearing how happy she sounded, he was certain she hadn't yet come across the offending internet article. Any grudge he'd had over her lending money to Connor was instantly dismissed from his mind.

"I miss you," she whispered as he moved the phone piece closer to his ear.

"It's killing me, being apart from you for so long. I tried to get a flight out tonight."

"You did? Why? Is everything okay with the hotel?"

It was you I was thinking of.

He scrubbed a hand over his forehead. "The hotel is fine. I wanted to come home to you."

"Aaaww." She made that squealy noise he so loved. "That's nice to know. I want you home too. I can't wait to see you again. Andrea and I were planning one final girlie night, so there's no need to worry. You take your time and get back safely, at a reasonable hour." She giggled and he heard Andrea having words with her again. She obviously hadn't seen the article, and he felt a wave of relief wash over him.

In the end, there were no available later flights and so that evening, he took them all out; Elsa, Carlos, Rona, Tori and Kim and her son. They went to a local family run restaurant that Elsa had mentioned. Until he'd met Ava, Nico would have thought nothing of choosing the most expensive restaurant in town. But being with Ava had taught him something he'd never realized before; that his good intentions might be perceived as showing off and that taking people to places they would not normally dine out at might come across as a way of making them feel less. Or as Ava had often told him, 'it was too showy'.

They had the most amazing evening. And even though it had been late and was way past Tori's bedtime, he'd insisted on her coming along even though Rona had been willing to leave the toddler with one of her friends. Not only was Carlos against this idea, but so was he. Nico wasn't used to being around children and he knew this would change soon enough.

He enjoyed the evenings he'd spent with Ava's family. Sitting with Elsa and the others reminded him of how great his loss was, as well as his gain. His father would have loved to have had such evenings with him and Ava and his grandchildren but this was something Edmondo would never know and the truth of that reality hurt Nico hard.

In enjoying the warmth of being part of Ava's family, he was brutally reminded of his own loss. He didn't want to do what Edmondo had done—spend so much of his life building up his business and only enjoying family life later on, when Nico was older. He vowed never to make the same mistake, even though he was aware that his obsession for the new hotel was leading him into dangerous waters.

As soon as the hotel was open, he would slow down, at least that's what he told himself.

CHAPTER FORTY-ONE

"He knows," said Ava, hanging up the phone and walking back to the dining table.

They were having dinner late in the evening because Andrea had stayed later at work.

"About the article?" Andrea clutched the unopened bottle of wine in her hands. "How can you tell? I didn't hear you talk about any article."

"Trust me, Nico knows," sighed Ava, sitting down slowly. She'd already shown Andrea the offending piece.

"Are you psychic?"

Ava shrugged. "I can tell from his voice and the fact that he was trying to change his flight so he could come home sooner. And that he called in the middle of the day when he usually waits until the evening."

"You need to write a book on relationships. I'd buy it," said Andrea, twisting the cork out. "I know nothing about the art of subtle clues."

Ava laughed. They'd dissected more past romances, although she'd noted that Andrea didn't discuss Riley again. She took this to mean that he must have hurt her too much and the pain of that relationship was still like a raw flesh wound. It would take time to heal. She was convinced that Andrea felt something for him, despite her denial.

"But," said Andrea, pouring wine into her glass and frowning. "Leo seems to know each time I need a sugar rush."

"He does?" Ava warmed to the idea of a possible connection between Andrea and Leo. She'd already concluded that he was worthy of having Andrea through the conversations she'd had with him. And she remembered that he'd been worried when Andrea had missed the wedding.

Her friend frowned as if in deep thought. "We take it in turns to get coffee in the mornings, but when the mood strikes, I'll go and get myself a pastry and more coffee in the afternoon. Right now my body craves that kind of comfort food. It seems that Leo knows just when I need a pastry," she murmured. "More so lately," she added, as an afterthought.

"Or maybe he knows you have a sweet tooth," suggested Ava, tucking this little snippet of conversation away for future use.

"How are you going to deal with the nasty stuff?" Andrea asked.

"Nasty stuff?"

"The internet article."

"*This* internet article?" asked Ava, hoping that Andrea hadn't seen the previous one with the risqué photos.

Andrea nodded. "You guys have also been in the local magazines and papers a lot. But you'd have been on honeymoon around that time."

"I'm glad we were away," said Ava, letting out a huge sigh. "I hate being in the public eye."

"I'd love it," gushed Andrea.

"You wouldn't. You think you might, but until it happens to you, you don't understand how intrusive it can be, and scary too." She looked out through the French doors of the dining room. "Someone could be out there watching us this very moment and you wouldn't know it."

Andrea turned and stared out of the window. "I didn't think of that," she whispered, her voice shaky. "That's scary."

"It's Nico they're after, and he's used to this. It comes with the territory, but it's not something I will ever get used."

"It's not just about Nico now. You've added a certain glamor to his reputation, what with the way you both met, and now with the baby, and the wedding, and of course, your business."

"My sales will start to slide down again," said Ava, miserably. "Just when I was beginning to get my momentum back." With a month to go before her due date, she didn't have the mental or physical stamina to fight the negativity. Her plan was to continue as usual by doing the best she could for her customers but she always put her baby and Nico first.

"No way," Andrea insisted. "Things will get better." She ran her fingers slowly along the thin stem of her wine glass. "More water for you?"

"I've had enough water," said Ava, wishing she could have a glass of wine. It wouldn't be harmful, but she had mostly adhered to a no alcohol policy as soon as she'd found out she was pregnant. With the sort of morning she'd had, a glass of wine would have been sweet comfort, but she refrained.

"Listen to me," said Andrea, "There is no such thing as bad publicity."

"Me being a struggling waitress and abandoning my customers and my business while I cavorted around Amalfi with my playboy husband—that's *good* publicity?"

"It's *free* publicity and you mark my words, interest in you and your store will go up. You'll come across some people who will love you, and some who will hate you. Haters will hate, but mostly, people are nice, if you give them half a chance."

Ava didn't share Andrea's positive outlook, but marveled at her ability to sound so upbeat given her recent circumstances. "I love that you always look on the bright side. Listening to you makes me feel cautiously optimistic. I am positive, or I used to be more than I am now, but these recent intrusions into my life make me see the world less through rose tinted glasses and more with the blue-gray filter of reality."

"We all go through ups and downs, Ava. One minute we think life is wonderful and nothing can get us down, and then when something bad comes our way, we sink into the depths of misery. You'll come out of it. It's not the time for you to dwell on the crap that others dole out to you. You're about to give birth and maybe you should slow down and take things easy."

"I *have* slowed down. I slowed down after we returned from our honeymoon. It's not just for my sake, it's also more because I know how stressed out Nico is. We can't have both of us in that same state. He won't say it, he thinks I need him more but there are times when he needs me more. He won't ever admit to it, and he busies himself in so much work, taking on the world and everything—even going to Denver, when it 'could' have waited until December or January—it could have. It would have been hard but not impossible to get by until then, even if Connor booted us out. But Nico is still grieving over Edmondo. This has been a hard year for him, and he's nursing his wounds in silence. He thinks he's invincible but he's not, he's just a man, and they sometimes fall down too."

Andrea smiled at her. "You're the only one who can help him. You're the only one who he'll allow to help him. We all need support," she agreed. "Men are lousy at asking for it. I if

I worked alone, it would have been harder for me to claw my way out of the darkness I've been in but Leo has been the greatest help. He's so positive and so dynamic. It's as if the fire never happened and we're marching forward at warp speed regardless."

Ava wasn't sure if she detected signs of admiration from her friend, but she liked what she was hearing. "I created an order for d'Este for five hundred cribs earlier."

Andrea squealed with delight.

"But then I deleted it because, despite what you say, I expect my sales to tank until this latest news dies down."

Andrea shook her head vigorously, and her dark ringlets bobbed ferociously around her shoulders. "No, no, no. You raise the order again and you put out a press release announcing the facts. You get Nico to get his lawyer to come down hard on the perpetrators of these lies—"

"It doesn't really do anything," Ava protested. "New lies spring up soon enough."

"Who cares? Soon those assholes will realize it's not worth printing more lies because they'll suffer the consequences. You just keep on keeping on. You're a hard-working woman, Ava and your love story is beautiful. The fire wasn't your fault and you didn't let your customers down—it was me and Nico not telling you. Maybe you could have dealt with it better, if you'd known from the start. But I still maintain we did the right thing."

"Maybe you did," replied Ava. What good would it have done? She'd have had a miserable honeymoon, and instead she now had the most beautiful memories to look back on. Aside from these ugly rumors, the only other spot on her cloud was Connor and the money he still owed her. More than anything she hated keeping this secret from Nico. A couple of times she'd been tempted to tell him, but she could see he already had more than enough to deal with and not wanting to give him another thing to fret about it—for she instinctively knew that this news would annoy him— she thought it best to leave him in the dark. The sooner she got her money back, the better. "Thank you. You're a great friend. Talking to you always makes me feel better. You're almost as good as having Nico around."

They laughed together.

"Almost?"

Ava dipped her head from side to side, contemplating it. "He's irreplaceable, but you come a close second best."

CHAPTER FORTY-TWO

Andrea was right. Ava found that her website traffic exploded in the subsequent weeks as the article went viral.

On Nico's return they had both discussed Andrea's advice and decided to let the blatant lies fester for a while. Pelosa didn't clamp down on it immediately.

Ava's temporary notoriety as the 'struggling waitress out to ensnare the playboy' resulted in more visitors to her website and, after the initial flurry of haters and trolls jumping on the bandwagon passed, a beautiful thing happened. She started to see positive reviews and comments on mommy blogs from satisfied customers. One website even printed the newsletter she'd sent to her customers on her return from the honeymoon, where she'd explained about the fire.

Slowly and silently, her own army of happy customers were coming to her defense. It renewed her hope and made her feel better about the whole situation. And she'd been more than relieved that her worst fears—pictures of her naked or in compromising positions, albeit with her husband—hadn't surfaced again.

But she still lived in constant fear of that happening again. As time passed she found herself looking forward to her baby's arrival, hoping that a focus on something other than her online business and the interest of others' in her life might bring her more peace.

With her hospital bag packed and ready, they were biding their time, or rather, she was biding her time, having slowed down at work, and Nico was trying to give her the appearance that he, too, was slowing down.

The reality could not have been further from the truth.

Nico's life went from frenetic to chaotic and as the days crawled into the first week of November, Ava cut back drastically on her hours in the office at the Casa Adriana and chose to work from home more. The pressure on Nico was immense and there were days she felt his mood simmering as things reached boiling point and last minute problems with the hotel came to the fore. Now that her due date had come and gone, he tried to work from home as much as possible.

"Happy?" Nico asked her one evening as they sat in bed. She was reading and he had his laptop balanced on his legs.

"I'm always happy," she said, distracted, and reading about the timetable she was going to put her baby on. Sleep, two hour feed, sleep, two hour feed. That seemed to be the gist of it during the first month. It would be a breeze.

"How are the d'Este cribs doing?" He stopped typing and gave her a split second of his attention. She noticed he did this frequently. He would often be working away on something then he would stop to make sure she was fine. But with three weeks to go until the hotel opened, she knew he had weightier matters on his mind.

"They're selling like wildfire," she said, looking at him gleefully. "I'm going to have to place another order."

Nico tilted his head down and kissed her on the lips,

laying a gentle hand on her stomach. "Andrea was right. There's no such thing as bad publicity."

"She was right," Ava conceded.

"She knows her stuff."

"I'm going to order another five hundred cribs."

"Double it," he advised. "No, actually, triple it." He looked serious and it got her thinking.

"Triple it?" With his recent cash injection into her business, she would be able to do that.

"They're obviously selling well."

"They're flying out of my store."

"Triple it."

She seemed hesitant. "Fifteen hundred cribs?"

"What are you scared of?"

Success.

Scaling up too fast.

Taking too much on.

"It seems like a lot," she said quietly. But, the five hundred had sold. She recalled there had been a time earlier on when a manufacturer had made a mistake with an order and had nearly sent over one hundred cribs when she'd ordered ten.

She'd come a long way in a short space of time.

"Okay, I will."

The business in Denver was moving along smoothly, and heeding Nico's advice, she kept a close eye on Rona now that her sister had ended her employment with the college and was working full-time for her.

Rona worked two full days at the warehouse and three days from home. Ava wouldn't have been able to keep her on full time, but Nico had insisted on injecting money into her business, 'to help until the baby comes out and grows up' he told her, cheekily.

He'd insisted on it as soon as he'd returned from Denver,

telling her that it would help Carlos, and he felt they should do what they could to help him. Rona had been a help while she'd been in Verona, and Ava knew that going out to work with a toddler meant expensive childcare arrangements. She accepted Nico's generous offer after sleeping on it. It still didn't sit easily with her and the only thing that convinced her was the knowledge that it would help her sister and her husband.

If she could help her family now that she was able to do so, why not? After all, she'd helped Connor—something that she was beginning to regret, especially since he hadn't yet paid her back—and he certainly wasn't family, or much of a friend.

"I'll pay you back the first quarter of next year," she told Nico and had known, from the hard line of his jaw that he had other ideas, that he didn't want anything back but also that he was letting her have her say. "As you wish," he'd responded.

Nearing the end of her pregnancy, she went back to sharing her thoughts and asking his opinion with all things to do with her business—as she had done when they had first met.

Accepting his investment allowed her to place bigger orders. She knew, judging by the way Nico's face sometimes tightened, that the pressures of adding the finishing touches to the hotel weighed heavily on his mind. She didn't want to add to his troubles and so she backed down much quicker than she normally would have.

Returning to work after the baby was born would be a big enough point of contention between them and she was going to save her ammunition for then. She already had plans in place regarding her online store. Lizzi would be home for Christmas and was eager to earn extra money. Ava had decided to take a month out after the baby's birth to get through Christmas and the New Year. By then the baby would be nearly two months old and Ava was fairly confident of having a routine in place by then, according to this latest new baby book that she'd been reading.

She planned to work from home until the baby was six months old, coming into the office whenever she needed a break, maybe even working one or two half days at the Casa Adriana. She imagined she'd have a lot of time on her hands if the baby slept all day long. Apparently, they only became more demanding at six months old.

Nico had mumbled something about taking on a nanny, but she didn't consider herself a royal by any means and knew she was more than capable of bringing up their child as well as running her business. So, that idea was blown out of the water long ago.

"Any signs?" he asked, sliding his hand over the mountain that now passed for her stomach.

"Not a thing." She let out a heavy sigh. Other women dropped babies early, why couldn't she be one of them? Sleeping was difficult, and the need to constantly pee was more than annoying, especially when it interfered with her sleep.

"Sex is known to bring on labor," suggested Nico, in a low voice.

"So is castor oil," she retorted, pushing the thought away.

"But sex is more fun."

"For you, maybe. Right now, that exit is a one way street. And the baby's coming out of it."

"You can't be serious." Nico whispered in her ear, biting her earlobe gently.

"You want sex, now?" she moaned, when usually she

would have heated up at the thought of it. "Do you really find me attractive even now?"

"I can't imagine a time when I won't find you attractive." His hand moved to cup her watermelon sized breasts. She heard him sigh deeply, heard the animal moan of his voice as he squeezed what was more than a handful, and let his mouth claim hers slowly. She moaned too, and pushed her book out of the way. They kissed and stroked, and sighed with pleasure that built up slowly and deliciously—until Nico's cell phone rudely interrupted their tender moment.

At this time of night it had to be important. He stopped and scowled at the name on his screen. "Bruno?"

Ava slid her head onto the pillow and stared at her stomach as she listened.

"What?" Nico barked. She directed her gaze at him, saw his face redden, saw the angry veins jut out along his neck and temples. "They can't do that!" he yelled. "We're opening in two weeks. They. Can't. Do. That."

He belted out of bed.

Ava sat up slowly.

He started to pace around the room. "You told me we'd passed, that the wiring wasn't a problem anymore."

She saw the color fade from his face. "Not negotiable. You hear me? *Not* negotiable. It has to open. Who's behind this?" he shouted. "You get me the name of the guy who refuses to sign off the safety checks."

She didn't like the sound of this.

"Tomorrow?" He looked over at Ava. "I can't come—"

"Go," she told him. Whatever it was he had to do, she wanted to him do it. "Go," she urged, again. "The baby's not coming anytime soon." She was four days over. According to Elsa, she and Rona had both gone over by a week.

Nico hung up and wiped his hands all over his face. It was

when he didn't shout, when his voice turned deathly quiet, that she understood the rage he tried to contain. "The officials aren't signing off the safety checks on the staff quarters."

"I thought everything had been signed off?"

"Me too." Nico scrubbed his face, and suddenly, he looked so tired and haggard, as if the news had aged him a few years. "They need me in Ravenna tomorrow."

"Then you must go."

"But you need me here. I don't want to leave you. Not like this."

"I'm hardly in labor, Nico. No twinges, no Braxton Hicks, no show, no nothing. This little one isn't ready to come out yet, I promise you."

He attempted a smile, but when his lips failed to turn upwards, she knew he was beat. He looked like a man defeated, and it broke her heart to see him this way.

"Come here." She held out her arms. He walked over to her and she lay down, letting him rest his head on her chest. "It's going to be alright. Everything's going to work out just fine," she promised.

CHAPTER FORTY-THREE

"I don't want to leave you." Nico kissed her on the lips and she could tell from his solemn face that he was torn between needing to go and wanting to stay by her side.

"Go," she said, sounding extra cheerful, hoping to put his mind at ease. "We'll still be waiting for you when you get back."

"I'll be back by the afternoon."

"Take your time and get all these last-minute problems sorted out so that you won't have to think about them."

He kissed her once more then left. She felt the pain of his departure more sharply now than ever before. It wasn't only because the baby had gone over its due date. But she could see he was troubled, and it pained her to see him so down when he'd been so buoyed up recently by the way things had been progressing.

She went back to bed and tried to get some rest, mostly because she hadn't slept properly last night. It wasn't only because she was so heavy and uncomfortable but because Nico hadn't slept either. It was better for him to go to Ravenna when she was still feeling fine, than to have him tense and strained at home beside her. Once he'd fixed things there, he'd be back by her side and then they could focus solely on the arrival of their baby.

But her attempt at resting failed as sleep eluded her and restlessness overpowered her to the point where she was forced to get out of bed. She wanted to take her mind off worrying about Nico but also to stop thinking about the slow dull ache that seemed to have started along her back.

It was nothing, she told herself, convincing herself that she was being paranoid. But the tightness along her lower back slowly worsened. Was it a labor pain? She couldn't be certain. It wasn't a sharp shooting pain, more like a dull ache, and since she wasn't sure what labor pains were like, she didn't want to have a false alarm and worry Nico unduly.

So she ignored it again.

Not now, she told herself. *You can't come out now,* she told her baby. *Not while your Daddy isn't here.*

With renewed effort she set about working from her office at home, but even the news of selling twenty three cribs yesterday did nothing to inflate her mood.

As the day wore on at snail's pace, she became steadily restless and found herself staring at the clock, watching time seep away. Even the afternoon nap she usually had did nothing to put her at ease.

Nico said he would be back soon, but it was a four hour round trip to Ravenna and she estimated that it would take longer than he had envisaged.

She had already decided that she would wait until he got back and that there was no point in calling him now to tell him about a pain she wasn't sure about. And she also didn't want him to race back like a lunatic.

But by late afternoon the twinges became more

pronounced and she prayed that these were the false Braxton Hicks pains.

Nico will be here soon.

She checked her hospital bag for the third time, then Googled 'Braxton Hicks' but was none the wiser. When the pains were fifteen minutes apart and stronger, her worry deepened. Home alone and with no idea of whether she was in labor or not, she knew she had to call someone. But the nurse she spoke to at the hospital told her that unless her pains were so severe that she couldn't move, it was likely to be nothing.

Ava breathed easier. She didn't want to be in labor, not without Nico by her side. Her tolerance for pain was low anyway, and she didn't want to put anyone out by turning up at the hospital when she was only experiencing false labor.

So, she forced herself to put up with the pains and reminded herself that Nico would return as soon as he had resolved everything. He was only taking longer because he wanted to make sure he'd tied up all loose ends. This thought comforted her and she tried to take a walk in the grounds outside, clutching her cell phone tightly.

But the pain that now struck made her stop and she froze, paralyzed as she squeezed her eyes shut. She grimaced, as the contraction cut through her like a hot poker stick in her lower back, sharper, and stronger than those preceding it. Her stomach hardened like concrete and she breathed in and out slowly.

When it had passed she still wasn't sure whether to call Nico. She decided against it, thinking this couldn't be the real thing because in films women screamed from the tops of their lungs.

Surely, *this* couldn't be labor?

She was in extreme pain but she wasn't forced to making

loud noises. But another pain shot through her body like shrapnel, forcing her to gasp loudly. It was so strong and so sharp that she had to bite her lips together.

What if she ended up giving birth alone?

When the pain had passed she dialed Nico's number only to find that it went straight to voicemail.

And that was when she panicked.

CHAPTER FORTY-FOUR

Nico tore down the rural roads that lead away from Verona, past Montova and down the motorway to Ravenna, his face like thunder when he arrived at the hotel building site before eight.

Bruno was already on the scene looking a paler shade of his former self. "I don't understand, Nico."

"How could this even happen?" Nico demanded, charging through the mobile unit where his managers where gathered.

"It's not technically a problem. The wiring works. It passed the test."

"Then what *is* the problem?" Nico growled, refusing the offer of a cup of coffee.

"The laws are getting stricter, especially when it comes to workers, and safety. What they're saying—"

"Who exactly?"

"The officials, the people who pass these—"

"I want his name—whoever refused to sign it off."

"It's a department, Nico. It's not one man's decision," Bruno replied.

"There is always someone at the top of the hierarchy who is responsible," Nico bellowed. "I need to talk to him. I have a hotel that's ready to open in ten days' time. Do you know how much money I stand to lose each day that it remains closed? You'll incur the penalty—are you aware of that?"

"Technically, we wouldn't," Bruno replied, bravely. "The project isn't late, or over budget."

"But clearly it's in danger of not opening." Nico wasn't interested in excuses, he wanted solutions.

Bruno scratched his chin. "The point of contention appears to be that you replaced the wiring in the hotel rooms, and you could have done so for the staff quarters."

"Except that we only replaced the wiring in the main building because of the mold problem, right?"

Bruno nodded.

"Listen up," ordered Nico, addressing the team of three men who sat quietly before him. "I want you all to tell me how we can move past this." He didn't want to spend too long here but now that he had come he wanted to visit the department concerned. It was better to deal with this shit now than to keep coming back and forth while Ava was closer to having the baby. He sat down and checked his cell phone—no calls from Ava. He breathed a little easier.

It was almost late afternoon when Nico and his men arrived at the offices of the department of safety. It took a while for him to find anyone from that team who would agree to see them. He wasn't accustomed to hearing 'No' and he had no plans to pay another visit, or to be away from Ava for much longer. After much discussion and his refusal to move, one of the officials gave in and another suited official with a forgettable face finally turned up and begrudgingly agreed to hear their concerns.

After the official had informed them of the department's

ruling, Nico relayed his side of the facts as he understood them.

"We cannot agree to sign off the safety checks on the building. The staff quarters are deemed unsafe," the official told them, turning the pages of the report he was referencing.

"It's not unsafe," thundered Nico. He had to stop himself from slamming his fist on the table. "It was passed before. What's changed all of a sudden?"

"You're endangering the lives of the employees."

"How am I when the wiring was shown to be safe at the initial inspection?" Nico demanded.

"You replaced the wiring in the rest of the building, and you should have replaced it everywhere. We have stricter laws in place these days."

"That's all I keep hearing, but if I provide a safe working environment for my employees, then surely the only thing that will hurt them will be the fact that they will miss out on their earnings?"

"We are not changing our decision." The official's tone was final.

"What do you expect me to do?" Nico demanded. "I'm supposed to open in two weeks' time." He stole a glance at his cell phone again. There was no goddamn signal in this musty old building and he was anxious to hurry this along.

"The only way you'll be able to open the hotel is if you get those quarters rewired."

"Are you playing games with me?" growled Nico, his voice deathly. He eyeballed the official with a cold stare.

"I'm giving you a solution."

"You're being an—" Nico started but Bruno cut him off.

"How about we have a quick five minute break to cool down and then we can work out a way forward?" Bruno suggested. "You tell us exactly what is needed for us to meet your newer, tighter regulations and we can discuss and move forward."

"Not negotiable," Nico started to say.

"Five minutes." Bruno gave Nico a hard stare.

"Five minutes," the official agreed.

"What was that about?" Nico asked, his rage simmering like lava as they stepped outside.

"He's not going to change his mind, can't you see that? You're dealing with a man who's stuck in bureaucratic government policy. The decision isn't his—he's telling you what he's been told." Bruno lowered his voice and leaned in towards Nico. "My contact says this guy's boss is brown nosing and he's in with one of the top guys. He's friends with Armando Vieri, one of the politicians who's lobbying for workers' rights and he's had—"

"Wait." Nico listened to a message from Gina on his cell phone. His face crumpled. "Shit," he spat out, and quickly dialed Ava's cell but she didn't answer. Frantic with worry, running his hand through his hair, Nico called Gina. She answered on the first ring.

"Ava's gone into labor, Nico. We're in the hospital. Hurry."

He raced to his car and thoughts about Bruno and the official and the spa hotel were quickly forgotten. Flooring the gas pedal, he raced off, driving like a maniac as he weaved in and out of the small roads in Ravenna. His chest felt tight, as if it had been clamped in a pair of pliers. But his thoughts were on Ava and how he'd left her alone.

Of all the days, of all the things that could have happened, why now, why this?

He sped along at breakneck speed, not caring about the rain that spattered his windscreen, or the speed limits he'd broken. In record time he'd cleared the motorway. His thoughts lurched between anger at himself, that he'd come here at all with Ava overdue, and seething rage for the official who refused to sign off the safety report on the hotel.

It was unbelievable bad luck.

One moment things had looked to be working out smoothly the next it all went wrong in a matter of moments. What was it that Bruno had started to tell him? About this Vieri guy? For some reason the name sounded familiar.

As the rain crashed down, Nico accelerated faster, desperate to reach the hospital where Ava was waiting. The hotel didn't matter anymore, but the birth of his child did. He hated that he wasn't by Ava's side at a time when she needed him the most. He hated that he'd not been the one to take her to the hospital.

There was no way he was going to miss the birth of his child.

The rural country roads near Montova told him that home wasn't too far away, and as he scrambled around a bend at breakneck speed, the car spun out of his control, and veered off the road.

The trunk of a tree, large and deadly, raced towards him and it took all his might to turn the steering wheel sharply to the left, narrowly missing the tree. But his relief was shortlived as the car spun around like a spinning top then hurtled down the grassy incline, overturning in its wake. The noise was deafening, before the world turned dark.

CHAPTER FORTY-FIVE

"You're not in labor but don't worry. You have a while to go yet, but we're going to keep you here," the second nurse had told her. This one had kind eyes and a soft face and immediately put Ava's mind at rest.

At least this one nurse was better than the first one who'd looked at her with disdain after checking her. "Two centimeters dilated," she'd sniffed. "But you have a private room. Let me see if it's ready." She'd left Ava, with Gina, in the reception area of the maternity wing.

All Ava had wanted was Nico. If she was only 'two centimeters dilated' and it hurt like hell, she was already petrified as to what the other eight centimeters might bring. She thought she'd been brave holding out as long as she had.

Unable to get hold of Nico, she'd called Gina, knowing that Gina was closer to her than Andrea would be. Within ten minutes, Gina had driven up and taken Ava to the hospital. Fear pricked her thoughts like a shock of electricity as she was helped into her hospital clothes and taken to her quiet room.

They waited together and Ava expected Nico to come charging through the door any moment now, thereby relieving

Gina. But as the afternoon wore on in a haze of pain and confusion, something about the strained look on Gina's face told Ava that something wasn't right.

"He should have been here by now," said Ava. The pains were coming, but they had slowed down and were longer apart, yet it still felt as if a hot knife sliced her back each time.

"He's on his way," Gina told her. But as the afternoon lingered towards early evening, Gina walked in and out of the room, frequently. Whenever she returned it was with a smile on her face that looked anything but natural.

The nurses continued to monitor her progress but did not seem unduly concerned, and even Ava felt that her pains were starting to subside again. She called Nico several times but it always went to his voicemail. The last few times she'd called his cell phone had rung for the longest time and when he still didn't answer, she became even more worried. "Have you heard from him?" she asked Gina again when she walked into the room.

"He's coming." Gina smiled widely. "I know he's on his way."

"You said that hours ago."

"I spoke to someone called Bruno at the hotel site. He told me that Nico had left a few hours ago. He says they're doing some roadwork along the way, so maybe Nico's been held up."

"But he's not answering his phone," Ava cried. She knew he wouldn't have let the whole day pass without speaking to her.

"Sometimes there's no reception in the rural areas."

"But it would go to voicemail, wouldn't it?" Something in the pit of her stomach told her that things weren't adding up, that there was no way in hell that Nico wouldn't have been here by now. There was no way in hell that he wouldn't have answered her call. She wasn't on any medication or oxygen and her brain wasn't addled.

She knew when two and two didn't make four.

She tried to focus on other things, as the pains continued to tear through her body, albeit in irregular patterns and with less force. She had walked, with Gina by her side, up and down the hospital corridors and outside, to keep mobile and to take her mind off the worry that filled every cell of her body. As the hours slowly passed, and there was still no sign of Nico, her anxiety started to rise and the pains started up again.

"Something's happened," she mumbled to herself, frantically wringing her hands together.

"You need to rest up a little," the nice nurse told her. "I understand you're worried, but I'm sure your husband will be here soon. You need to think of the baby."

"How can I rest?" Ava snapped, when the nurse left the room. "He wouldn't do this. Nico would have been here by now."

"I know. But do you remember your wedding car got delayed—after the accident? It could be—" Gina swallowed, "roadworks or an overturned truck, or something ..." But Gina didn't sound too reassuring.

Ava closed her eyes and forced herself to breathe deep, and slow. She wasn't ready to have the baby, not without Nico by her side and so she forced herself to relax, in an effort to slow things down. In time, the pains started to slow down again. "Stop start labor," the nurse explained. "The baby's spine is against your spine, and it might take a while."

A while would be good, thought Ava, staring into space. Her heart beat furiously. How could it be so late and still no sign of Nico? She kept turning her head towards the door each time she heard footsteps go by. Any moment now she expected him to come rushing in, his face flustered, his eyes dark and filled with concern. And he would kiss her, she knew, on the lips, while his hand stilled on her stomach. And he would tell her that everything was going to be fine.

The footsteps stopped outside the door, and she heard the sound of the doorknob turning. She waited in expectation of seeing that beloved face, of wanting to fall into her husband's big, strong arms, but Andrea walked in—her face somber, her eyes glassy.

Instantly, Ava knew that something terrible had happened.

"Hey." Andrea put on a smile.

"Tell me." Ava's heart was beating so fast and so furiously, she expected it to burst right out of her chest. She slowly sat up in bed with her hand protectively around her stomach, preparing herself for the worst.

"Nico's been held up," said Andrea. "He's on his way." Her eyes were dull and Ava didn't miss the quick glance she threw at Gina. The two women shared a look that they wished to hide from her.

"I'm not stupid," Ava exclaimed, her patience gone. "Tell me the truth. What is it?"

"That *is* the truth," Andrea insisted, moving quickly to her side. Ava felt as though she wanted to cry. It was getting late and Andrea was here and Nico was not. She could handle it, if they would only tell her the truth.

"As a friend Andrea, you *have* to tell me the truth." She swallowed the sob that was stuck in her throat. "I'm about to have his baby, for Christ's sake. I deserve to know." She felt herself wanting to break out into tears, but somehow she managed to keep it together.

Andrea looked at Gina, then at her. She took Ava's hand

gently between her own. "Nico's had an accident. He's alive," she said quickly. "But we don't know how bad it is."

She heard a scream, then realized the sound had come from her. She shrank back trembling, a wail escaping her lips, as she put a hand up to her face, feeling her breaths coming fast.

An accident?

Her Nico?

It had been hours, and they'd known all along, and they'd lied to her the whole time. It couldn't be good. It explained why Andrea was here too, why Gina wasn't leaving.

Ava panicked, wanting to vomit, wanting to fall.

And that's when she felt it.

Not the rush of water she'd read about, but a slow trickle, so slow, she wasn't certain whether she'd wet herself.

"I think my water just broke," she whispered, before she started to pant—not from the pains—but from the thought that Nico was hurt, and she had no idea how badly.

CHAPTER FORTY-SIX

When he came to, he was lying in the hospital with Leo by his side and a pain as sharp as if he'd been skewered through the chest.

Where was Ava? And why did Andrea keep coming in and out? Nico opened his eyes one minute and she was there, then he fell asleep the next. When he opened his eyes again she'd disappeared. But Leo always remained by his side.

What was he doing here?

The next time he opened his eyes he would try to stay awake long enough to ask about Ava ...

Sleep came swiftly, and it was deep, and heavy. When he next stirred, he opened his eyes to find the room dimly lit. It seemed quieter too. Leo was still here and Andrea walked towards him again. The pain still lacerated his chest, and hurt even more each time he tried to breathe.

What was this thing attached to his body?

Ava. The thought of her stopped him cold.

He had to find her. But when he tried to shift his body, the pain intensified. It was as though he'd been pinned to the bed, held in place by a large rod that impaled his chest to the headboard. Anxiety twisted his insides and he still struggled to breathe.

"It's okay, Nico. Don't move too much," Leo told him.

When he looked down, he saw a tube in his chest and gasped for air. "Where?" *Am I?* He couldn't get the words out all in one breath and speaking felt like an effort.

Ava. She flashed into his mind once more and as his thoughts began to gain clarity, shock turned his insides to liquid. "Ava?" he cried and tried to lift his head but shooting pain tasered his chest, rendering him immobile.

"She's fine." Leo said. "You're going to be fine, too."

"Where?" he whispered, trying to move his arms, the frustration getting to him.

"Here, in another room. She's resting, Nico. You need to rest, too." Leo's voice was soft yet firm.

"Want to see her."

"You will. She can't see you like this."

"Baby?" he muttered, anger stealing up his throat. He would never forgive himself if he'd missed the birth of their baby.

"No baby yet," replied Leo calmly, smiling at him. "She's in the maternity ward and things are going slowly but everything's fine. We need you to recover."

Nico gritted his teeth together. He needed to see Ava now. Anger coursed through him as he made another desperate attempt to sit up again. He would crawl out of here if he had to.

"No," said Leo, trying to get him to rest back gently. "Don't make things worse." The door opened and Andrea came in then, rushing to his side, her eyes filled with tears and she gave him a weak smile. "You're awake."

"And fighting to see Ava," Leo told her. Nico spluttered,

feeling bitter at the way things had turned out, hating that he felt completely helpless.

"You were in an accident, Nico." Andrea's voice was gentle and calming. "Your car went off the road and overturned as it went down a hill. The drivers behind you stopped to help. It took a while for the emergency services to cut you out and you've been here ever since. You've got two broken ribs, and internal bleeding in your chest. The tube is still draining the fluid, but you're alive and you're going to be fine."

He shook his head, anger mixing with frustration. Ava needed him, but what good was he like this?

An invalid.

His eyes turned moist. "Have to see Ava," he croaked. It hurt like hell.

"Try not to talk," Andrea soothed. "You'll recover faster but only if you rest."

"Want to see Ava. *Now*."

"She's sleeping, Nico. I've tried to keep her informed, but for a while there her blood pressure started to creep up. You have to let her get some rest, otherwise she'll be too tired to push the baby out. She's been in stop-start labor the whole day and she's exhausted. I told her you were here and that you were fine. She's just fallen asleep. She'll be up again soon and I promise I'll take you to see her."

His body steeled with anger. "Need to see Ava."

Andrea's eyes turned soft and she nodded. "You can, you will. But let her sleep."

CHAPTER FORTY-SEVEN

It was the dull pain that woke Ava in the early hours of the next morning.

She was surprised that she'd managed to sleep at all. The pains which had subsided earlier now started up again.

How long was this torture going to go on for? No wonder they called it labor. And then she remembered.

Nico.

She had to see Nico. The baby was fine, she could see that from the monitors they'd strapped onto her stomach. But how was her husband? They'd told her he was here and that he was going to be fine, but she didn't believe them anymore. Deciding that she needed to see for herself, she attempted to climb out of her bed but the movement alerted Andrea who sat in the chair close by. She opened her tired eyes and got up quickly.

"Where do you think you're going?" Andrea asked, gently trying to get her back into the bed. "You can't go anywhere, you're all hooked up."

"I want to see Nico," Ava protested. "I need to see my husband."

"Okay, okay," said Andrea. "I know you do." Her voice was softer. "You both make terrible patients. We've had to keep Nico in his bed and he's in no position to walk."

She froze, Andrea's words cutting through Ava like a machete. "No position to walk? How bad is he? Tell me the truth, Andrea. I'll hate you forever if you don't."

"He's doing well. He had to get some rest and so did you. That nurse you don't like warned us to make sure you both stayed put."

"Why can't he walk?"

"He's recovering," replied Andrea vaguely. Then her face softened. "Let me get him for you."

She rushed out of the room while Ava waited, her heart beating treacherously, her insides hard and empty all at the same time. She was scared to see him, scared to discover how bad he was, and yet desperate to see him again.

When Andrea returned, it was with Nico sitting in a wheelchair, pale and gaunt; a ghost of the man she'd last kissed goodbye. Tears brimmed in Ava's eyes, threatening to spill over, part sadness, part joy, part relief. Words weren't necessary as she held her breath, killing the cry that tried to escape from her throat, her gaze fixed on him as Andrea wheeled him towards her.

When he looked at her, her heart shuddered back to life, and utter gratitude crashed over her, in thanks for the life that had been spared, and the life she still carried.

Nico's gaze never left her face, and she saw his lips tremble as Andrea pushed his wheelchair right up against her bed. She got up slowly, not caring about the wires strapped to her stomach, and needing to put her arms around the man she loved with every fiber of her being.

There were soft moans, and desperate words, and arms

refusing to let go as they held each other tight, thankful to have found one another again.

"Careful, Ava, he's still weak. They've only removed the tube." She heard Andrea's words and immediately pulled away, and she saw the pain etched across his face. "Look at you," he whispered, sounding out of breath, as if the life had been kicked out of him.

"And look at you," she whispered, struggling to stay strong, to stop herself from crying. She couldn't fall apart, even though the tears threatened to fall from her eyes. She couldn't break down, because for the first time since she'd known him, he needed her more than she needed him.

"I'm going to be okay." He held onto both of her hands, and she was struck by a sharp searing pain. She squeezed his hands even tighter, then moaned as the contraction ripped through her body. He held onto her, watching her face, until the moment had passed.

"This one was different," she said, in a voice that was no louder than a murmur, and she braced herself, as another pain started to build up, almost on the tail of the previous one.

"I won't leave you again," he promised, lifting her hands to his lips and kissing them. She noticed that he didn't bend forward, that his face was tight and twisted, that he was in deep pain, even though he tried to pretend otherwise.

She gritted her teeth together as she waited for her pain to pass. "You're allowed to be weak, Nico," she said softly. "You don't always have to be the strong one."

His eyes misted over and his lips tightened. She shook her head. "Sometimes you have to let me help you. It's not a sign of weakness when you give in because you're so beat. Sometimes you just have to give in." His lips wavered just then, and his face softened. But a sharp pain torpedoed through her, almost splitting her body in half.

"It's ... time ..." she just about managed to say, then waited to catch her breath, waited for the wave to peak. She looked at her belly. "She ... waited ... for ... you ..." she told him, biting the words out as she forced herself to endure the pain. She hoped that his wish for a girl would come true.

The next contraction hit soon after, drilling down through her back and into her stomach. She couldn't speak, couldn't hear, couldn't move—only breathe, and feel his hands on hers.

When the contraction had passed, she opened her eyes and saw that Leo and Andrea had slipped out quietly leaving the two of them alone. She fell back against her bed, adjusting herself into position, their hands still connected. She could feel it coming again, barely a minute had passed since the last pain, she closed her eyes, knowing it started slow before peaking. The epidural which had slowed down her contractions initially had almost worn off. She'd been holding on until she saw Nico again. And now he was here.

There would be time enough later to scold him for driving so fast, for putting his life in danger, for almost leaving her. But it could wait. For now, she was thankful that he was by her side.

"I've got you," he told her, and she held onto his words as a new pain reached a crescendo, and she howled out in terror, clinging onto him for dear life.

Just as Nico had predicted, Elisabetta Rosella Elena Cazale made her grand entrance into the world a few hours later; named after his mother and maternal grandmother. She was a mini version of Ava.

The pain that had racked his body had melted the moment he heard his baby daughter, covered in slime and blood, utter her first cry. He forgot his own pain as love for this new life radiated through his body.

The labor had been slow and long and drawn out and had left Ava exhausted. He'd stayed by her side the whole time and after much screaming and howling on Ava's part, he felt as though the nerve endings in his hand had been severed as she'd clung to him each time a contraction hit.

A nurse had remained with him the whole time, monitoring him closely. He now sank slowly back into his wheelchair, exhausted, but jubilant, waiting patiently while the doctor finished checking the baby over. The nurse tended to Ava, who lay with her head back on the pillow, sweat streaking down her face, her eyes shiny and dark.

"You were right," she whispered, turning her head towards him.

"And you were amazing," he told her. "Thank you for giving us a beautiful little girl."

"I didn't do this alone," she moaned in a voice so low he barely heard her. "You had something to do with it as well."

Moments passed in quiet silence and then eventually a nurse walked over to hand her the baby. "Do you want to hold her?" Ava asked.

But he was afraid that he might accidentally let go of her. He felt weak, and worn out, as if he was going to pass out. "You first."

Ava cradled their daughter to her chest as he looked on, eyes shiny once more, remembering Edmondo, and knowing how overjoyed his father would have been. With determination he slowly got up from the wheelchair and held onto the side of the bed once more, looking down at the tiny bundle swathed in white. She had dark hair and red rosebud lips, and she slept peacefully in her mother's arms.

"Isn't she perfect?" Ava cooed.

"She is." He lifted his finger gently to his daughter's face. Ava smiled up at him, looking tired but happy; the pain of pushing the baby out seemed to have been forgotten. He placed a gentle kiss on her lips, saying nothing, but overcome with gratitude for the things that mattered the most to him. These two ladies in his life.

"We'll talk about your driving later," she told him. "The hotel? What happened?"

It wasn't that he'd forgotten all about it, but rather that he'd pushed the thoughts to the back of his mind while he'd been preoccupied with Ava and the baby.

But now that they were safe and well, he considered what Bruno had told him. At first he hadn't connected the dots, nor thought much about the mention of Vieri, or wondered why a lowly politician would concern himself with the safety regulations of a hotel and go poking his nose into workers' rights. Nico was confident that he hadn't done anything wrong, or illegal. But slowly it all began to make sense. He understood the interest, once the name came to significance.

Armando Vieri, Silvia's latest lover.

It almost made sense, were it not so sad and pathetic.

"We can't open yet," he said, "and it doesn't really matter anymore."

"But—" Ava stared at him wide-eyed.

He shook his head, putting his finger to her lips. "It's not important. It can wait. I'm not going to spend these first few weeks of *her* life," he nodded at his daughter, "or this new chapter in *our* life worrying about things that can wait."

"But Nico—"

He gave her a smile that came from the depths of his heart. "There's no 'but', Ava. This is my first Christmas with you and with our baby. I want to look forward to the New

Year and everything it brings. As long as I have the two of you, nothing else matters."

She smiled at him and he noticed her eyes had started to fill with tears. "Don't be sad," he said softly, shaking his head.

"I'm not sad." But a rogue tear fell anyway. "These are happy tears."

He knew from the smile that trembled at her lips that her happiness was deep. He had much to be grateful for himself, and knew how lucky he'd been to have made it back. That he was standing here, looking at this new life, when he could have hit the tree and worse, was a miracle.

The thought that he might never have seen his new daughter and that he might have left Ava alone in the world, lingered with him, black and heavy.

"They're the best kind, aren't they?" he murmured, wiping her tears away. "Happy tears."

It didn't matter what Vieri or Silvia tried to do. The real legacy Edmondo had left behind was not the string of Cazale hotels, but *this*. Nico looked at his wife and sleeping daughter, and felt truly blessed.

Thank you for reading HONEYMOON BLISS! Nico and Ava's epic romance comes to a final close in the last book, BABY STEPS.

Life is perfect ... almost ...

Juggling the demands of a new baby as well as a new business, isn't easy. Ava is thousands of miles from her family, making a new home in a new country with a new husband. It's not easy. The romance that began in Venice seems a far distant memory.

Is this true love, or another mistake?
BABY STEPS is available everywhere

SIGN UP FOR MY NEWSLETTER to find out when new books release!

http://www.lilyzante.com/news

I appreciate your help in spreading the word, including telling a friend, and I would be grateful if you could leave a review on your favorite book site.

You read an excerpt from BABY STEPS below.

Thank you and happy reading!
Lily

"Don't tell me there *might* be a problem," Nico snapped as he sat in his study, silently cursing to himself. He'd sneaked a call to his project manager, Bruno, while Elisabetta was sleeping. "Tell me you can do it, and then get it done." He coughed, and then instinctively touched the side of his chest where the tube had been inserted. He was on the mend now and back to normal but it had been a long six weeks since his car accident.

And he was still *pissed*.

Pissed that the Cazale Ravenna, his new spa hotel, still wasn't open for business, pissed because every moment it remained closed, it sucked up money, pissed because he needed to get back into the swing of things and it was impossible to concentrate on his work, to have conference calls, or business calls while everyone else was at home; his wife, his daughter, his mother-in-law and his housekeeper.

Now, only two days into the New Year, he was more desperate than ever to get back to the Casa Adriana, the main family hotel and his main place of business.

"All I'm saying is that we're on a tight deadline as it is,

especially if you still want to open next month. We've still got to re-paper, re-paint and re-plaster all the affected walls."

"We *will* open next month."

"We don't even have a date for the next inspection, Nico. Those people take their time."

"I don't care how difficult it is," Nico replied through gritted teeth. "I just want it done. Use your contact." Bruno's friend in the health and safety department was the one who'd alerted them to why the hotel might have failed its safety check. Armando Vieri—his malicious ex-girlfriend's new lover and a politician old enough to be her father—had meddled in things which were none of his business. Nico was sure of it, though he didn't have the hard proof to back up his assumption.

"Hear me out," Bruno insisted. "You don't want to mess up again." There was a slight pause before he back tracked. "Not that you messed up—"

"I didn't mess up." It wasn't illegal to have old wiring. Nico had been told by his architects and builders that it was fine, but in hindsight, he should have had all bases covered. His father would have. But Edmondo wasn't here now and this project—this supposed new offering in the Cazale chain of hotels—was something he had a lot riding on.

His reputation for one thing. People were watching him, the press and business people. Nico was certain they were all waiting for him to fall flat on his face and because of that he was more determined than ever to prove them wrong.

A lot had happened this year; meeting Ava, falling in love, his father's death, his marriage and the subsequent birth of their daughter. Thankfully Elisabetta's arrival had taken his mind off what had happened, and distracted him from the pain and inconvenience of his injuries. He'd nearly missed her birth because as he'd raced to the hospital upon learning that Ava had gone into labor.

The car accident—completely his fault—could have been fatal and he might never have seen Elisabetta.

All this he blamed on Silvia and Vieri. He had tried to put on a brave face about it but his resentment towards those vipers simmered not too far below the surface.

"The inspectors will be stricter this time around," Bruno warned, interrupting his train of thought. Nico pursed his lips tighter together. Forced to agree, he grunted. "Yes." Bruno had a point. "Which is why you must ensure it's done properly." Nico lowered his head, contemplating events. Bruno was damn good at his job and more importantly, he wasn't a 'yes' man. Nico didn't need any more of those around. He wanted results and he wanted people who could do the job and Bruno was the right man for it.

"Do your best," said Nico, knowing that his irritation was misdirected. It wasn't only the delay in the hotel's opening that annoyed him. He hated not being able to do things at full capacity. He wasn't used to being incapacitated. He was used to rushing around, being capable, having a body that was in peak fitness and while his recovery had been good, resting at home when so much needed to be done, had made him a brooding menace.

For the first two weeks he'd been too weak and incapacitated to ponder on the recent turn of events. He'd had trouble breathing but at least he was alive. Elisabetta's arrival had helped but those early weeks had been a blur.

Elsa, his mother-in-law had arrived soon after and had been a huge help to them both and yet he wasn't the only one who was trying to get back to normal. Ava was also recovering from the birth which hadn't been easy.

Their first Christmas together as a married couple had

been quiet and they'd ushered in the New Year without any fanfare. But now that the holiday period was almost over, he felt the pressure starting to build up again. Each day the Cazale Ravenna remained closed, it was costing him money.

He found himself caught up in the same vicious circle thinking the same vicious thoughts until Elisabetta's soft cries caught his attention.

"Is that Elisabetta?" Bruno asked.

Nico exhaled slowly, a softness melting his tense body. "Yes," he replied. It was his beautiful little girl.

"She's loud," said Bruno, laughing.

"She has a pair of lungs on her that would put me to shame," Nico said as the baby's cries grew louder.

Bruno chuckled.

"She can be a handful, sometimes, but she's a beautiful handful." These random bouts of crying that she would suddenly break into—Ava said it was 'colic'—these were hard to deal with. But for the most part, he had enjoyed being at home; though the resentment he felt towards what had happened tainted his enjoyment of being a new father.

Nico stepped out of his study and into the large hallway entrance, cocking his head towards the direction of the kitchen. During the day, Ava was usually downstairs and they would set the Moses basket in the part of the dining room that connected to the kitchen. Ava often set up her laptop on the large kitchen table.

His irritation rose with the pitch of Elisabetta's howls. *Where was Ava?* He hoped she wasn't back on her computer in her study upstairs, sneaking a look at her emails. There was no need for her to work and he couldn't understand why she insisted on it.

Nico flexed his fingers. He couldn't think amidst this noise and this, mixed in with him being cooped up at home for so long had made him jittery. Impatient. Frustrated. He walked into the dining room and Elisabetta's cries amplified.

"It sounds like you need to go," Bruno offered. "We can talk about this tomorrow."

Nico shook his head. How was he supposed to get his business back in order when he couldn't even think in peace? "We need to discuss this properly," Nico said making a decision there and then. "I'll come by on Monday."

"Already?" Bruno sounded surprised. "Shouldn't you be resting?"

"Any more rest will kill me," said Nico, just as Elisabetta's cries turned into a whimper.

"Don't put yourself through the headache, Nico. I've got everything under control."

"I'm sure you have."

"I can keep you updated."

"I know," replied Nico. "But I'll be over all the same." He wasn't surprised that his project manager didn't sound keen for him to show up on site. They'd had over a month without him and he was anxious to see for himself how they were getting on. The cellphone recordings of the work in progress that Bruno often sent him, and the daily updates didn't give Nico peace of mind.

"You're the boss," said Bruno and Nico wandered into the kitchen.

"And don't you forget it," he said. "I'll see you on Monday." He hung up and stared at Ava. She was sitting at the kitchen table with the laptop in front of her and the baby at her breast.

BABY STEPS is available everywhere

BOOKLIST

Honeymoon Series: Take a roller-coaster journey of emotional highs and lows in this story of love and loss, family and relationships. When Ava is dumped six weeks before her Valentine's Day wedding, she has no idea of the life that awaits her in Italy.

Honeymoon for One
Honeymoon for Three
Honeymoon Blues
Honeymoon Bliss
Baby Steps
Honeymoon Series (Books 1-3)

Italian Summer Series: This is a spin-off from the Honeymoon Series. These books tell the stories of the secondary characters who first appeared in the Honeymoon Series. Nico and Ava also appear in these books.

It Takes Two
All That Glitters

Fool's Gold
Roman Encounter
November Sun
New Beginnings
Italian Summer Series (Books 1-4)

The Billionaire's Love Story: This is a Cinderella story with a touch of Jerry Maguire. What happens when the billionaire with too much money meets the single mom with too much heart?

<u>The Promise (FREE)</u>
The Gift, Book 1
The Gift, Book 2
The Gift, Book 3
The Gift, Boxed Set (Books 1, 2 & 3)
The Offer, Book 1
The Offer, Book 2
The Offer, Book 3
The Offer, Boxed Set (Books 1, 2 & 3)
The Vow, Book 1
The Vow, Book 2
The Vow, Book 3
The Vow, Boxed Set (Books 1, 2 & 3)

Indecent Intentions: This is a spin-off from The Billionaire's Love story. This 2-book set consists of 2 standalone stories about the billionaire's playboy brother. The 2nd story is about a wealthy nightclub owner who shuns relationships.

The Bet
The Hookup

Indecent Intentions 2-Book Set

The Seven Sins: A series of seven standalone romances based on the seven sins. Emotional, and angsty romances which are loosely connected.

Underdog (FREE prequel)
The Wrath of Eli
The Problem with Lust
The Lies of Pride
The Price of Inertia
The Other Side of Greed
The Seven Sins Books 1-3

A Perfect Match Series: This is a seven book series in which the first four books feature the same couple. High-flying corporate executive Nadine has no time for romance but her life takes a turn for the better when she meets Ethan, a sexy and struggling metal sculptor five years younger. He works as an escort in order to make the rent. Books 4-6 are standalone romances based on characters from the earlier books. The main couple, Ethan and Nadine, appear in all books:

Lost in Solo (prequel)
The Proposal
Heart Sync
A Leap of Faith
A Perfect Match Series Books 1-3
Misplaced Love
Reclaiming Love
Embracing Love
A Perfect Match Series (Books 4-6)

Standalone Books:

Tomorrow Belongs to Us
Love Among the Ruins
Love Inc
An Unexpected Gift

ABOUT THE AUTHOR

Lily Zante lives with her husband and three children somewhere near London, UK.

Connect with Me

I love hearing from you – so please don't be shy! Email me (lily@lilyzante.com), message me on Facebook or connect with me through these different platforms:

Instagram | Facebook | Twitter | Website

Follow me on Bookbub
Follow me on Goodreads
Follow me on TikTok
Join my FB Reader Group

ACKNOWLEDGMENTS

I would like to thank the following ladies for taking the time and effort to help make my books better. They find the errors and typos that I have completely missed:

Marcia Chamberlain
April Lowe
Dena Pugh
Charlotte Rebelein
Carole Tunstall

A big thank you to Tatiana Vila for creating my awesome covers: **www.viladesign.net**